⌐HE UNCHANGING HEART

⌐rake is a woman in love who lets no
       of all her young sister, Stella,
.n the way of her happiness, or what
 ceives to be her happiness. Stella –
    ˙ithful heart – and husband alike
       ˙en on the ruthless wheel of
       ʀcpentance comes ... and with
       ˞ of all that life was to mean.

THE UNCHANGING HEART

The Unchanging Heart

by

Sonia Deane

Dales Large Print Books
Long Preston, North Yorkshire,
BD23 4ND, England.

British Library Cataloguing in Publication Data.

Deane, Sonia
    The unchanging heart.

    A catalogue record of this book is
    available from the British Library

    ISBN   1-84262-453-9 pbk
    ISBN   978-1-84262-453-1 pbk

First published in Great Britain by Hutchinson & Co. Ltd.

The moral right of the author has been asserted

Published in Large Print 2006 by arrangement with
The estate of Sonia Deane, care of Rupert Crew Ltd.

Dales Large Print is an imprint of Library Magna Books Ltd.

Printed and bound in Great Britain by
T.J. (International) Ltd., Cornwall, PL28 8RW

TO
CATHERINE

Whose constructive criticism, helpful ideas and infallible judgment, have meant so much to me.

I offer her this story in appreciation and friendship.

S.D.

CHAPTER ONE

I could not help knowing as I walked down the main street of Milbury that all eyes were turned in my direction, that any newcomers were nudged by local inhabitants and told: 'That's Lydia Drake, daughter of the headmaster of the village school'. I smiled greetings in all directions, paused to give little Willie and Tommy Small a pat, and to admire their harassed mother's latest effort – her fifth in as many years. It was very pleasant, I reflected, to feel that among all the villagers I was regarded after the manner of a Ministering Angel; it gave life a purpose and had an exhilarating effect upon me. And even though I longed to reach out and touch greater heights than those provided by the shabby, straggling village, nevertheless, I appreciated that to do the work nearest at hand, and do it well, was, at least, something of which to be proud.

I thought of father as I walked along. He had served in his present capacity for over twenty years. It was a pity he had not been more ambitious: I'd always dreamed of his achieving eminence in his profession and had endeavoured to spur him on towards that end. The words: 'A man of honour and integrity', came to my mind. They were used frequently in his praise. My thoughts stopped there as if modesty forbad my adding that: 'Self-sacrificing and noble' were used in mine.

I went a little deeper into my personal problems as I indulged these reflections, tearing aside that 'seventh veil' from the mind and peering within it more closely. What did I want from life – personally. Difficult to say, since the happiness of others had always been more important to me than my own. But I was not ashamed to admit that I craved something better than the mediocre existence which had been my lot for so long – if I viewed that existence outside the framework of its service to others. I drew in my breath sharply; the warmth of the June day, with its soft, fragrant breeze, stirred me; the taut, blue sky was as a mystic world in which I could trace my destiny. Music poured into my soul as I confessed that it was marriage I wanted; marriage which I saw, not only as an outlet for repression, but, since I should crave only to help the man I married, then it would, also, be as a stairway to success.

So engrossed was I in my thoughts that it was not until a voice challenged me gaily, that I realized the presence of Stella, my sister, beside me. I glanced at her lovingly:

'You startled me, darling.'

'So deep in thought.' Her laughter was gay, infectious and my affection for her seemed to envelop me in that second almost as a vital physical attribute. How absolutely reliant she was upon me; how very responsible I was for her, and how carefully I had guarded her since mother's death some while before; a death which had placed upon my shoulders all the burdens of running a home and looking after father and her. Stella was beautiful, both in disposition and appearance. She had a passionate sincerity, a vitality and vivaciousness which endeared her to everyone with whom she came in contact. And beneath it all was a sensitivity as of a soul illuminating every simple act. To me she was a child to be nurtured and protected; my instincts towards her were almost fiercely maternal.

She walked along beside me, her soft, bronze-gold hair fluttering gently in the breeze; her eyes expressive and eloquent of her every emotion as she said:

'You're tired, Lydia.'

'Nonsense.' I laughed, and tucked my arm through hers.

'I'm serious,' she persisted. 'I've been thinking very earnestly about things. It's time I stood on my own two feet a little more and relieved you of some of the responsibilities for a change.' She spoke with solemn impressiveness. 'I told Daddy so the other evening.'

'And what did he say?' I held my breath as I waited for her answer. A violent resentment stirred within me at the thought of losing control over her.

'Oh, he didn't give me any support; just smiled that gloriously vague smile of his and said that we'd both be hopeless without you, and that you were the mainstay of the family.'

I said lightly:

'But you don't agree with him – is that it?'

Instantly, her face clouded.

'Agree with him! But of course I do, darling. What worries me is that we seem to impose on you. From the moment mummie died you've – well!' She looked at me. 'Honestly, I don't know what we should have done without you.'

I drew in a deep breath. That was better.

'You just weren't intended to bother your head with responsibility,' I said. 'I don't think you'll ever quite grow up, Stella – it's your most lovable trait... Are you going to the Marshall party to-night?'

We had reached the small, double-fronted house that hung in rather Dickensian style over the pavement and looked as shabby as the buildings around it. My key went into the lock.

Stella said:

'Yes, I think so. It might be fun. The West-burys are going to be there.'

I found myself tensing.

'You like Allan?' I walked ahead of her and flung back the faded chintz curtains that had been drawn in the living-room to keep out the sun.

'He's awfully kind, Lydia.'

'Damned by faint praise, darling.'

Stella flung back her head and laughed.

'I like him – but not romantically.'

'Is there anyone whom you do like – romantically?'

'Shouldn't I have told you had there been?'

'That is a question and not an answer,' I admonished. Something in her expression arrested my attention. Suppose she had been keeping something from me. The very idea made me feel slightly sick.

Again she laughed.

'Can you like a person whom you've never met and seen only once?'

I stared at her.

'Who is it?' I tried to keep my voice very steady, but my thoughts were racing.

'The new Doctor – Stephen Ashley. I saw him for the first time yesterday. Awfully attractive, Lydia. Something friendly, tender about him.' She gave a little self-conscious grin. 'He's promised to go to the Marshalls to-night.'

'I see.' I smiled at her.

Stephen Ashley... I'd heard of him, of course; he'd just moved into 'Stoneleigh', one of the ugliest houses in Milbury, and put a brass plate up outside. The typical, struggling young doctor ... the very last person on earth for Stella who needed to be spared the hardships of life: she was altogether too fragile and sensitive to be buffeted. I consoled myself, however, that careful guidance would protect her – even from herself.

'They say,' she rambled on with enthusiasm, 'that he's brilliant and simply wonderful with children.'

'Then,' I said swiftly, 'he should be in his element here. The place swarms with them.'

She gave me a querulous look:

'I thought you loved children.'

'So I do... But, at the moment, I prefer a cup of tea.'

She relaxed; I knew she hung on my every word.

I went out into the kitchen, put the kettle on, and called to her:

'What are you going to wear to-night, Stella?'

'I've only my blue frock *to* wear,' came the reply.

'You look lovely in it, darling.'

She joined me and stood resting against the jamb of the door.

'You are such a generous person Lydia.

Never any pettiness of jealousy with you. I couldn't bear it otherwise. Somehow we're a tradition. If we ever quarrelled it would be like – like hurting, desecrating Mummie's memory... Is that very sentimental?'

I shook my head.

'I feel that, too... Stella, how do you think daddy's looking these days?'

She raised her eyebrows in surprised alarm.

'What do you mean?'

'I've been worried,' I said slowly, 'and didn't intend mentioning it to you.'

Instantly she protested:

'But I'd hate you to keep things from me.' Her brows puckered anxiously. 'He certainly hasn't been too well lately.'

I nodded, and said:

'I shall try to persuade him to have a thorough overhaul and go right away this summer. A change is what he needs badly. It's the wretched money business that's the trouble.'

Stella was setting the cups on the tray and she suddenly burst forth:

'I still say it's high time I did some work, you know. I'm just a passenger in this outfit. Just because I had a bad pleurisy that has fluffed my lungs a bit, there's no reason why I should be put in a glass case, and I'm jolly well going to begin and earn some money.'

I turned and looked at her. Her face was eager, yet determined. It struck me suddenly, sharply, that Stella had a decided will of her own and that any kind of challenge, or open opposition, would strengthen her resolve. The idea of her leaving home appalled me; she didn't realize how totally unfitted she was to face the world alone or how, away from my care and eternal vigilance, her health would suffer. Nevertheless, I knew I was treading on thin ice and I said lightly:

'Meanwhile, suppose you justify your existence by taking the tray into the sitting-room. Then we can have some tea.'

I always loved the tea hour with Stella. She would sit curled up at my feet and with almost child-like simplicity recount little items of news, local gossip, and I felt in those moments that we were shut away from the world and all alien influences.

She remained in her chair, however, after having finished tea; her expression was thoughtful and yet inexpressibly tender. I waited, conscious of tension; of an atmosphere suddenly projected into the room and the hateful premonition came to me that this moment was fraught with destiny; that in its seeming innocent and inconsequential exchange of words, lay drama, even suspense. Stella said abruptly:

'It must be dreadfully hard work for a doctor like – like Stephen Ashley.' Faint colour stole into her cheeks.

I knew that she wanted to talk about him

and a sickness, as of jealousy, consumed me. She was lost to me in those seconds, rather like someone who had travelled beyond me into a new world.

'Oh, I don't know,' I said casually. 'Doubtless he likes it or he wouldn't have chosen medicine as a career.'

'I was thinking of just starting like that' – her eyes met mine – 'without buying a ready-made practice.'

'Obviously he hadn't the money to buy one.'

'You don't sound very sympathetic, Lydia. It isn't like you.'

I hastened:

'But darling, I am most sympathetic; no one admires courage or ambition more than I – and he must have both.'

She warmed to that.

'Allan said he was a wonderful person... Rather an idealist who has very little time for money.' She studied me intently: 'Would you marry a man who was penniless and struggling, Lydia – if you loved him?'

I felt instinctively that she was seeking my approval for that which she, herself, would be prepared to do. I said guardedly:

'The circumstances would determine my course of action, darling. If I felt that I was strong enough, mentally and physically, to cope with the hardship and privation of poverty, without being an added burden to him – once the first flush of romance had subsided–' I paused effectively. 'Then, yes. I hope I should be sufficiently helpful to him to enable him to rise in the world and become anything but penniless and struggling. But, it is not noble to marry merely because the man is penniless, unless you have the stamina and type of character to battle against things.'

She said softly:

'You always think of everybody's point of view – don't you? Never your own?'

'I try to be fair,' I said, thrilled by her praise of me.

'And,' she said gently, 'you think I'm very irresponsible – all heart and no head – and very young for my years?'

'If I do, darling, then I think, also, that it is your most lovable and attractive virtue. I would not have you changed – not one scrap.'

I studied her as I talked, watching the play of expression upon her face; the light and shade of a deep emotion which radiated from her – rather as a magnetic beam, drawing all within its power.

She gave me an affectionate gaze:

'You might really be my mother, you know Lydia – oh, not in years,' she hastened, 'but in your attitude, your solicitude, I mean.'

A thrill of pride and delight surged through me.

'We're very close,' I said quietly. 'Aren't we?'

'Very, Lydia. I know you'd always understand; that I could tell you anything – good, bad, or indifferent about myself. It's a lovely comforting feeling.'

I glowed inside. The somewhat shabby room in which we sat – a room of faded chintz and well-worn furniture – took to itself an importance. It was my universe and that universe revolved around me. It was balm to my spirit. After all, I had done a good job – I'd nothing to be ashamed of; Stella and father leaned on me, relied on me; I had steered the somewhat frail ship that was our home through many rough waters... Stephen Ashley. The thought of him obtruded; it was rather like a nail-file drawn over fine silk; a disturbing element. Of course Stella would marry one day; but someone of my choice because I knew what she needed. But a penniless doctor! I was far more the type to be suitable for such a position. My thoughts hovered uncertainly. Did I, in truth, want a perpetuation of the respectable poverty I had always known? The scheming and the scraping to keep up appearances; the 'going without' and the longing for money to spend without thinking about whether or not it could be afforded; to say nothing of the immense power that accompanied it. No, I saw myself in very different circumstances. I knew my own capabilities to the last degree; I could dominate and hold sway in a world vastly different from that to which I had been accustomed. Asserting my authority, giving orders and seeing they were obeyed, filled me with exhilaration. I should be just, but never weak; Stella would think of a dozen reasons for being over-generous and gave, not only materially, but spiritually, to everyone. Hers was a warm, impulsive nature; she ran to meet people like an eager child with arms outstretched. Mine was the temperament to walk slowly, forming my judgment as I did so; assessing their virtues and vices and never taking anyone on trust. That, in my opinion, had to be earned.

Father came in and interrupted the conversation, rather to my annoyance. I watched him, conscious of faint impatience. There was a faraway look in his quiet, grey eyes; his shoulders had begun to stoop – even though he was still in the early fifties – and his clothes hung on him as from a peg. The note of cheerfulness in his voice was, I knew, assumed and calculated to inspire confidence and to deceive us about his true feelings. When mother died that vital part of his heart had died, too. He was not, however, a man to parade unhappiness, but it went very deep.

What, I asked myself, were my reactions to

him as a person – apart from the dutiful aspect of our relationship? I was fond of him; but he was not in the least degree as important to me, or as close to me, as Stella. On the other hand, I knew that he held me in very great affection, even esteem. I could influence him as I could influence Stella. But his acceptance of his unadventurous life was a continual frustration to me. I had dreamed of his moving up the scale – leaving the restricted life of Milbury far behind him. Now I knew that hope would never come to fruition and, at times, fury assailed me because of my own impotence: for once there was nothing I could do to further those ambitions.

I said gently:

'You're tired, Father.'

His lips twisted into what was intended for a smile. He looked at me from the very level eyes; his features were sensitive, even æsthetic.

'Just the heat... But if anyone has a right to feel tired, it is you, my dear. Always doing something for us – eh, Stella?'

Stella moved to his side, as though she would comfort him by a gesture. I noticed it with a pang akin to envy. There was a bond between father and Stella, subtle, indefinable; she knew and understood how he felt about mother's death far better than I, even though I pushed the very suggestion away from me as being absurd. There was a spirit of infinite gentleness in their approach to each other; a silent sympathy. Possibly, I argued to myself, all this had its inception in the fact that Stella had felt mother's death far more acutely than I; not, I insisted, because I cared any less for mother than she, but because I had been plunged into responsibility and sacrifice as a result of it.

Stella exclaimed:

'I've been saying that Lydia does far too much, Daddy, and that I ought to do far more.'

I smiled at them both.

'We do not think in terms of who does most, only of what is in the best interests of us all. And so long as I can keep you both well – happy–'

They exchanged glances and then looked again, at me.

'I wonder if you will ever think of yourself, Lydia,' father said admiringly. 'Just like your mother – always ready to sacrifice yourself for others.'

'Suppose,' I answered, thrilled by their eulogies, 'you began to get ready for your party, Stella – or you'll be late.'

Father raised his eyebrows inquiringly.

'I'm going to the Marshalls,' Stella confided to him. 'I wish you'd both come with me.'

I detested the Marshalls; but they were

wealthy and important landowners in the district, and to be accepted by them meant a great deal to the daughters of a local schoolmaster and constituted a major triumph. We had been introduced to them by Diana Westbury, Stella's god-mother whom, also, I heartily detested, although I had to admit she had been awfully generous to us both. But on one occasion she had made a very odd remark to me. I never thought of her without a sensation of annoyance creeping back with the memory of her words: 'You know, Lydia, there is something about you that is just a little too good to be true, my dear. I never feel you are quite real.' Possibly she had intended it as a compliment, but I could never be sure. And since she knew all I had been through and sacrificed for Stella and father, I considered it ungenerous and in poor taste.

Father, as was his custom with all suggestions involving his going out, said hastily:

'Not to-night, Stella: I just want to stay here and rest.'

I reinforced that with:

'And I must get down to the mending, darling, or neither of you will have anything fit to wear.'

'But–' Stella's protestations were very real: 'the mending can wait.'

'Perhaps, darling; but, apart from that, I never feel quite happy in my mind when father is alone all the evening.' I smiled at him as I spoke.

A few moments later I went up to Stella's room where she was dressing.

'Anything I can do?'

She was struggling with hooks and eyes and gasped:

'Please do me up, Lydia. I'm sure I'm fatter; I just can't make the darn thing meet.'

'Nonsense!' I fastened her frock with ease and appraised her. Her skin had the sheen of velvet; her figure was firm and rounded, her waist slender.

'You look beautiful,' I said softly.

She glanced in the mirror, but gazed at my reflection.

'Not half so beautiful as you, Lydia… Oh, I'm not – you know I'm not. You have poise, dignity – oh, everything. You command where I beg.' She laughed. 'Everyone admires you and says how wonderful you are. I'm awfully proud. Why *won't* you come to-night?'

'I've already told you, darling,' I said smoothly.

'Then next time I shall stay with daddy while you go.' She puckered her brows. 'Although he doesn't really mind being alone you know; there are times when he prefers it.' As if aware that she might be misunderstood, she added swiftly: 'Alone, and he is with mummie; I sometimes feel that we intrude on his solitude, Lydia.'

I stood back from her; my heart was racing.

'I think,' I said firmly, 'that I know father's state of mind pretty well, Stella. You're younger; it is natural that he should confide more in me so as not to burden you with his troubles. I don't mind staying; so long as you have a good time–'

She flung her arms around my neck and kissed my cheek.

'Dear Lydia! You're the most wonderful person in the world. And I love you very much,' she added with almost childish simplicity.

I held her closely for a second and let her go. Everyone would love Stella – everyone did love her. I almost grudged the smiles she turned upon others.

She left the house – seeming to float out of it like a pink, fluffy cloud shimmering in a silver light. I watched her go and then returned to father, who was sitting slumped in his chair. At the sound of my footsteps he pulled himself together instantly. I said firmly:

'You're not well, Father. I've known it for some weeks, but I didn't want to distress Stella by mentioning it. Now–'

He cut in:

'I'm perfectly all right, Lydia; you fuss too

much, worry too much about me.'

'You need advice,' I insisted. 'That is why I'm asking Dr Ashley to come around to see you this evening. Stella is out and–'

'Dr *Ashley!*' He stared at me.

'Have you anything against him? Since Dr Younger is no longer here... Well, we must have someone. I have good reports of this new man and I intend to get in touch with him,' I added with a half smile. 'That cough of yours – oh, Father, I don't ask much of you – do I? See him – if only to set my mind at rest. You know you are not well; thoroughly run down. Oh, I'm not blind, and you've been living on your nerves ever since mother died.'

He winced and was at once helpless, vulnerable. He had not the strength or the energy to argue with me.

'Oh, very well,' he said resignedly. 'It is, I suppose, the least I can do to satisfy you.'

I smiled and said briskly:

'I'll try to get Dr Ashley now.'

He looked at me pleadingly.

'I'd much rather not see him to-night, dear. Make it to-morrow, if you can.'

'Just,' I admonished smilingly, 'like a small child putting off the visit to the dentist. I'll not pander to you.'

And with that I went into the dining-room and got through to Stephen Ashley. After a few seconds his voice came to me – a voice

26

reassuring, without any of the abruptness, or even terseness, employed by many of his profession. I found myself tingling and in the grip of a new and strange sensation as I told him who I was, and explained how vitally necessary it was for father to have advice. And I added: 'If you could *possibly* see your way clear to come this evening—'

He said instantly:

'I'll come with pleasure. After Surgery.' He took the address. And when the conversation had ended I remained at the 'phone almost as one mesmerized by some invisible presence; some spiritual force which he projected over the wires. So that was the man by whom Stella had been attracted.

He arrived soon after eight. I opened the door to him and our eyes met.

'Miss Drake?'

'Yes.' He was far more attractive than I'd been prepared for him to be. His dark eyes were keen, penetrating and yet disarmingly friendly, even frank. He was tall, broad shouldered without having any suggestion of bulk and a virility stamped him as a man of power, forcefulness. 'I feel that I've imposed on your kindness by bringing you here to-night,' I said, as I led him into the dining-room. I looked up at him. 'But as a psychologist I'm sure you appreciate that, sometimes, the mood of the patient is all important.'

'Vitally important.' His voice enthralled me; it was music – soft caressing and yet deep, haunting.

I built up father's case, going back briefly to mother's death and ending:

'I feel certain you will help.' I added as a safeguard: 'Of course I may be taking altogether too serious a view of his condition, even exaggerating it, but if that is so, then I can plead only my anxiety for him.'

He was studying me intently, but it was impossible to read his thoughts. As a hazard I might have said that he was admiring me; that in a single look he had taken in every line of my face and body and formed a reasonably good idea of my character as far as it was possible for him to judge me.

'I will do my best,' he assured me.

The clock struck eight-thirty.

'Would it be impertinent of me to ask if you have dined?'

He smiled.

'Not in the least. My meals are slightly irregular.'

'Then perhaps coffee and sandwiches would not be amiss?' I hesitated. 'Or perhaps you are in a hurry?'

'A doctor is always in a hurry and yet must never be in a hurry,' he commented. 'I am due at a party but–' He shrugged his shoulders. 'I am perfectly happy at work. That's what I'm here for.'

I took him into the sitting-room and left him with father. I felt suddenly composed. My plan had worked – to the advantage of everyone. I knew, instinctively, that for Stella to have met this man at the Marshalls without my steadying influence, would have been fatal and made it dangerously easy for her to claim him as her especial and personal friend, in consequence. Now, his introduction to us in a medical capacity would create a family atmosphere and preclude the possibility. I realized more than ever the responsibility imposed on me in preventing anything of a serious nature ever developing between them.

Emotion started deep within me, bringing me curiously to life. Stephen Ashley's eyes meeting mine for the first time had injected a heady intoxication into the atmosphere. Excitement swelled like a soft, warm tide as I went out into the kitchen and began, rather feverishly, to cut sandwiches. But the picture I saw, in my mental eye, was of the rather frayed edges of Stephen Ashley's shirt; the suggestion of an uncared for existence. How easy to determine the type of woman he needed beside him; a woman who could take the reins of his home, run it efficiently and economically ... a woman who would revel in moulding the clay and building it up as a monument the world should acclaim... The country doctor emerging into the eminent

Harley Street Specialist... And finally – why not – becoming Sir Stephen Ashley. It would need a woman of physical and mental strength and infinite resourcefulness; a woman prepared to sacrifice the pleasures of to-day for the glories of to-morrow. He and Stella would be tragically unsuited; he would break her heart on the altar of his work and the duties it involved; she would break his with her sheer inability to cope with domestic problems and her delightful impulsiveness which would, inevitably, cause him acute embarrassment.

My heart beat faster... Could I deny that I was the woman he needed? That I possessed all the ingredients necessary to fill that niche in his life which would transform it? Few women, I argued, would relish being the wife of a penniless, struggling doctor; he would not find it easy to win the right type in a district such as this... For the life of the doctor's wife was, at all times, fraught with disappointment, frustration, loneliness. I could endure all that: had I not always done so? And ... wouldn't wealth without any attendant conquest or fighting to achieve it, bore me?

I was hardly aware of having cut the sandwiches; they seemed, finally, to appear of their own accord. I heard laughter coming from the sitting-room. Of course I'd known there was nothing really wrong with father, but, all the same I had been anxious for him to see a doctor... And, this way, quite apart from any other issue, Stella had been spared the suspense of waiting for the 'verdict'. Dear Stella ... I thought of her with infinite tenderness. How fanciful she was, and incapable of balanced judgment; just the lovable child to be protected at all times. Pray God I might always be in the position so to guard her.

I carried the tray into the sitting-room.

'I'm afraid,' said Stephen Ashley, 'that I have given you added work to do.'

'We all,' I said lightly, 'have a job to do in life. I love mine – and that is everything. A woman's place is the home and it is up to her to run it efficiently and without expecting a halo for reward... Black or white Dr Ashley?'

'White, please.'

What was he thinking, I wondered, as he took the cup from me. Almost impossible to tell and yet there was a light of approval in his eyes as he said:

'It is very refreshing to find a woman who is prepared to remain in the home and not regard it as an affront or drudgery.'

I remained very calm.

'Isn't the answer to be found in the degree of the love that the woman has for the person for whose welfare she is responsible?'

'Ah.' His voice was deep. 'But how many

women to-day think in terms of love?'

I shook my head and gave my shoulders an imperceptible shrug.

'One can but speak for oneself; I'm afraid there is always the danger of bringing any discussion down to the particular.' I added quickly: 'Material things have never impressed me very much – in fact not at all. Success, after all, lies in the simplicity of happiness, service; there cannot be such a word as "sacrifice" when one cares deeply for a person. Anything one does for them gives such infinite pleasure as to rank almost as selfishness... I hope those sandwiches are eatable?'

'Delicious.' He took another one. 'They have reminded me very forcibly that I've not had a meal since breakfast.'

'Ah,' said father, 'which just goes to show that we men all need looking after.'

Stephen Ashley commented:

'I most certainly do, but I cannot imagine anyone wanting the task at the moment.'

My heart missed a beat. I said swiftly:

'How do you like Milbury?'

'I don't; I like my ideal of what it could be,' he said and his voice rang with conviction. 'There's enough work here to last a man a lifetime, and he still wouldn't have done half the things he hoped to do. That is, of course, what makes it so interesting.'

So he was the crusader – exactly as Stella

had painted him. I watched his every shade of expression as he sat in the deep arm-chair opposite father. His features were clean cut, etched; I saw him as a man who needed me; a man who would be thankful to creep into the domestic harbour I could provide for him, before inspiring him to reach the very heights of his profession. And I saw him, too, as the man whom one day I should love... His arms would be strong, yet tender; his kisses thrilling. Here was no sickly senti-mentalist, but a man who would know how to love and, without shame, or any sense of immodesty, I dwelt on that possibility. Never before had any man roused me physically; never had I been moved to this state of feverish excitement that was like a fierce tide upon me. Even as I talked to him a series of mind pictures projected themselves on the screen of those thoughts... He would be my husband; we should be married in the little church on the hill... I had been born for that Destiny... Once more to give, to help, rather than to receive... I felt that we were allies already. I refused to contemplate the thought that such a hope was wishful thinking, self deception. I knew I was the type of woman he obviously admired and that the views I expressed – and emphasized as the time passed that evening – struck a chord of sym-pathy within him, particularly when I said with feeling:

'It is the children here that touch me most. Their plight in some cases is pitiable. I do as much as I can but–'

Father interrupted:

'They come to Lydia with all their troubles.' It was said with a laugh. 'I marvel how she finds time to cope with everything here and still help in the village.'

Stephen Ashley studied me with great intensity.

'Then you are interested in social problems, Miss Drake?'

'Very.' I smiled at him. 'I think I must have been a crusader in a previous life. I want to revolutionize the world – make it fit to live in and, as you so rightly said, this place is such fertile soil.'

I knew that impressed him. I could, accurately, I was certain, gauge his thoughts, the process of them being: 'Not often you find a young, attractive girl concerned with such problems, or content to live as she is obviously doing, looking after her father and sister, yet in no way being the domesticated dullard'.

'You must,' he said, 'know a family called Small?' He smiled and added: 'Although if ever a surname was a misnomer!'

We laughed together.

'Yes, I know them; squalor personified: I give her a hand with the children; get them scrubbed one day and–'

Our eyes meeting silently completed the sentence. I will him in that instant to see *me,* the woman; to forget social problems and think of romantic ones and felt that, up to a point, I had succeeded.

The clock struck eleven; the mood of the hour enveloping us in a luxurious sense of restfulness and ease.

Stephen Ashley said sharply:

'Good heavens!'

Father exclaimed:

'We're flattered you haven't rushed away. Conversation, discussion, is a dying art, alas.'

It was some minutes later that Stella and Allan Westbury arrived. They came into the room, blinking in the artificial light. Then:

'Dr *Ashley!*' Stella's voice was breathless.

He arched his eyebrows.

'You know me?'

'Isn't the new doctor always a source of interest?' she said with that ease and naturalness that was a part of her charm. Alarm took the place of pleasure. 'But, is there anything wrong – I mean–'

'Nothing.' He spoke gently and I noticed that a certain light came into his eyes as they rested on her flushed face. 'Your father is just going to do as he's told – that's all.' He turned to Allan who stood silently beside Stella. I made the necessary introductions while father disappeared to get the remainder of a bottle of sherry that was kept for such occasions since, normally, we could not afford to drink it.

Allan said:

'I understood that you were to have been at the Marshall's to-night, Doctor?'

'I was; but Miss Drake's call was more important and I did 'phone Ella Westbury. She is one of those understanding women of whom one is never afraid!'

Stella laughed.

'I can't imagine your ever being afraid of a woman.'

'I wouldn't like to make any rash statement,' he countered, and it was as though they were the only two people in the room; as if between them flowed some sudden and rare affinity.

Stella said abruptly:

'I think your profession must be the most satisfying and absorbing in the world.'

His interest deepened: I knew it and emotion churned within me dangerously as I said indulgently:

'Stella's a darling: she thinks in terms of the films – the white-coated surgeon and gleaming hospital.' My smile took the sting out of my words sufficiently for them not to be resented.

'Lydia can never quite think of me as grown up, you know.'

Allan teased her.

36

'Lydia is quite right – you're a babe.'

Stella looked at Doctor Ashley.

'Do you think that, too?'

He chuckled softly.

'This is where I hide behind professional discretion!'

Allan put in:

'And to change the subject! We're glad to have you among us, Dr Ashley. If I may say so, we've needed someone like you here for a very long while.'

'I heartily agree,' father exclaimed stoutly.

'And I hope you will be very happy,' Stella said quietly.

I felt a pang as I heard the wistful note in her voice and wished that I could spare her any of the hurts that life might inflict. It was essential that her love should be given to the right man for she would, I knew, blossom like a flower under its influence and pour the richness of her own character upon the object of her affection – selflessly and that would be her doom were she not protected by material security and all that went with it.

I looked at Allan. How insignificant he looked beside Stephen. Allan was in love with me; faithful, docile, the type that, while I could appreciate to the full his sterling qualities, I deplored his lack of fight and ineffectual approach. I had been absolutely honest with him, inasmuch as I had told him I was not in love with him, or with anyone else. I know he cherished the illusion that I might *learn* to care. How ridiculous! Love never consciously grows; it flares to life in a split second even though the two people concerned may have known each other for years. Meanwhile, I encouraged his friendship with Stella; in his hands she was perfectly safe. His financial standing was excellent; his position in the district enviable. He was the man who would give Stella the tender devotion she needed. And, already, his regard for her was deeply sincere. Now more than ever their relationship must be encouraged.

Stephen (I had already begun to think in terms of his Christian name) and he left together some little while later. Stella called me to her room as I was passing to mine. She was already in bed and, unpowdered, her face had a freshness, a bloom that was warm and appealing; her soft, grey eyes rested upon me lovingly, trustingly.

'Are you too tired to talk, darling? But I'm bursting to tell you – oh, so much... The party was wonderful, but I just held my breath hoping for Stephen Ashley to appear. What made you send for him to-night?'

I was very calm as I sat down on the edge of the bed beside her. Stella would never doubt my word, or question my intentions. What I did was right in her eyes, and that fact alone was going to be my greatest asset in the fight ahead – my fight for her future happiness and to save her from a folly she would regret for the rest of her life. My own feelings, or possible happiness, were of no account at that moment.

'Father seemed so utterly worn out, darling. But I can set your mind at rest – there is nothing really wrong with him – although he is, Dr Ashley said, in a highly nervous state. A rest, later on, is what he needs and must have.'

'So long as you are satisfied.'

'I am.'

'Lydia?'

'Yes, darling.'

'Do you like him?'

'Whom do you mean?'

'Stephen Ashley.'

I kept my voice very steady.

'As far as one can after such a brief meeting – yes.' I felt sick with apprehension for her.

'I'm glad... Will it sound utterly wild and crazy and – and presumptuous, almost immodest, if I say that I think, one day, I shall marry him; that he'll love me?' She drew her knees up to her chin as she talked, and rested her cheek on her folded arms. 'Because I love him. I knew it before tonight, but seeing him and talking to him here–' Her eyes were like stars; she radiated all the beauty and quivering loveliness of a child merging to womanhood; suddenly she was complete, fulfilled, and very wise.

I said, curbing my emotion:

'Darling, you can't love him, the *person;* you can love only love. That always happens at your age.'

She shook her head.

'This is quite different,' she said solemnly. 'It was just as if he had reached out and drawn a thread from my heart and tied it to his. Utterly natural. I felt that if he had put out his hand and asked me to go with him to the ends of the earth I would have gone without question.' She added with a sweet, confiding smile. 'I can tell you all this, darling, because talking to you is rather like thinking aloud; you understand.' A sigh. 'Oh, Lydia, I'm so happy; it is as if I've suddenly been rocketed to a mountain top and life is spread out like a carpet at my feet. I shall make him such a good wife – oh–' she screwed her nose up into a delicious smile – 'not in the dull sense… It won't matter how hard I work, or what I do, or if we never have any money. I know all that he hopes to achieve here and to help him – to *help* him–'

I dare not betray my hand; cross her, criticize. My only chance was to retain her confidence so that, at all times, I was fore-warned and forearmed.

'Then,' I said softly, 'I hope your dreams come true, darling.' I clasped the hand she generously stretched out to me. 'But suppose he shouldn't feel as you.'

Her expression smote me; it was anguished. Then she said softly:

'Somehow I believe that he does; that to-night a spark was lit between us, Lydia ... but if I am wrong and he chooses someone else–'

I waited tensed as she paused.

'If,' she repeated, 'he chooses someone else, then his happiness would mean more to me than my own.' She flung back her head with a rather voluptuous abandon. 'But I've an idea that I shall be the "someone else"; that even at this moment he is thinking of me. Would I seem quite mad if I said I can almost feel his thoughts?'

I smiled tenderly.

'No, darling, I don't think you are mad – just very sweet and lovable.'

'Ugh,' she made a wry face. 'You make me sound like a lollipop.'

I moved to her side as she slid down in bed.

'Bless you, Lydia,' she whispered. 'It's so lovely to have you to talk to; you're so good to me.'

I tucked her up, turned off the bedside lamp and went from the room. Her thoughts of Stephen seemed so vivid, so intensely real as to accompany me like a ghost.

It was some few days later, after I had tried

unsuccessfully to 'run into' Stephen, that Stella said as we sat together after tea:

'Stephen took me into Dornsford this afternoon – gave me a lift in his car. He's asked me to go out to dinner with him – confinements permitting – on Friday. Oh, Lydia, I'm so *happy*.'

I felt ill as I sat there, sick with apprehension for her.

'What did he say?'

'Oh, everything, and yet it didn't seem to matter; we were together. I know he's almost in love with me, Lydia – if not quite. And I think he knows it about me, too. Atmosphere? A look; the way he spoke my name. It was as if all of summer, its warmth and richness were drenching us in its glory; we just were happy beyond thought. He told me about his work, his ambitions … little intimate things that mean so much when a man of his type tells them. He spoke of his family, too. His father died in the last war.'

'And you're going out with him on Friday?'

'I'm counting the hours… I want him to kiss me; I want to feel his arms around me–'

'Aren't you rather rushing things, darling?' She would never know what superhuman effort it required to keep my voice steady.

'No,' she said honestly. 'I'm not ashamed of how I feel and I wouldn't have it any different. I don't have to pretend to you where to anyone else I'd die rather than breathe a word. But love is so gloriously free from hypocrisy and stupid convention.' She lay back in her chair and then tucked her legs – long and slender and beautifully shaped – under her. 'I want four children,' she went on eagerly. 'A real *family*... Lydia, you're not shocked?' Her voice sounded almost a-mused; she became the elder in that moment.

'I was just wondering how you proposed to keep four children, my dear innocent, on the money Stephen Ashley would earn! Or how you'd cope with their upbringing.'

'We'd cope together and I'd soon learn the rest. I'm not really the helpless type, darling: you just think I am. If I had to do it I should despise myself if I didn't do it well.'

'I'm sure,' I said soothingly, 'you would... Did you see anyone else while you were shopping?'

'Diana.'

Allan's mother always insisted on the use of her Christian name.

'What had she to talk about?'

'Generalities; but she asked us all to go to tea on Sunday. I said I thought we could. I know daddy always enjoys talking to her... Do you feel any different about Allan these days?'

'No; just the same.'

'Poor Allan. He's so terribly fond of you, Lydia.'

I said carefully:

'I think he *was,* darling, but that now you are far more to him.'

'I!' It was an outraged sound of denial. 'But we're just good friends, Lydia; whatever put that idea into your head?'

I knew that overstatement could be fatal. And I changed the subject.

The following day Stephen called to see father, and both father and Stella were out.

'I'm awfully sorry,' I said, as I admitted him; 'but father's watching the local cricket... I was just going to have tea. Will you join me?'

He laughed.

'A case of always feeding the brute,' he said gaily. 'I'd love to join you if I may.' As he stepped over the threshold he glanced around as if expecting, and hoping, to see Stella, and I had the instinctive feeling that both the professional call and the acceptance of tea were designed to that end.

We chatted together and every nerve in my body seemed to be throbbing as I looked at him. His dark suit and white shirt added to his attractiveness; the faint smell of disinfectant came closely to my nostrils; and I knew that, suddenly, I was a woman in love. And with that knowledge came the conflict of Stella. Yet did the mere fact of my loving Stephen alter the moral issue where she was concerned? For her to marry Stephen

44

would be a tragedy for them both and my love for him in no way altered that fact. My duty was plain enough and no sentimental self-sacrifice on this occasion must deter me from my avowed object. I must do everything within my power to prevent Stella being plunged, through sheer infatuation, into a life that would destroy her.

Inevitably, her name was mentioned. I said quietly:

'Stella is in Dornford. She and Allan Westbury have gone to visit friends there.'

A shadow crossed his face.

'She is very lovely – so refreshing. Vital and yet restful.' He stopped abruptly as one fearing to betray himself.

I said with great tenderness:

'Stella is everything to me. I've been mother and sister, too.'

'You must,' he said gently, 'have had a pretty tough time of it – the responsibility – since your mother died.'

'I suppose I have – in a way.' I kept my voice well modulated. 'But Stella more than atones for it all. I won't deny that I have missed quite a bit; been tied but, what is that?'

'A very great deal to anyone of your age.'

'I suppose,' I said carefully, 'my greatest concern has been Stella, but I must not weary you with my family problems.'

'Please do–' It was an urgent, breathless sound.

'I have always dreaded lest she might fall in love with the wrong person; she is so impulsive, so generous and warm hearted that, in a moment of infatuation, she wouldn't stop to think. And yet, for her to marry into hardship, or even our kind of genteel poverty, would have spelt tragedy. She's just not cut out for such sacrifice: she hates going without, and I've always seen to it that she has had as little of it as possible. It isn't that she is a materialist – but–'

He interrupted me with an almost desperate impatience as he said:

'I notice that you use the past tense... Does that mean your fears are removed?'

'I think so,' I told him and smiled confidentially. I realized that this was a moment when Stella's life, and all that was embodied in the word, hung in the balance and that if I would save her from a reckless marriage – for which she was ill-suited and which would involve misery not only for herself, but for him – I must lie in order to achieve my objective. I felt no stirring of conscience, no sense of guilt, as I made the decision; the issue at stake more than justified the means. My voice was very steady as I added: 'Stella is very much in love with Allan and I have every reason to believe he cares deeply for her. Waiting for her to tell me that he has asked her to marry him is agonizing suspense, for if my own future were involved it could hardly mean more to me.' I paused. 'But I've no right to be betraying her secrets to you … and yet, somehow, I feel that you understand and that we speak the same language.'

His face was dark, inscrutable, and it was obvious I had dealt him a bitter blow. But since it could only be for his good I knew that to strike before his feelings became more deeply involved, was to lessen the degree of his pain, and thus I endured the state of wretchedness in which I found myself with a semblance of fortitude.

He said slowly:

'I should have thought your sister would have been capable of great courage.'

'Oh, that I wouldn't deny for a moment. But Stella has never quite grown up: I think that is half her charm, and she would go blindly and whole-heartedly into a thing and then, when it was too late, begin to count the cost. And, of course, I suppose I am more vigilant than ever because of the fact that she was so very ill last winter. Pleurisy, with the fear of complications.'

'T.B?' Consternation showed in his eyes.

'Suspected; but the X-rays show only a fluffy condition of the lungs. Stella needs a smooth pathway, every comfort and care; she is the child to be spoiled and kept happy – not because she is weak *or* spoiled, but because she was made for that kind of life.

47

We all have our niche, don't you think? The tragedy is when we step out of the right one, or choose the wrong.'

He said almost grimly:

'I never think it fair for a doctor to marry at all. Particularly if he happens to have very little money.'

I said stoutly:

'I couldn't agree with you less – provided he chooses the right woman. You are merely bearing out my theory about Stella: to give that argument point, I would say, for instance, that for Stella to marry a doctor, or a schoolmaster, or anyone who had to fight both materially and spiritually, would mean disaster for the reasons I stated just now. But that doesn't do her any discredit whatsoever.' I laughed and sipped my tea. 'Whereas for me! I shall probably marry a penniless artist and starve happily in a garret! That wouldn't be any great hardship to me, because I'm used to struggling and fighting and making ends meet – I've lived in that atmosphere all my life. And tried to keep it from touching Stella too closely.'

'Meaning that if you loved a man you would be prepared to make any sacrifice for him?'

'I hate that word "sacrifice!" – as I think I said the last time you were here. If I loved a man his happiness and welfare would be my only concern; his life, mine. And I shouldn't care if he never made any money provided he in no way regretted making me his wife. But' – I paused – 'I'm not putting that forward as representative of how all women should look at things; many people think it exceedingly foolish not to demand the moon – because if you ask for nothing,' I laughed, 'that is all you'll get!'

He nodded and got to his feet.

'You're a most unusual woman,' he said softly.

My heart raced; I smiled at him.

'But all the talking won't alter things – will it?' I suggested.

'Sometimes,' he answered gravely, 'a word can change a man's whole life. Emotion can so easily deaden reason, make one utterly blind to the facts.'

I felt that my lungs had been put into a vice in that moment. I had done my best to protect Stella and, also, to spare him. I knew the day would come when they would both thank me, or have cause to do so. And I was content.

Nevertheless, there was a certain unendurable suspense about the days that followed, as I waited for Stephen to cancel his appointment with Stella for the following Friday; but no message came from him. Suppose, after all, I had not convinced him? Suppose he was far too deeply in love with her – selfishly in love with her – to be deterred by anything I had said. It was like being poised on the brink of a precipice.

Meanwhile, Stella counted every moment of the time, and when Friday came there was about her that excitement which was like some invisible ray. Once, almost as though the suspense were killing her, she cried:

'Pray that the 'phone doesn't ring, Lydia. Oh, *pray* it doesn't ring.'

But at six o'clock that ring echoed shrilly through the house, smashing the silence almost sinisterly. Her gaze leapt to mine as one who hardly dares to answer it. Then she flew from the room and, a few seconds later, returned and as I gazed upon her anguished face, I felt a pang of remorse.

'I knew it in my bones,' she said dully, 'that something would happen to prevent our going.'

I said tensely:

'There are other nights, darling.'

She looked at me with a stricken expression darkening her misted eyes:

'He sounded strange, Lydia ... almost as though he were saying – good-bye.' And with that she rushed from the room.

I sat very still. I needed all my courage and resolution in that moment. But I knew that I had done my duty.

CHAPTER TWO

I waited a few minutes before going to Stella. It would be an ordeal, and I searched my heart seeking further justification for the step I had taken in her interests and finding, on closer analysis, that I was more convinced than ever that my actions were her safeguard and her future salvation. This impulsive infatuation would die a natural death and she would be spared untold misery in the years to come.

She looked up at me as I entered the bed-room, and dashed a hand across her eyes with appealing, childish gesture.

I said gently:

'I wondered if you would like to go into Dornford, darling. A film perhaps... There's always something very blank about–'

'No.' It was a cry. 'I couldn't. I'm sorry, Lydia: it's sweet of you to think of it, but I'd rather be here.' She added: 'I'm afraid I'm being childish, but I had counted on this evening with Stephen.' She looked at me very directly, and with great earnestness: 'I wish I could rid myself of the feeling that he was deliberately getting out of it – as though he didn't want' – her voice faltered – 'to take me out, or be with me.'

I felt that my lungs were bursting; that my heart was dangling on a slender thread as I asked:

'What possible reason could you have for such an idea?' I infused a note of incredulity into the question.

'That "something" which comes over the 'phone, Lydia. He didn't give any explanation whatsoever. If he had–' She broke off, mastering her emotion before continuing with: 'It would have been simple if he'd been called out on an urgent case.'

'What,' I asked, 'did he say?'

'Simply that he was afraid he wouldn't be able to see me to-night as arranged. And that he was sorry. He didn't make any attempt to suggest another, or alternative, meeting.' She got up from the bed on which she had been sitting and walked restlessly up and down the room. Then, despairingly: 'There must be something,' she said. 'Oh, Lydia, you're so wise, what do you think? Am I building it up because it means so much to me or what – all I know is that, in my heart, I felt that he cared for me.' Faint colour stole into her cheeks. 'And that, by his attitude, I was not without justification for thinking so.'

I appreciated that half measures were useless; that this was the moment in which to be cruel to be kind and I said gently:

'Listen, darling, I must be honest with you...'

She stared at me, a stricken look coming instantly to her eyes, her lips parting as one who waits in an agony of suspense for a blow they know to be imminent.

'Please, Lydia. I want the truth: you are the one person on earth I can trust; I know that what you say will be right. Don't, if you love me, hold back anything for fear of hurting me.'

That made it a little easier and I went on:

'Don't you think that Stephen might have been afraid lest your feelings for him were becoming serious? That, on reflection, he realized he had no right to encourage you by paying you attentions that so easily might be mistaken for something deeper?'

Stella uttered a cry of dismay.

'You mean that he sensed my love for him and–' Colour flamed into her cheeks.

I hastened:

'Not necessarily that, darling; but that to do anything calculated to win your love– Oh, Stella, don't you see? It is so terribly easy for a man's attentions to be misjudged by any girl – particularly when she wants to believe that those attentions are serious. Stephen is not, I am sure, the type to do anything that might, conceivably, hurt you later on. Far better that he should be honest now, before any damage has been done, than wait until your affections were irrevocably involved.'

Stella smoothed her hands as one renouncing a dream. Her eyes became inscrutable for a second and then, as if she could no longer remain behind that mask which was as a protection of her pride, she murmured plaintively:

'My affections were "irrevocably involved" at our first meeting.'

'Stella!' I felt slightly sick.

She looked at me.

'Every word I have said to you about my regard for him is true, Lydia. I suppose I was just deluding myself when I imagined that he felt the same way; building up a picture, a dream that wasn't there.' She stopped. 'And yet–'

'What?' I held my breath in suspense.

'I'm the last person really to flatter myself about that kind of thing: there seemed to be something instinctive between us – as I told you.' A note of despair crept into her voice. 'And now–' She caught at her breath: 'It was as if I had done something to displease him; as if some misunderstanding had arisen.' She gave me an inquiring gaze. 'I think I shall ask him – try to–' She finished dismally: 'You don't approve of that?'

I said gravely and my words lent strength to my own beliefs.

'When a woman has to ask for reasons and

explanations, darling, her position becomes pretty invidious. Let things take their course. Stephen may 'phone you again very soon; you may meet him and his attitude and actions will speak for themselves. If he cares–'

'I know,' Stella said quietly, 'he will come to me and nothing will keep him away.'

I dare not argue that point. Better to leave the situation as it was, even though it hurt me bitterly to realize that Stella was suffering. I looked at her as she sat there. How delicate she was; how unsuited for life's battle. Didn't all this prove it? A word from Stephen and she was in the depths of despair. What a tragedy it would be were she to have married him in that first impulse of infatuation, which might so easily have fired him with the passionate belief that he returned her regard when, in truth, he would discover that she was no more than a child to be petted and spoiled, and far from the type he needed so desperately as a helpmate in his struggle for existence. How they would – without knowing it – have cause to thank me later on. And if it so happened that, ultimately, Stephen realized that I was the woman he needed to share his life, then I should have no regrets. For me to be squeamish, or weak, now, because, up to a point, I could not divorce my own happiness from the issue, would have been criminal and lead them both to destruction.

'I think,' I said gently, 'that if I were you, Stella, I should turn the pages of this story and begin again. Don't, darling, I beg of you, build it up beyond its rightful proportion. Your happiness means so much to me; I'm so terribly anxious that you should find the right man.'

She stared at me rather challengingly:

'And you don't think Stephen is the right man – in any case?'

'No,' I said firmly; 'since you ask me – I don't. You were not cut out for the hardship that being his wife would entail.'

She gave me a strangely appealing look:

'If you love a man enough, Lydia, you can rise to any heights and endure anything, for his sake. No one can be proved until they are tested.'

I smiled inwardly. Sometimes she tried to be so very wise, but I knew the real Stella and what she most needed from life. I had not cared for her and guarded her for nothing. And even though my heart was sad as I left her, nevertheless a sensation of proud thankfulness overwhelmed me. I had not shirked my task – distasteful though it had been.

We all went to the Westburys, as arranged, that following Sunday, and it so happened that not only Stephen, but his family, were there, also.

It wasn't easy to describe the Westbury home. My antipathy towards Diana was, in fairness, apt to colour my impressions of it. The atmosphere was unruly, undisciplined and Bohemian. Everyone pleased themselves what they did, the clock was an ornament and not a necessity, and Diana held court after the manner of a Queen – and if it suited her to receive people in her bedroom, and while she was in bed, then she did so. Her daughter, Felice, followed in her mother's footsteps and, now an art student, wandered through life somewhat blankly, remembering very little of what went on around her, but appearing thoroughly to enjoy every moment of her existence. Their position in Milbury amused them; for they had an uncanny and disarming knack of seeing through a thing – and that thing might be animal or vegetable. I always felt that Diana was probing her way in a single glance, to my innermost mind and to my heart; that she was endeavouring to fault me because she resented the fact that – even though I had to admit it myself – I had more than pulled my weight and achieved a good deal since mother's death. Stella she openly adored. Father was her 'old friend' and friendship to Diana was above rubies. I deplored the fact that she chose them from such a wide, and varied, field and that one literally never knew whom one was going to meet at her parties. Somewhat enviously – I admit – I coveted the wealth that enabled her to be thus eccentric. Allan, sober, solid, but always the good mixer, was different entirely from Diana, and had taken after his father, now dead.

When we arrived the room was already full of people, most of whom I knew. Stella whispered breathlessly:

'Oh, Lydia! Stephen's there.'

My heart missed a beat. I had seen him the moment I crossed the threshold, feeling the thrill of his presence and yet filled with anxious concern for Stella. Was it my imagination, born of fear, that their glances leapt together and the very atmosphere became tense.

Diana Westbury, a striking woman in her late fifties, with silver hair and rather handsome features, moved instantly to our side, welcoming us with a smile and a warm:

'How lovely to see you all… Stella, darling, you look pale.' A glance at me. 'No need to inquire after your health, Lydia, you always look well.'

'Hard work,' I said, feeling on edge, as always I did in her presence, 'is the best tonic.'

'I doubt,' she countered, 'that Stephen Ashley, here, would quite agree with you, or he'd be out of a job tomorrow. You have all met, I understand.' She paused, adding:

'But not, I believe, Stephen's mother and sister ... Dora and Monica... No surnames here – just can't bear them. Always muddle them up, and it makes life so simple when you dispense with them.'

I don't know why, but I felt a strange depression as I gazed at Stephen's relatives. Had I foolishly imagined that he had no roots. Absurd, because Stella had told me that his mother and sister lived in Hertfordshire; but my mind had not absorbed it as a fact. I found myself looking into a pair of very level, and very critical, blue eyes as Mrs Ashley said:

'Lydia; I've heard my son speak of you... And Stella.' She looked at father. 'Nice to have such charming daughters.'

'Equally nice,' he answered, 'to have a son and a charming daughter.' He glanced at Monica as he spoke.

Antagonism welled within me. Monica was modern to her finger-tips which were a brilliant red. I judged her to be brittle, self-centred, and probably outrageously frank. We looked at each other and declared silent war – almost as though aware of the fate that would force us into each other's company. Ardent dislikes, I thought, were precisely the same as ardent loves – equally instantaneous. I hated her sleek, gleaming head with its up-swept hair style; the full, blue gown which reeked of Bond Street. She looked predatory and oozed that appeal which, to me, was cheap. Not in the least like anyone I should have imagined as a sister of Stephen.

At that moment he joined us, avoiding, I noticed, Stella's gaze and moving to my side, saying laughingly:

'Lydia, so far, has "fed the brute". This is the first occasion on which she had not to do so. Some man is going to be most awfully lucky.'

I saw Stella wince, but she said:

'I couldn't agree more. Lydia does everything perfectly and without any fuss. I wish I were half as clever or efficient.'

Monica's eyes seemed to meet mine in challenge:

'And I'm sure, Lydia, you are the exception to the rule that perfection is very dull and not to be trusted.' A smile. 'I have very few domestic virtues; but I shall get by, no doubt. One can do anything in this life – if one wants to.'

I bristled.

'Then,' I countered, 'it is a great pity so many things are done so badly, by so many amateurs.'

I knew that Stella wanted to leap to my defence, but I cautioned her with a look.

Allan interrupted the conversation. I managed to speak to him alone for a few seconds and said:

'Do something for me – give as much attention to Stella as you can, Allan. She's not herself to-day; I'm rather anxious about her, in fact. And you are such a tower of strength and she has great regard for you.'

He looked at me.

'Trying very hard to get me to put Stella in your place, aren't you, Lydia?'

I started. Had I been so transparent.

'If I am, then I can pay you no greater compliment,' I replied softly. 'Stella means the world to me – and you know it. Just as I know she needs you and that together – well, it would be absolutely right. I'd be hopeless for you.'

'Perhaps; human nature being what it is we mostly like the things most calculated to hurt us.'

'And do I hurt you?' I spoke regretfully.

'Not deliberately,' he answered. 'But you're so strong and firm. I feel that I am trying to break down iron doors in order to reach you, and shall never succeed.'

I sighed. This was getting us nowhere.

Nevertheless, he did as I asked and monopolized Stella almost exclusively from that moment onwards. Stephen made no attempt to break into their conversation, but remained slightly aloof from the noisy throng until, finally, we found ourselves alone in a suddenly deserted lounge.

Everyone at Diana's parties roamed at

will, overflowing into garden and reception rooms, converging only for meals. It didn't appeal to me. I preferred a more formal, orderly pattern with a hostess gracing the procedure. I knew that in her position I should endeavour to entertain and observe all the rules in the process. This Bohemian do-as-you-please attitude, was alien to my instincts and I shuddered at Diana's love of keeping open house, without realizing the status she missed, and the waste it was of her wealth which could have been put to so much more effective account.

Stephen said:

'Mrs Westbury' – a smile – 'Diana, has an amazing flair for this kind of thing. What a youthful spirit and what personality.'

I despised myself because jealousy shadowed my heart. I said breathlessly:

'You like such parties?'

His eyes met mine and a strange thrill went over me.

'Normally – no! Here, yes. I feel that I've known Diana and her family for years.' He paused. 'I have that same curious feeling about you, Lydia. You don't mind if I use Diana's ideas to suit my own inclinations, and use your Christian name?'

'Not in the least.' I didn't want to talk of Diana and allowed my glance to wander to where Stella and Allan were walking on the lawn immediately in front of the room in which we were sitting. I knew that Stella had deliberately gone outside to avoid Stephen, whose attitude made it obvious that he had no intention of singling her out. I could tell by her expression that she was not hearing a word of that which Allan was saying, and that only one thought obsessed her.

Stephen said abruptly:

'Your sister and Allan seem to be very engrossed. I hardly think you have any cause to fear the ultimate result of their relationship.' He added, almost harshly: 'It seems a foregone conclusion.'

'I think so,' I said swiftly. 'The emotional strain is telling on Stella. I shall be so thankful when she is married and settled. I shall feel that I, then, can begin to think in terms of myself.'

He looked at me with a strange earnestness:

'You are the most beautiful woman I've ever met,' he said slowly. 'Don't you ever think of yourself in the ordinary way?'

I smiled, my heart warming to his praise.

'You could hardly expect me to answer that question, Stephen, could you?' I used his name unconsciously and it sounded sweet on my lips. 'I'd hate above everything to appear as the self-sacrificing martyr! Heaven forbid.'

'That's what makes you more unusual than ever – most women love that role.'

I laughed, my spirits soaring.

'I think you libel my sex.'

Again, his gaze turned to Stella as if he could not help himself.

'I thought,' he said tensely, 'that when I first saw her to-day, she looked strained.'

The words smote me. Was that anxiety based on the fugitive hope that his behaviour might have had an emotional reaction upon her? And that his 'phone call on Friday night might not have left her entirely unmoved. A dangerous notion for him to harbour. I said quietly:

'I'm afraid she is living on her nerves at the moment. In fact, I tremble for her if this uncertainty continues much longer.' I tried to speak brightly, but knew that concern seeped through to acquaint him with my anxiety. 'I shall have to call you in professionally if this goes on. But' – I shook my head – 'there is no medical cure for love, alas.'

'No,' he said grimly. 'None.'

I added:

'You would never allow her to suspect that I had confided in you, Stephen – would you?' My eyes sought his, and he held my gaze as I added: 'Looking back on it, I don't quite know why I had the temerity to burden you with my troubles.'

'I'm honoured that you did,' he said softly. 'I'm sure you've shouldered them alone quite long enough.'

'If I can see Stella happy–' I drew in my breath sharply. 'This environment would be so right for her, too. She'd blossom like a flower in the sun.' I took the cigarette Stephen offered me and, after he had lit it, said: 'Father and I just cannot give her the things she loves and needs.'

It was at that moment Stella and Allan joined us. I knew that Stella was drawn back to Stephen rather as a magnet. Her voice when she spoke to him was smooth, her small, shining head held a trifle higher than usual, although only I was aware of the fact.

'I'm sure it isn't often you take a few hours off, Dr Ashley.' She added: 'A doctor's life must be frightfully exacting.'

Stephen's gaze was upon her with great earnestness; I watched him with a desperate anxiety as he said:

'I seem to remember your saying, on the occasion of our first meeting, that you considered my profession to be the most satisfying and interesting one in the world.'

Stella wavered. I could almost 'watch her' – being able to read her innermost thoughts as I could and always had done – thinking as she stood there; feel, too, that mental clutching at the crumb of hope because he had remembered what she had said and, then, smarting at his rebuff of Friday, and his remoteness during the afternoon, finally falling back on her pride to support her as she answered:

'I still hold that view; but it doesn't make it any the less exacting, does it?'

Allan put in cheerfully.

'I've always thought that it was the doctor's wife whose life was exacting.'

'As a bachelor, I wouldn't know,' Stephen countered lightly. He glanced at his watch. 'I must be getting along.' He glanced at me. 'You were speaking of Mrs Small the other day: she's in a pretty bad way; I expect you know.'

I didn't know. I hadn't been for my usual visit the previous day.

'How bad?'

'Pneumonia and that heart of hers–'

Stella spoke:

'Has she anyone to help her, look after her?'

'Only the family – that's the tragedy of these cases.'

'But I could do something,' she cried, her eyes wide with sympathy.

That was so like Stella, always ready to help and quite incapable of the task or the strain imposed.

I said firmly:

'Of course I'll go. If I'd known–'

'Could you come along now?' Stephen asked.

'Yes.' My heart thudded wildly. I had

never hoped for such an opening as this, such a chance to help – even if in a very small capacity. I looked at Allan. 'I can leave Stella in your care... Father is far too absorbed with Diana, talking politics no doubt, to be concerned with my absence.'

Stella pleaded:

'But I could do something–'

'Darling–' My smile embraced her lovingly. 'You'd never stand the atmosphere of the place – let alone anything else. I'll be home probably before you are. Explain to Father.'

I appreciated that to see me leave with Stephen was torture to her and it pained me immeasurably that I, of all people, should be placed in the position thus to inflict it. But, instinctively, I knew that this was the turning point. The idea of her helping in a sick room brought a loving smile to my lips: no one was less suited to the task than she, and I dreaded the very thought of her coming into contact with the germ-ridden atmosphere of the Small home.

Stephen said as we reached his car:

'This is awfully good of you, Lydia.'

'Not in the least.' I smiled. 'They would have sent for me sooner or later, in any case.'

'It's a pretty grim place to which to take you,' he said ruefully.

'I'm used to squalor, too,' I said. 'If one is

genuine in one's desire to help people, one just cannot afford to be squeamish... It was sweet of Stella to offer to help. She's like that but–' A smile. 'Life to her is so very much a matter of pretty pictures, illusions; she has never come up against reality.'

'Do you think,' he said with directness, 'that you are wise thus to protect her, prevent her from trying to grapple with life?'

A tiny flame of resentment flared within me. I answered quietly:

'I think that if I had ever prevented her from trying it would have been most unwise.' I met his gaze very levelly: 'As it is, she is perfectly free to do as she pleases. I hope you don't imagine that I would, in any way, dominate her life.'

'No, no; of course not,' he said hastily. 'Just that, sometimes, it does everyone good to be thrown on one's own resources.'

'Stella would loathe that. One is either the clinging vine or the pioneer; and to change the one into the other merely spells disaster.'

'I understand.' A pause. 'And, of course you are right. Free will, the right of choice, enables us, for the most part, to be ourselves unless circumstances weigh us down with obligations that prevent our life taking its normal course.'

I said softly:

'Above all, I should hate you to misunderstand my solicitude for Stella. It would, obviously, have lessened my responsibility considerably had she been a different type … and yet her very lovableness, her impulsive childishness, more than atones. She reminds me of a playful kitten that will never grow up, and needs cherishing and looking after. Thank heaven for the Stellas: they colour and decorate life and make it eternally gay.'

Stephen looked at me.

'You have a lovely way of looking at things, Lydia.'

'If I have then you must give the credit of it to the capacity I inherited for loving.'

'All or nothing?'

'Yes, Stephen. All or nothing.'

'A dangerous formula, because one stakes all on a throw.'

'So be it,' I answered.

We had reached the Smalls' cottage by this time. It was a tiny, two-storied house containing four rooms and a kitchen which almost opened out on to the street so short was the passage that led to it from the front door. A faint, stale odour permeated the air – a mixture of unwashed bodies and bad cooking. Steam poured from an old-fashioned copper where Silas Small was endeavouring to do the weekly wash and I suspected that every garment had been pushed into the fearsome-looking contraption. He came forward to greet us after the eldest boy, Willie, had admitted us. His unshaven face, and lank hair, completed a picture of dirt and dejection. He wore no collar and his shirt, open at the neck, was no less filthy than his greasy suit.

'She's wus, docter,' he said. 'Coughin' somethin' awful. Fair gives me the creeps it does... Willie, I'll tan the hide off yer if you meddle with that byke agin.'

We went upstairs. Stephen gave the sick woman an injection; I, when his duties were complete, set about the task of washing and attending her, and of cleaning up the room as best I could. An hour later we were ready to leave.

Out in the fresh air – the soft, fragrant breeze of a summer day – we looked at each other.

'You see,' he said, 'what I mean. There's enough work here to last a man a lifetime – as I said before. When I go into those filthy dens I want to tear them down with my hands. But–'

'What?' I prompted.

'Who will listen? All that people are interested in to-day is money, power, success. The voice of a country doctor! Bah! And yet, if it takes me that lifetime I'll have this place made-over before I'm through.' His voice rang with sincerity. 'Someone has to start it; it might just as well be me.' He looked at me earnestly. 'Are you on my side?'

'You know I am. I've always felt the same; that's why I've worked as I have among these people.'

He didn't speak, merely opened the door of the car and handed me in, then moved to his seat beside me.

'I've some drugs to pick up at home,' he said quietly. 'Would you mind if we called there before I take you back?'

'Not at all. I'd love to see inside "the doctor's house".'

'You will hate it,' he said abruptly. 'It's grim and old and wants hundreds spending on it – a barn of a place.'

'But you like it?' I waited, tensed, for his answer.

He gave me a sudden, appealing look.

'Frankly, yes; how did you know?'

'Just your vehemence; had you really disliked it so much you would have left it.'

'You can read people's minds very well, Lydia Drake,' he said with a light laugh. 'You scare me a little.'

I allowed my laughter to mingle with his. A strange affinity flowed between us in those moments. We had been drawn together across that bridge which narrows between life and death; he was beginning to realize my strength, and I knew that was what I wanted most. Just as I wanted him to realize that he could never complete the task upon which his heart was set – at least not alone. And that the woman he chose to help him must be as strong as he and of the same indomitable spirit and courage.

His description of Stoneleigh, his home, was by no means an exaggeration. It was shabby, crumbling with age, old-fashioned in design. I noticed, with satisfaction, however, some exquisite furniture adorning it; antiques that in their rightful setting would look superb and, in imagination, I could picture that setting.

'My grandfather left me the furniture,' he said easily. 'It's rather good – some of it. Come into my den. Useless my apologizing for anything you see around. I haven't the time to be meticulous – except in my work.'

'But you have servants?'

'One; she nearly drives me crazy, but I must have someone to answer the 'phone and take the messages and she *is* efficient at that.' He saw my gaze wandering to a pile of mending that was adorning an arm-chair. 'Yes; pretty sight, isn't it? Pity I didn't learn the art of sewing while I was at school.'

My heart went out to him. Oh, what a change I could make in such a house; what scope there would be. And how fantastic it was that a man of his calibre should be wasted in Milbury...

I said casually:

'The mending problem can soon be

solved. I might just as well do it for three as for two – as I do now.' And with that I stuffed it into a large bag that was the type to stretch to almost unlimited proportions.

'But–'

'No "buts",' I said practically. 'It's time someone took you in hand.'

He showed me around. The rooms were inclined to low ceilings; the cream distemper was chipped and some of it, put over the original paper, now curled back leaving gaping white patches of plaster. A faint smell of disinfectant deadened the mustiness of age. His surgery was austere, white, efficient, and newly decorated. I took in every detail of the instrument cases and drug cabinets. Adjoining it was a one-time dispensary used for the making up of prescriptions which he no longer carried out. I caught his gaze upon me – a reflective gaze.

'Stella,' he said suddenly, 'was intrigued by the X-ray. It's the only one for many miles around – apart from the hospitals, of course. I spent my last bean on it, and it cost over a thousand pounds.'

So Stella had been in that house.

'I can imagine Stella loving that,' I said easily. 'Rather like a toy to her.'

'I suppose so.' His voice sounded flat. It was easy to realize that he was seeing his surroundings as he imagined Stella would judge them and was depressed in consequence.

Suddenly, almost sharply, he asked: 'Lydia – you're quite sure about her and Allan, aren't you?'

My heart sank. Had I to endure that ordeal yet again.

Before I could speak, however, he added: 'Forgive that. It was a foolish and unnecessary question.' I knew that could he have expressed his thoughts he would have added: 'No woman could be expected to live here, anyway – least of all Stella.'

A pang shot through me. How fantastic it was to picture Stella as his wife, enduring the hardships and disappointments of such a life as his, and how thankful I was that my intervention had spared them such a tragedy. I said evenly:

'I think this house could be made quite lovely with a little imagination and distemper. You wait until you marry, Stephen, and see how a woman will transform it. She'd revel in it. No fun in having everything just *there;* the fighting is the fun; the climbing together.'

'Aren't you rather flattering your sex by judging them by yourself?' he said impressively.

'Of course not,' I admonished. 'I'm just average. Obviously you wouldn't marry the helpless type and any other – well!' I managed to smile. 'You see if my words don't come true. Just think of all the things she will be able to do for you? Look after your accounts, case sheets; do a hundred and one things so unobtrusively that you will not be aware of their being done. Manage everything. To a woman with spirit and character who doesn't mind the struggle to reach the stars ... well! I envy her, that's all.' I laughed. 'I could, of course, apply for the job – on a purely platonic basis!' I didn't allow any time to elapse that allowed of his comment as I said: 'I *must* be getting back.'

He exclaimed:

'It's been marvellous to have your help, Lydia. And so encouraging to listen to your views.'

'I'm glad.' I picked up my bag.

'But I do feel it an imposition for you to–'

'Forget it,' I said. 'You just can't go around in rags, you know.' It struck me that his mother and sister might have done something towards looking after him, and it was almost as if he sensed my thoughts as he said:

'Mother and Monica would do them but' – a wry smile – 'I'm afraid they are not exactly fond of needlework – or expert at it, either. Monica did mend some socks for me once and I thought I'd a stone in my shoe when I began to walk!'

He drove me back to the house and then went off on his rounds to those patients in need of a late visit. Standing beside me on the pavement before leaving, he said:

'Thanks for everything, Lydia. May I look in when I've a moment? I get rather weary of my own company sometimes – not that I've time to be alone much.'

'That,' I said quietly, 'is no criterion since your being with others invariably means work. Of course, look in any time: we'd love to see you.'

He moved away then, stepping back, said swiftly:

'I hope Stella will be better; I know you're worried about her. If there's anything I can do – call me up.'

'I will ... but I think that Allan will have to be the doctor in this case.'

'I suppose so ... good-bye, again.'

Stella said to me that evening after father had gone to bed.

'Well, Lydia, you were right. Stephen doesn't care – this afternoon proved it. He seemed to look right through me; it was just as if he were twisting a knife in my heart. And when you went off together I had that shut out feeling, as though I were just an incompetent child... Why is it you never think I can be helpful?'

'Darling!' I tried to sound indulgent. 'For you to have gone into that house! You can't imagine what it was like.'

'I'd appreciate seeing,' she said resolutely. 'Oh, I know how you want to protect me, but it gives everyone such a wrong impression of me. I'm not helpless – I know it deep down inside.'

'Of course you're not,' I said, pandering to her mood. 'But I fail to see that because you are unfitted to tackle an offensive job such as I undertook this afternoon, that it is any reflection upon you.'

'Stephen probably thought so.'

'I'm quite sure he didn't.'

'Meaning that he didn't mention me?'

I said:

'Oh, darling; I'm sorry, but–'

'It's you he likes,' she said softly. 'That's the truth – isn't it?' She leaned forward. 'Please, Lydia, we've never lied or had secrets from each other.'

CHAPTER THREE

Stella's question was one that could easily precipitate a crisis. Everything depended upon the answer I gave her: her future; mine; and Stephen's. It was as if Fate had dealt me a hand and challenged me to play it fearlessly and boldly. My mind went back to that afternoon at Stephen's house; I saw again the chaos that surrounded him, and his desperate need of help – help such as I could so freely and adequately, give. He was a man poised perilously in space, needing some magnetic force to harness the power within him, so that he might, in turn, re-distribute it to a suffering world.

Could Stella – assuming that Stephen returned her love – possibly be that force? Could she do other than complicate his life even to the point of smashing, or retarding, his ambitions to serve humanity? I knew that for him to marry her would encompass his ruin; that his affection could not hope to survive her helpless incompetence, her childlike inefficiency.

And what of her? Could I honestly say that such a marriage would not bring about her doom, also? Could I, through cowardice and squeamishness, turn back from my avowed objective. Deceit and lying were abhorrent to me; the very idea of indulging either caused me acute distress and yet what, now, was the alternative? Here was the crisis: I could separate her from Stephen for ever and, thus, save them both... Or I could, weakly inspire fresh hope in her mind and undo all the good work previously done.

Her question was simple enough. I searched my heart. Didn't I know, already, that Stephen was falling in love with me? That he realized his need of me, and had been drawing closer to me from the moment of our meeting, almost as though our regard were pre-ordained? And I had been selected as the one to inspire him in humanity's cause, and enable him to fulfil ambitions that were noble and of the highest order.

I looked at Stella; she was sitting tensed as she waited; her face pale, even drawn; the thought of hurting her turned that knife once more in my heart and I asked myself why I should have been called upon to bear such an affliction – I who loved her better than anyone in the world and would have sacrificed anything in her cause. The clock ticked into the silence; long afterwards I heard its sound as though imaginary wings were beating as the seconds lengthened, and the suspense became unbearable. She cried:

'Lydia; answer me – answer me. It's you he

likes – isn't it? Don't you see I must know – once and for all.'

I felt that the air had been squeezed from my lungs; that my heart had replaced all the other organs and thumped as in some hollow cavity. I was trembling. And then, as if aware of the responsibility placed upon my shoulders, suddenly I was composed; the conflict was no more. I knew what I had to do. My voice came slowly, but every word was measured.

'I'm afraid it is, Stella. But, don't you realize how terrible this is for me. You're in love with him and that he should choose *me*–'

She started; anguish shadowed her eyes; her lips quivered and then were still. It was like being condemned to watch something that one loves, die. I told myself that I must not weaken; that in a little while she and Allan would find happiness, and she would be secure for all time – secure in that world for which she was made and in which she belonged. This was no more than an adolescent infatuation and I had to treat it as such, no matter how hard it might be.

Her voice was husky; it cracked as she whispered:

'So you *know* that he cares.' She shook her head. 'And I imagined–'

'Darling–' I spoke soothingly. 'Nothing is settled. I've been so torn–'

She cried:

'Because of me?'

'Of course – knowing how you felt. I could never take my own happiness – in any case – at your expense. Although it doesn't lie within the power of any human being to inspire love. And just as if Stephen had loved you, nothing I might have said or done would have prevented it … so it is in reverse.'

Stella leaned forward.

'I've behaved childishly,' she whispered. 'Seeing the reflection of my own love in his eyes, imagining things were as I longed them to be.' She paused. 'But if I thought that my foolishness might in any way spoil your happiness–' She drew in her breath sharply: 'Oh, Lydia, that would be tragedy to me: sheer hell. Don't you see? After all you've done for me, all you mean to me. You must promise – *promise* that–'

I said softly:

'Stella– Oh, Stella.' And my vision was blurred; I felt humbled by her generosity, her love for me.

She came and knelt at my feet.

'You're right for Stephen,' she murmured. 'And I love him well enough to know it; you'll help him achieve all he wants to achieve in Milbury. He'll need your strength, your support, Lydia.'

I felt slightly sick and hastened:

'But you, Stella. I–'

She knelt back on her heels and faced me.

'I don't come into it,' she said with supreme courage. 'I was just – foolish. Don't let's talk of it again.'

'But,' I insisted, 'we must. Oh, darling, I want you to be happy; taken care of. All these years I've been here, and there could be no happiness for me unless you were secure, settled.' I paused and went on significantly: 'If you were to marry Allan, now... Ah, then, *then* I could begin to think about myself.'

Stella said very quietly:

'Meaning that you would refuse to marry Stephen unless I were settled?'

I hesitated.

'That would be intimidation, darling.'

'What we call it doesn't matter,' she said sombrely. 'If it is the truth.'

I felt trapped and exclaimed almost desperately:

'Do you imagine I could marry Stephen knowing you were miserable and–' I broke off.

'And what of Stephen,' she said swiftly. 'Don't you owe him your first consideration.'

I hedged:

'We will think of that when there is something more concrete to go on, Stella. At the moment my concern is you. Even loving Stephen would not divorce me from that loyalty to you and I couldn't snatch my happiness at your expense – desert you in any way.'

She spread her hands appealingly:

'But don't you see the folly of such reasoning. What good would it do me to know that because Stephen *didn't* love me, you and he were to be made miserable? There's no logic, no sense in that anywhere, Lydia. Oh, darling, I know it's just like you, and that you'd always be ready to sacrifice yourself, but only you and Stephen count – you must see that.'

I wanted to force home upon her how closely her actions impinged on mine; and I answered her steadily:

'Put yourself in my place, Stella. If you were happy with someone else and Stephen asked me to marry him I will be quite honest with you and admit that I shouldn't hesitate to say yes... But with your ghost haunting me – oh, you must understand.'

Stella was very quiet; there was suddenly a stillness about her that almost alarmed me. I loathed the part I had been forced to play. She said impressively:

'Then you have nothing to fear, Lydia. I think I can promise you I shall never be that ghost, darling. I may have behaved foolishly, even childishly, over Stephen... But now that I know the facts, I hope I've enough sense to realize that adjustments will have to be made, and that life does not stand still.'

I held my breath. Did she mean that she would marry Allan? That she could, already, see the wisdom of such a marriage.

'On the other hand,' I insisted, 'I could not bear you to feel that any line of action was forced upon you through anything I had said. Oh, it is so difficult to explain.'

She looked at me very levelly, her expression inscrutable:

'We all have free-will, Lydia.'

She had drawn a veil over her feelings, intending to keep it drawn; and I sensed that this was the last conversation we should ever have about Stephen in relationship to her emotions.

'That,' I said, 'can cut both ways, darling.'

She held my gaze almost masterfully:

'If you refused to marry Stephen on my account then it were better you should not marry him – for you wouldn't love him, Lydia.'

Had she turned the tables? I couldn't be sure. My voice was low as I commented:

'Although I might claim to be the only judge of that, I will concede its truth – up to a point. There are degrees of happiness according to one's peace of mind. Suppose we leave it at that, darling. I cannot say more and I can only pray that, eventually, you will understand my point of view.'

She asked, almost abruptly:

'If I married Allan would you give everything to Stephen and be content?'

My heart raced.

'Yes: I should know, then, that you would share my joy and find in Allan that one man most capable of providing you with the things you most need.'

'I see.' It was a solemn sound. A strange smile twisted her lips. 'It's funny, Lydia, how little security means to me. To fight with a man, struggle with him, work by his side and inspire him – that is my idea of true fulfilment.' She laughed but there was a catch in her voice as she added: 'I know – I'd be a hopeless failure.' She laughed cynically: 'Perhaps you're right.'

'I think I know you pretty well,' I said gently. 'You'd not be a failure in the dismal sense, darling, but you could, very easily, wreck your life. I can perhaps see farther ahead than you.'

'Yes,' she said spiritlessly, 'perhaps you can.'

Her mood had changed; the exultation of urging me towards happiness had died, leaving the blank of grim reality from which, now, even hope had been extracted. I argued that I had saved her from herself, and had nothing whatsoever with which to reproach myself. Nothing could be gained without effort. Now, Stella would begin to build along different lines; in a matter of weeks she would have recovered from Stephen completely. And instinct told me that she would turn to Allan – as was intended and right. And it went beyond that to Allan himself. Stella would more than atone for the loss of me; she was fitted to be his wife where I was not. His mild acquiescence would bore me; his family drive me insane; there was no scope in such a marriage for one of my temperament. But for Stella... Yes, I had done well. Out of this crucible of temporary suffering would rise content and happiness for us all. But without my hand to steer the frail ship into harbour, tragedy would have struck, even though the mirage of happiness might first have quivered in its path. It hadn't been easy; but the victory was mine. I breathed deeply as one who has run a hard race. And thought of Stephen. He would never know from what I had saved him; but if he wanted me for his wife then my life would be dedicated to his service. Through me he would rise to great heights; his burdens would be mine...

Stella left me a few seconds later, saying:

'I'm tired, Lydia; bed for me.'

'Anything you'd like brought up?'

She shook her head.

'No thanks.'

I watched her go. Much of her conversation coming back to comfort me. Her eagerness that Stephen and I should be happy...

Stephen and I… How naturally those names linked themselves together seemingly without volition. I sighed and relaxed and allowed myself to dream. And in those moments I knew peace.

Father said at breakfast the next morning:

'Where's Stella?'

'She overslept; she'll be down in a moment.'

He glanced at the door as if expecting to see her standing there. Then:

'I'm afraid that isn't true, Lydia.'

I said sharply:

'What do you mean?'

'That,' he said firmly, 'she hardly slept at all. If she told you she did, then she had good reason for wishing to save you worry.'

'But–'

'I didn't sleep,' he said wearily; 'and my hearing is very acute. Stella was sobbing half the night. What is it, Lydia? She's looked strained and pale, lately. You know her so well that–'

My heart thudded.

'Sobbing! Oh, nonsense, Father! You imagined it. What possible reason has she? We talked together before she went to bed and I can assure you she was perfectly cheerful then.'

He wasn't to be put off.

'I'm sorry, my dear; I know you don't want to believe me, but that is not a matter about which I should be mistaken… Do you think Stephen has anything to do with it?'

I kept very calm, knowing that his peace of mind depended upon my being thus.

'Why – Stephen?… No; if it is anyone, it is Allan. But I think I can set your mind at rest that things will soon be different.'

'Allan! But it was you that he–'

'Isn't that explanation enough?'

'You mean that Stella cares for him?'

'Yes; and that he cares for her – far more than he realizes. I'm not the wife for Allan and he's beginning to see it.' I put out my hand and patted his. 'Don't worry, Father dear; everything will work out. And if Stella were crying … she is really like a child – laughter so soon follows the tears.'

He nodded and relief came into his eyes.

'I don't know what we should do without you, Lydia – you are such a tower of strength and if you assure me that Stella is all right and that there is no need to worry–'

'I do tell you so… Ah, Stella!'

I watched her closely as she came into the room, and beamed at father as she said:

'Ah, Daddy; you should scold me for being late. It's shameful – and you at the marmalade stage, too… No Lydia, no cornflakes; I'm dying for coffee. Not very hungry… Isn't it a heavenly day? I've been thinking that if you are sure there is nothing I can do to help you, that I'd go over to Diana's to-day – just laze in the garden. And perhaps go out with Allan in the evening.'

I flashed father a knowing look to which he responded.

'Darling, of course – you go. Nothing that I can't cope with here. And, in any case, I must go down to Mrs Small this morning...'

Did she flinch? Or was it my imagination. Her eyelids were swollen and although I knew she had rouged her cheeks, the colour in no way concealed the look of strain that defied all make-up. Stella could not hide anything from me: I know her too well. But I hardened my heart; sympathizing would be useless and, indeed, hypocritical in the circumstances; better by far a few tears now than a broken heart later.

Father said anxiously.

'You'll crack up, Lydia, if you go on at this rate. In fact we all need a change, and I'm going to see that we have one. Diana offered me her cottage at Rottingdean for the summer holidays. We could all have a complete rest. And' – he looked at me – 'there's a daily woman who would look after us, Diana said.'

I felt my heart sink. Rottingdean – away from Stephen. I couldn't bear the idea.

'Moving from one house into another isn't a real change, Father,' I said smoothly. 'And, without being selfish, that still leaves the housekeeping to do. I know what you need: a peaceful hotel where you would have companionship and a different life altogether. That is just as vital as the rest for you.'

'But I hate hotels, Lydia.'

I smiled at him indulgently. How hopeless he was – incapable even of appreciating his own tastes or peculiarities.

'That is what you say, Father; but you always enjoy yourself when you get there.'

'And there is the money.' He looked troubled. 'This would be an ideal way out and give us all pleasure.'

I said firmly:

'That is beside the point; the question is what is best for you.'

Stella said with a smile:

'You've lost, Daddy.'

I said sharply:

'What do you mean, Stella?'

She answered me very composedly:

'Only that you always know the right medicine to prescribe for us, darling – even if it tastes unpleasant.'

I felt hurt.

'Is that quite fair?'

'Fair?' She looked at me blankly. 'It was quite fair as I meant it... Heaven knows we need the medicine and are the better for it.'

My heart stopped its racing. I could not bear to feel that I was misunderstood. It wasn't an easy task always to do the right thing for two people who were rather like helpless children.

'You, Father,' I said swiftly, 'need to get away even from us. No one to think about but yourself. As likely as not if we took that cottage, Diana would descend upon us with her host of friends and–'

'Diana would never intrude or take advantage of the fact that she had lent it to us.'

'I'm sure of that,' I hastened; 'but she is so irresponsible. The things, in any case, for which one pays are free from all strings... I'm sure I'm right.'

'I told her we'd be delighted to have the place,' he said awkwardly.

'Then suppose you don't bother about it any more– I'll put that right with her,' I said calmly. 'But, of course, if you want to go down there: it's entirely up to you; I wouldn't persuade you for the world.'

Stella said:

'No, Daddy, if you fancy that kind of holiday–'

'No,' he said swiftly. 'Lydia knows best. Perhaps I do need to get right away.' He turned to me. 'If it isn't leaving you to do all the dirty work... I mean Diana might think it ungracious–'

'She won't,' I said blithely.

'Leave it to Lydia,' Stella said warmly. 'She can arrange anything. If only I had half her power.'

I laughed.

'You have, darling – in a different way...
How about the Atlantic coast of Cornwall –
or–'

'I don't fancy the distance. I'm too tired,'
he said wearily.

I looked at him, admonishingly.

'You cannot hope to get really fit without
some effort, you know.'

He nodded.

'You shame me,' he said gently. 'Very well,
Lydia: I'll do anything you say.' And as if having reflected upon the possibilities, added: 'I
can see your point, my dear.'

I poured Stella out her coffee. Life seemed
suddenly to have levelled itself out. I was
happy as one joying in the care of others and
seeing the fruits of my labours reflected in
the content and happiness that resulted
from those labours. In a little while Stella
and Allan would be settled and, if Fate so
decreed, so would Stephen and I.

It was that same evening, on her return
from the Westburys', that Stella said – in
answer to my observation that she was
home early:

'Allan had a masonic dinner engagement...
By the way, Stephen brought me home from
there.'

A strange tingling went down my spine.

'Really.'

'He looked most dreadfully tired, Lydia.'

92

'Overwork.'

She traced a pattern on the arm of her chair with the end of a piece of paper she had nervously twisted into shape.

'I can't quite understand him; I can't explain, but he talks in riddles to me.'

'Darling!' My voice was indulgent.

'I'm serious, Lydia. He said he hoped my life would be very happy and all my wishes be fulfilled.'

'Is that so strange?' My heart was thumping rapidly. It was as if all the suspense returned and with it the ghost of danger.

'Not in itself; only his inflection made it so: he is like a man keeping something in check all the time. I just can't explain.'

I said softly:

'Perhaps he wanted to confide in you.' I stopped, for she could not conceal the sudden pain that was reflected in her eyes. She said, with an attempt at carelessness:

'Of course – about you. Now I understand what he meant when he spoke of a man's hands being tied and his position not allowing him to fight to win a woman's love.'

'And what was your answer?' My lips felt dry; a hollow sensation struck at the pit of my stomach; a certain unbearable tension crept into the atmosphere.

She said unevenly:

'I told him that a woman was always in a far more invidious position because, in no circumstances, could she betray her love to the man, and had to bear the torture and suspense of waiting for him to speak.'

Relief came mercifully as her words died away. Nothing she could have said was more likely to substantiate my story about her regard for Allan and the situation between them.

My voice was husky, unlike my own as I prompted:

'Did he agree with you?'

'I don't know.' She rested her head back against her chair in a gesture of infinite weariness. 'He just looked at me very strangely and said in an odd kind of voice: "You will not have to endure that for very long I am quite sure."' She added shakily: 'Just for a terrible moment I thought he had guessed.' There was an abrupt pause. Then, lightly, as though the subject were closed, she went on conversationally: 'Don't you think it would have been rather nice for us to have accepted Diana's offer of the cottage for the holidays? Why don't you want to go – is it Stephen?'

I stared at her.

'My dear girl, just as if I should allow my own feelings to stand in the way of anything likely to benefit either father or you. No; I gave my reasons. Father should really get away – right away from us. It would do him good. And … if we can avoid being indebted to Diana so much the better.'

'I can't quite understand why you don't like her, Lydia.'

'It isn't a question of not liking her–'

'But you don't like her – do you?'

I hated to appear ungenerous or critical and replied:

'I don't like some of the things she does – but that is a different matter... Darling, you look awfully tired. How about going to bed early?'

She sighed.

'Not a bad idea, Lydia... And what of you?'

'I am rather weary,' I admitted. 'I've been on the go, every second since I got up.'

'Stephen said how wonderful you'd been to Mrs Small... I wish I'd said something different to him to-day; something that–'

I cried:

'Never mention me – hint in any way that–'

'All right,' she said gently. 'I shouldn't have done but, after all, I could have reassured him that, since he loves you, his position would only add to your love and give you the additional joy of helping him... That's someone at the door.'

I went swiftly to answer it. Then:

'Stephen!'

He looked at me.

'Could you come right away. Mrs Small –

I can't get a nurse for love nor money.'

'Of course; but–'

'Miscarriage,' he said briefly. 'I've just left her; but there must be someone–'

Stella came and stood framed in the doorway; the light shining behind her gave her an almost unearthly beauty; her dark, slumberous eyes going straight to Stephen as if finding their only natural resting place. I saw a muscle in his cheek twitch; the line of his jaw tighten, and felt the tension mounting between them as if some magnetic force had been released. She said:

'I could help.' And her words were quiet but firm.

He said almost curtly:

'No, Stella; this isn't a job for you.'

'Then,' she persisted. 'I'll wait up; you'll need coffee, sandwiches. I'd like to feel I'm not quite a sawdust doll... Lydia, better take something warm; you'll want it later... I shall,' she said resolutely, 'sit up' – this in answer to my request that she should go straight to bed. And for the first time I knew that argument was useless.

Stephen and I left the house together. I tried to concentrate on the task ahead; but the vision of Stella and the look I had intercepted between them lingered to haunt me.

He said crisply:

'Do you know anything about these cases?'

'Quite a bit; they're not infrequent in Milbury. This is one time I cannot feel sorry; heaven knows she can do without any more children.'

'The problem is to pull her through, Lydia – in her state at the moment. There are the others; without her... It's grim,' he added gently. 'Unpardonable of me to come to you; I've no earthly right to drag you into all this but–'

'You know there is nothing I wouldn't do,' I said and my voice was low. 'This is the life I love, and for which I was intended – serving humanity, as you do, only in my own humbler way.'

'Strange,' he mused; 'I remember asking you that night we first met if you knew of a family named Small–'

'And said their name was a misnomer–'

'You have a good memory, Lydia.'

'So have you.'

He glanced at me swiftly and swerved the car into the pavement outside the house. A light burned from the upper window and the whimpering of a child came mournfully to our ears.

For the next hour Stephen fought to save that flickering flame of life and I did all that lay within my power to help him. But I knew, even as he looked at me across that still, inert figure, the battle was lost. He shook his head, his fingers creeping up the almost lifeless arm in the hope of finding the pulse that was to beat no more…

I said shakenly:

'Oh, *Stephen!*'

He led me away, down the stairs, to the front door.

'Wait for me in the car. The children are asleep, thank God; and you've done enough for one night.'

I sat tensed, watching for him to reappear; longing for his presence, unable to concentrate even on the tragedy of death, because so vital and insistent was the pulse of life and of love beating within me.

And at last he came, throwing his bag on to the back seat in a gesture of unutterable weariness.

'Afraid I shall have to take you out of your way– I promised I'd call at the Undertaker: Small, poor devil, can't leave those kids.'

We drove back into the town. Cool, soft air fanned our cheeks, refreshing and re-vitalizing us. I thought and it was as balm to my soul: this is an experience shared; an experience drawing us ever closer…

It was just before we finally reached home that Stephen said jerkily:

'It's so trite to say that you've been wonderful, Lydia. But you have. There's something about you – a calm, a resourcefulness–'

I said softly:

'Perhaps ... but you inspired both, Stephen.'

The car slowed down almost to a stand-still.

'I'd like to drive and keep on driving,' he murmured.

'I know... I'd love it too.'

'Then–' He turned to me abruptly.

Our nerves were taut; emotion surged between us. I think my heart must have shone in my eyes for him to see. Almost without volition, I put out my hand and felt his strong, firm grasp.

'Lydia,' he whispered.

The car stopped. We were home. But the spell was not broken, and the darkness lent it wings as I turned and pressed closer to him and it seemed that the very night itself offered us sanctuary.

'You need me, Stephen,' I murmured. 'I want to help you so much.'

'Need you,' he echoed, and I knew that this was the moment when Fate might give him into my keeping; a moment when, tired, weary, he would realize all that I had to offer, and find it impossible to resist the temptation to turn from the harbour and battle, alone, against the turbulent sea of his own loneliness.

'Oh, my dear,' I breathed.

I could feel his body tensed beside mine and I waited in an agony of suspense for him to continue.

His voice came breathlessly, urgently:

'Lydia, if I asked you to marry me... We could do so much, you and I–' He stopped as one living in a dream. Then: 'I'd no right to say that. I–'

'You've every right,' I whispered triumphantly. 'And my answer is yes, Stephen... Yes, I will marry you.'

He looked at me a trifle dazed, uncertain. Then, almost fiercely he said:

'I've nothing to offer you except–'

I silenced him.

'I love you,' I said slowly. 'I loved you from that first moment ... and you are the only man in this world who has anything to offer me, Stephen; the only man I have ever wanted to marry – the only man I shall ever love.'

At that second, the door of the cottage opened and Stella stepped on to the pavement.

Stephen said involuntarily:

'Stella!'

'I thought I heard the car... I've been so worried about you... Lydia, are you all right?'

Something about me as I moved beside her arrested her attention for she jerked her head up and looked at me – almost in terrified inquiry.

I said shakily:

'Darling, I want you to know – to be the very first to know – Stephen has just asked me to marry him.'

CHAPTER FOUR

In the moments that followed there was an atmosphere impossible to describe. It was as if the very pulse of life itself stopped while Stella drew in her breath sharply before saying in a voice curiously shaken:

'All the happiness in the world' – she glanced swiftly at Stephen – 'to you both.'

We moved from the flickering shadows of the night into the light of the sitting-room. A sense of unreality stole upon me, as if the reaction of recent events, and the nervous strain attendant upon them, took their toll in the face of victory. I was going to marry Stephen; to look after him and give him the help and inspiration he so sorely needed: I should be indispensable to him. It was an exulting thought.

His silence was a little unnerving and I looked at him with faint apprehension as he sank down into the nearest chair, as one dazed by the impact of sudden emotion. He was watching Stella as she began, rather feverishly, to pour out the coffee already awaiting us. It was a wondering, baffled look in which was the unmistakable reflection of pain concealed. I intercepted the glance she gave him, and found that my heart-beats quickened. The dark intensity of her expression smote me; she reminded me of a wounded bird trailing a broken wing and hoping that none might realize her hurt.

'It has,' I said, suddenly hating the silence, 'been an exhausting evening.' I smiled at Stephen. 'And a most unusual one in which to become engaged.'

'And Mrs Small?' Stella handed Stephen the coffee as she spoke.

He raised his gaze to hers.

'She's dead,' he said dully.

Instantly, she exclaimed:

'Oh!' It was an eloquent little gasp. Then: 'It must be dreadful for you.'

I said indulgently:

'For Stephen?'

'Yes,' came the quiet reply; 'I can almost imagine that the death of a patient is curiously a doctor's loss – no matter how impersonal he may be.'

Again, it was as if some strange understanding flowed between them that brought me perilously near to the edge of jealousy as Stephen answered:

'That is exactly it. One always feels a sense of helplessness and as if something more should have been done – even when one knows it wasn't possible.'

I moved nearer to him. Our glances met and he smiled, rather as a man drawn back to the realization of his personal happiness.

'Lydia has been marvellous,' he said swiftly. 'I think she should have gone in for my profession.'

My hand touched his and a thrill went through my body.

'Marrying you is the next best thing, Stephen: in fact a far better thing than any career in the world.'

'I'm honoured.' It was a clipped sound.

His attitude puzzled me slightly; rather as if he had withdrawn himself from me, changed his mood as his spirits revived and the effect of the evening's ordeal lessened. The hateful fear stabbed lest his proposal had been merely an impulse which could easily be regretted in the more sober light of reflection. A weak moment of strain and emotionalism, even loneliness and he had turned to me as he might, conceivably, have turned to any other woman in my place, whom he had liked. I resisted the insidious lie. Stephen was in love with me; he was not the type to make a false move and, obviously, he had intended asking me to marry him; any reluctance was purely on account of his material insecurity. Had he not expressed that view even to Stella, quite apart from me?

Nevertheless, it was as if the elation and thrill of my victory had fallen flat; as if both Stella and Stephen were averse to commenting upon it: the announcement had been made and the matter ended there. Somehow I felt cheated. It was, however, easy to account for the atmosphere which, I argued, was created mostly by me. Knowing of Stella's regard for Stephen was a distinct handicap, because I could not bear to rub salt in her wounds by any undue hilarity. And wasn't it conceivable that Stephen, believing her to be in love with – but not yet engaged to – Allan, might feel the same reticence?

It was as if Stella read my thoughts and felt it encumbent upon her to revert to the subject of Stephen and me, as she said glibly:

'So we are to be related, Stephen. A doctor in the family. So convenient!'

'But not,' he said tensely, 'unwelcome, I hope.'

'On the contrary.' She spoke swiftly. 'More sandwiches? I'm not such an adept at them as Lydia, but I think they are eatable.'

'You have made them very nicely,' said Stephen.

'Thus speaks elder brother to little sister,' she challenged laughingly. 'Thank you.'

I saw him start and then, almost with determination, draw her gaze to his master-fully, almost possessively, as he replied:

'You know I didn't mean it that way.'

I could see that she was trembling; her

eyes were no more than dark smudges in her pale, flower-like face.

'I'm sorry,' she murmured softly and, composing herself, added: 'When is the wedding to be?'

I answered her.

'Very soon; Stephen needs looking after.'

He interposed.

'It is rather early to make decisions.'

A tiny flame of fear flicked across my heart. There was a certain quiet resistance in his attitude, as of a man who would be unlikely to have his plans made for him. I knew, instinctively, he resented the fact that, materially, he had so little to offer; and I argued that no matter what I might say, his outlook and intentions would be coloured and affected by his position. Confidence returned however: I should be able to make him understand how little that phase of things counted to me.

'I,' said Stella, 'should hate a long engagement.'

Stephen looked at her and then abruptly glanced away as he commented:

'Circumstances alter cases.'

'But,' I said, with a light laugh, 'adjustments can always be made.'

Stella said quickly:

'I think it's time I went to bed.' There was something in her manner which suggested that we were anxious to be alone.

Stephen got to his feet.

'And I must be going; I'm keeping you both up.'

A sharp disappointment assailed me. I wanted him to myself; I wanted his kiss and his words of devotion; everything, now, had the strain of an anti-climax. It struck me that Stella could have left us alone immediately after wishing us happiness and, then, I despised myself for the ungenerous and unwarranted thought.

Stephen moved into the hall. Stella put one foot on the stairs and said hastily:

'Good night.'

She was, I knew, perilously near to breaking point. The next second she had vanished; we heard her bedroom door close and, suddenly, I had a tormenting vision of her standing pressed against it, fighting the sobs and the emotion that engulfed her. That was, I chided myself, pure weakness on my part; a sentimentalizing of the situation – the one thing I must guard against at all costs.

Stephen looked somewhat anxiously up the stairs.

'Her nerves are strung to breaking point, Lydia.'

I didn't want to talk of Stella just then. But I said:

'Things will work out; it is inevitable that our engagement should emphasize her regard for Allan and all that goes with it.'

He looked grim.

'He must be a blind fool,' he said with sudden vehemence.

'Stephen!'

'Sorry.'

My heart was racing. I felt slightly sick. The shadow of Stella seemed to fall between us. I mastered the emotion and looked up at him; my voice was low, suggestive as I murmured:

'Stephen?'

'Yes.'

'Do I have to *say* it?'

For answer, he put his arms around me and bent his lips to mine. I clung to him, thrilled, ecstatic; my senses swimming. Then, abruptly, he released me.

'Good night, my dear,' he said thickly and almost before I had time to speak, the front door had opened, and closed, behind him.

Was it my imagination, the over-anxiety to be loved, that made me feel his caress had lacked all passionate fervour? Was it that I had underestimated my own emotionalism which would prove insatiable without an equal fervour from him? I thrust the conflicting thoughts aside. What else was important beside the fact that I was to be his wife. Why seek to rush matters before he had been given time to adjust himself to the step he had taken. Adjust himself … I resisted the idea. What was there to adjust? My mind went back over the events of the evening. I heard again his voice saying: 'Lydia, if I asked you to marry me ... we could do so much you and I–' My spirits soared. How absurd to allow fear to impinge upon my happiness. Stephen was not the type of man to waste words, or indulge in any effusiveness.

Father took the news with a quiet acceptance that was slightly irritating. It was as if he had not wholly refuted the idea that Stella cared for Stephen. Or was it, I asked myself, that, knowing the facts, I projected them into his mind. I found myself saying a trifle sharply:

'You don't seem very elated, Father.'

He stared almost guiltily.

'My dear, of course I am. Stephen is a fine man.' He glanced anxiously at the door. 'Does Stella know?'

Impatience possessed me.

'Yes. Why?'

'No reason but–'

'Don't tell me you still imagine–'

He interrupted.

'I imagine nothing, Lydia; all I'm interested in is your happiness and hers.'

I persisted.

'And could you ever seriously believe that Stella would be the wife for a penniless, struggling doctor?'

'I made no such suggestion.'

'But you were thinking it, afraid, shall we say, lest Stella's feelings were involved and that she, too, cared for Stephen – despite the fact that I've already told you it is Allan whom she really loves.'

'If I was guilty of that,' he replied, 'it is no reflection on you, my dear. We cannot help what we feel.'

I wasn't satisfied; I could not live with that ghost in his mind.

'You have no need to be concerned for Stella: she and Allan will be engaged before many weeks are over your head – you'll see. I thought you had more respect for my judgment.'

He looked at me very earnestly:

'I have infinite respect for your judgment.'

'Then believe me, now,' I said urgently.

He hesitated then:

'I do. You lend such strength, such force, to any argument.'

Stella appeared in that second. Outwardly, she was blithe, even gay, as she said:

'Well, Father, we're soon to have a doctor in the family. Good news, isn't it?'

'Splendid.'

'Puts ideas into my head,' she said calmly and, for once I could not fathom her mood. 'My turn next.' A laugh. 'But being less noble than my sister, I think I shall seek the comforts of life.' She smiled broadly.

I plunged.

'Allan?'

Her face was a mask in that second; there was something inscrutable about her expression; something withdrawn in her attitude. She glanced at father and then said lightly:

'You know, Daddy, the very worst thing about Lydia is that one can never keep a secret from her. She's always a jump ahead of us – isn't she?'

He laughed and met my gaze. I knew that he was satisfied I was, after all, right. Stella could not have said anything better in her desire to hide her hurt and save her pride.

'Always,' he said gaily, relief in his voice. 'That is why she's so invaluable.'

I handed them their tea and served the breakfast.

'Would you care to write me out a testimonial, you two?' I said banteringly.

'Love it,' Stella said smoothly. 'Shall we give it to Stephen? Or maybe that would be superfluous since he knows your virtues, as you know his.'

'Stephen,' said father, 'will go a very long way.'

Stella sipped her tea.

'Stephen isn't interested so much in going a long way as in the right direction,' she said quietly. 'His ambitions are not material: but idealistic. I wonder if he will ever realize them; ideals aren't easy to live up to.' She looked at me. 'But with Lydia beside him he should achieve all that upon which he has set his heart.'

There was something intimate in the way she spoke – after the manner of one who knows instinctively what Stephen's innermost desires were, and I felt that I might be pardoned the faint jealousy that stirred within me.

Father nodded.

'He's a lucky man ... are you thinking of being married quickly, Lydia?'

I said very deliberately:

'Yes, if we can ... but, you know, I can hardly desert you two – can I?' I paused. 'I could never be happy unless you were settled and looked after.'

Father gave a lovingly impatient sound.

'I can soon fix that.'

My gaze turned to Stella.

'And Stella?'

Stella answered swiftly:

'What is to prevent my carrying on in your place?'

I smiled indulgently.

'Darling, it would be far, far too much for you – wouldn't it, Father?'

'Yes,' he said quietly. 'Far too much. But, you must not think of sacrificing yourself for us, my dear. We'll manage and–'

I shook my head.

'I shall not marry until my mind is at rest about you both – that is definite. Of course,

Father, you couldn't do better than move in with Mr and Mrs Lane; they've plenty of room and you could take your treasures with you, and be spared any further bother with a house. There, with them, you'd have the boon of companionship and, at the same time, privacy and since she and Mummie were such devoted friends–'

Father said:

'That would be a solution, but not until Stella is settled.'

I looked at Stella.

'She will be settled,' I said softly. 'I could never be happy unless my charges were well taken care of, you know.'

Father gave me an indulgent smile.

'Thinking of us, even when you're on the threshold of your own great happiness. But we cannot have you making any more sacrifices.'

I glowed at his generosity and said:

'I'm going to see Diana about the cottage this morning.'

Father hastened:

'Don't you think that, after all–'

'Now,' I said severely, chidingly, 'no more argument on that score! You've got to get right away and I mean to see that you do.' I glanced at Stella. 'How do you feel about going with father?'

She started almost guiltily and I knew that the thought made no appeal. Was it because she hated being away from Milbury – and Stephen? That, even though she knew he was going to marry me, she still preferred the torment of seeing him to the torture of being away entirely. It occurred to me that it would give me a much needed respite to have the house to myself for a week or two; to be free from responsibility, yet, at the same time, to know that both father and Stella were enjoying themselves and that such freedom imposed no loss on either.

She said with some directness:

'No, Lydia; there's the expense and–' She stopped, faint colour coming into her cheeks.

'And Milbury,' I said slowly, 'has its attractions?'

She stared at me and winced. I realized that, while I had spoken thus for father's benefit and peace of mind, my words were open to misconstruction from her point of view, since I was aware of her regard for Stephen. I managed to change the subject. Father was, I knew, reassured and that was, after all, the vital issue.

Stephen called an hour or so later, after Surgery, and on his way to his first patient.

'Darling,' I murmured softly, thrilling to his presence. 'How lovely to see you.'

Stella, on her way upstairs, paused in the hall.

'Good morning, Stephen.'

His voice was low as he answered her.

'Good morning Stella…'

She made no attempt to intrude, but passed us and went up to her room. I said swiftly:

'Stephen, I want your help over Stella.'

He started.

'*My* help?' He followed me into the sitting-room. 'In what way?'

'In the professional sense. You can see for yourself just how she is. Not sleeping, very little appetite. Something must be done to save her from herself,' I added firmly.

A rather hard note came into his voice as he said:

'I'm a doctor – not a magician. No doctor on earth can prescribe the cure for what you believe to be Stella's complaint.'

I frowned slightly.

'What I *believe* to be?'

He lowered his gaze.

'Very well: what you know to be.'

'Stella,' I insisted, 'must be forced out of her present mood.'

'And how do you propose to achieve that? Human beings are not puppets, Lydia, to move as one pulls a string, you know.'

'I was not,' I said, feeling slightly on edge, 'suggesting they were. I think that it would do Stella all the good in the world to get out of Milbury for a while; go away with father, for instance.'

'A "change",' he said somewhat cynically. 'One takes one's misery with one, my dear. I'm afraid I don't subscribe to the prescription of a bottle of tonic and a holiday as the panacea for all ills.'

I looked at him very levelly.

'And I hoped you would give me credit for having more intelligence than to suggest you do... My reasons for getting Stella out of Milbury are far more subtle. I think that Allan would follow her; that her absence is just what he needs to make him realize how deeply he cares for her.'

'The woman running away in order to be brought back – eh?'

'If you like.'

'Don't you think it is rather Stella's affair? If she is so much in love with Allan surely she would think along such lines – were it in her interest to do so.'

It was like hitting myself against a brick wall; I felt instinctively that Stephen was not in sympathy with my views and said, aware of a certain wrankling sense of injustice, because my concern for her welfare was not given the consideration it merited:

'Stella is wholly incapable of knowing the right course to adopt, Stephen. You must give me credit for understanding her weaknesses.' I added with conviction: 'What is more, I am in her confidence.'

He sensed my attitude and spoke gently:

'My dear, I do understand; but I wonder if you quite realize how dangerous it is to try to live other people's lives for them.' Hastily, he added: 'Even though your motives are the most worthy and unselfish.'

I protested:

'The last thing I want to do is to live her life for her, Stephen, but even being the very poorest psychologist teaches me that for any young girl to mope about–' I stopped. 'However, if you don't see things my way, I wouldn't try to influence you. Stella must take her chance. I just felt that she needed a little help, direction, if you like, and that it would be so very much more effective coming from you than from me.'

'Does she want to go away?'

'She doesn't know what she wants.'

'Beyond Allan, I presume.'

'Exactly.' I hated being forced to pretend, but I was fighting for Stella and felt that fact absolved me.

'I'll see what I can do,' he promised. 'Perhaps you are right, after all.'

Stella came downstairs just before Stephen left; she was dressed in readiness to go out. Stephen said:

'Can I give you a lift anywhere?'

'No, thank you,' she said politely. 'I'm only going to the shops.'

I watched her very carefully; it was as if some power emanated from her as she looked at him; as if her love was some vibrant force drawing him to her and I knew that it hurt me. Just as I knew how bad it was for her to encourage, and dwell upon, her own unrequited emotions. There was no question about it: her salvation would be to get away... I might persuade Allan to join her and now that Stephen and I were engaged such persuasion might carry more weight.

'I want to go to see Diana,' I put in swiftly. 'Could you run me near there, Stephen?'

'Of course,' he replied. 'If you don't mind starting right away.'

I had the stupid feeling as of not wanting to leave him and Stella alone together and it was as if she read my thoughts as she murmured:

'I'll be going, Lydia... Anything you want?'

I felt better.

'Nothing darling, thank you. Don't tire yourself... I've been telling Stephen that I'm worried about you–'

Stephen took my cue.

'As the doctor in the family,' he began.

Stella forestalled him. I had a strange, uncanny and curiously disturbing feeling that she had shut me out as she said:

'You wish to give me advice – is that it?'

'Have you any objection?'

'None.' Her smile was inscrutable. She looked at me very directly. 'Lydia wants me to go away with father and I'm quite certain you agree with her.'

I said, puzzled by her attitude:

'It isn't a question of my wanting you to go, Stella, but of feeling that the holiday would do you good. And–'

Her voice was calm, almost too calm, as she said:

'It's all right; I'm going. That will spare you so much persuasion, darling – won't it?'

'I don't quite follow,' I said sharply. 'What has persuasion to do with it? I was only looking at it all for your good.'

'I'm sure you were ... good-bye, Stephen... I'll be back for lunch.'

She went out of the house, leaving me oddly upset.

Stephen said quietly:

'Well, that problem has solved itself apparently.'

'I just don't understand her attitude,' I said in bewilderment.

'Was there an "attitude"? She merely told you she was going to do as you wished.'

I protested.

'But it was as if I had imposed that wish and she had resigned herself to it with a martyred air.'

He gave me a swift glance.

'I rather think you're imagining things, my dear.'

'I know Stella.' I hated being forced into such a discussion, and knew the extreme danger of making her an issue.

'I should stop worrying about her,' he suggested.

I sighed.

'Stella has always been an anxiety, Stephen … but now that I have you it will seem so much less great and–'

He interrupted me.

'I'm afraid I must hurry you, Lydia.' He looked at his watch as he spoke.

'Sorry … I'll just get my hat.'

My emotions were churning within me as I sat beside him on that journey to Diana's. The vision of Stella kept obtruding; was it defiance, challenge, in her voice or was I, even as Stephen had said, worrying unduly about her? Usually it was all so simple; this time, however, there lingered that faint uncertainty as, for the first time, I found it impossible to gauge Stella's thoughts, and hated being at such a disadvantage which, after all I had done for her, seemed so unfair.

Silence fell between Stephen and me as we drove together. I was aware of a certain strain not altogether divorced from disappointment; his rather phlegmatic and almost un-loverlike attitude puzzled me. I found myself saying:

'What have you in mind for our future, darling?'

'You mean – our marriage?'

'Yes.' I smiled. 'What else? I want to help

you – oh, so much.'

'I've no right to impose on you,' he said, and I felt his mood changing. 'Everyone leans on you and–'

'For you to do so, would be heaven to me,' I said, and my voice shook with emotion. Then: 'Of course, I'd hate to set the pace, but to waste precious time when we might be together, doing so much for humanity. I know just how I could smooth things for you, Stephen.'

'Bless you.' He was moved and I knew it. But nothing more definite was said. He left me at Diana's and promised to 'phone me later in the day.

Diana Westbury heard the news of the engagement and said very bluntly:

'You surprised me, Lydia. I thought Stella was–' She stopped and eyed me with obvious suspicion. I writhed under her scrutiny. This woman had always hated me, I told myself, for not loving her son. Never had my dislike of her been more intense or, I felt, more justified. I refused to discuss the matter with her as I went on coldly:

'I've come about the cottage, Diana. It was most kind of you to offer it to us for the holidays, but father feels, on reflection, that a complete change would be more beneficial. He and Stella have decided to go to Cornwall.'

'I see.' Her voice was clipped, calm. 'And

are you quite sure that the decision is theirs and not yours? And that, in truth, you are the only one who doesn't want to go to the cottage?'

I stared at her aghast.

'What do you mean?'

'I can,' she retorted, 'tell you in a very few words, Lydia. You are probably the most dangerous hypocrite I've ever had the misfortune to meet, because everything you do, while appearing to be self-sacrificing and for the good of others, nevertheless always turns out to your own advantage and as you wish it. You've dominated your father's life and now you are dominating Stella's in precisely the same way. They think that you wear a halo and you smugly allow them to do so. Well, I see you as you are; you've never fooled me for an instant. One of these days life will catch up with you and you'll be forced to pay your debts.'

I felt suddenly very sick as I cried:

'You must be mad. Every moment of my life, since mother died has been devoted to father and Stella; my concern has been wholly for their happiness... Stella to me is as a daughter–'

'For whom you'd sacrifice anything?'

'Yes, what is more, everyone knows that to be true,' I said confidently.

She stared at me.

'Everyone knows precisely what you want

them to know,' she said firmly.

My conscience was clear; nothing could shake me. I was justified in the knowledge that, at all times, I had done my duty, never shrinking even from the most unpleasant task if it was for the ultimate good of those dependant upon me and whom I loved: thus would it always be. Very quietly I replied:

'I can forgive you all this, Diana, because I know that you are bitter and prejudiced against me for not marrying Allan. Otherwise I might be tempted to argue in my own defence. As it is–' I shook my head. 'It would be beneath me.'

She gave me a swift, critical glance as she answered:

'If there is one thing more than another I thank God for, it is that you refused my son, Lydia. In your heart you know that to be true. I pity Stephen: little does he know what lies ahead for him.'

I refused to discuss the matter. This episode bore out the truth of all I had felt about Diana. She was an unbalanced person, not to be taken seriously for a moment; a person of violent antagonisms and pre-conceived notions, who wasn't capable of knowing the meaning of the word sacrifice.

'I hardly think that remark bears comment from me. I am more than fortified by the knowledge of how greatly Stephen needs me in his work, and of what use I can be to him.'

Diana's eyes seemed to burn into mine, but they in no way unnerved me. I could stand the fire of her criticism and I told myself that she appreciated the fact. I knew my duty and if, in pursuing it, I was subjected to injustice and unwarranted criticism from those incapable of seeing beneath the surface, or of giving me credit for all that had been achieved, then so be it.

She said slowly:

'You are a very, very clever woman, Lydia. But one day others will see through you – as I do.'

I smiled, almost exhilarated by my own immunity from her barbs. And at that moment Allan came into the room. I told him my errand and the decision about the cottage. To my delight he said:

'I think your father is perfectly right. Nothing like getting right away among the atmosphere of fresh people. The cottage is fine, but it would merely be a home from home... What are you going to do?'

'Remain in Milbury,' I said firmly.

Diana said, and her voice rang through the room:

'Lydia has some news for you: she and Stephen are to be married.' And with that she went from the room.

'So,' Allan said, 'that is final, Lydia?'

'Yes.' I gazed at him earnestly. 'Allan, I want your good wishes. You'll look back on all this one day and realize–'

'Stella again?' It was a strangely arrested sound.

'Yes – Stella. You're so fond of her Allan.' I lowered my voice. 'If I could see you two happy; Stella secure–' I shook my head. 'But perhaps such joy is not for me.'

He studied me with great earnestness.

'You're a strange woman, Lydia. You know I'm in love with you and yet you want me to marry your sister.'

'Because,' I said resolutely, 'I firmly believe that you and she belong together and that already you care for her very deeply. I should make you most unhappy. Oh, Allan, if only you could realize–'

'It means a great deal to you – doesn't it? I mean Stella's happiness.'

'Everything.'

'But unless she happened to care for me in return – in any case–'

'She does care... Allan, promise me something.'

'What?'

'Go down to Cornwall while she and father are there. See how things go, how you feel.'

He sighed. Then:

'Very well.' It was a resigned sound. 'But I'm too fond of Stella ever to deceive her, or undertake any step unless I know I can make her happy.'

I nodded. Now that Stephen and I were engaged Allan's emotional response to Stella would be very different and he would, I knew, turn to her. Proximity; a holiday together... I had no fears.

Stella was very subdued on my return home. I said:

'Darling ... what is it?'

She started, then:

'Have you and Stephen decided when you will be married?'

'That depends entirely on you,' I said quietly. 'I could never leave here unless you were secure and settled. You convinced me, darling, that I had every right to accept his love, despite your feelings, but this is different.'

'But—' It was a cry. 'That's absurd. Stephen needs you and—'

I smiled at her tenderly.

'So do you.'

She moved away from me and then turned back to me saying sharply:

'Are you suggesting, Lydia, that only if I were to marry Allan—'

I interrupted instantly:

'That is the last thing, Stella: such an attitude would savour of an ultimatum: we've touched upon all this before.'

'Nevertheless,' she persisted, 'the fact remains that if I were to marry Allan – assuming he asked me to do so – then you would feel free to do whatever Stephen might wish?'

I didn't hesitate.

'That's true enough; but–' I added: 'I want only your happiness, darling.'

Her eyes seemed to darken in pain and, then, to become strangely resolute of expression as she said:

'Then if Allan asks me to be his wife, I shall say "yes".'

CHAPTER FIVE

The conflict and tumult died within me as I heard Stella's words; the possibility of her happiness and future security increased the tempo of my own joy and gave to my engagement to Stephen the full measure of radiant satisfaction. To be torn between two loyalties was the most distressing of all positions, and it seemed that my life had been a succession of such hardships, even though I had steadfastly refused to regard them in that light. I said gently:

'You will find great happiness, darling – I know that. Allan will take care of you and–'

She interrupted with what seemed to me to be a certain abruptness:

'Security in marriage, Lydia, is something that has never appealed to me. I prefer the romance and uncertainty that so often accompanies it.'

I smiled into her rather solemn eyes. How very young she was; how full of pre-conceived ideas and notions about herself which bore no relation whatsoever to the fundamental truth. That was the greatest danger and I had always known it and vowed that, so far as it lay within my power, I would safeguard her from herself. Now, if things took their normal course, that would no longer be necessary: Allan would guide and restrain and care for her even as I had done and, as I, would love her deeply and devotedly.

'One has, darling, to be suited to the gruelling test of uncertainty; you were made for something better, gayer.'

She looked at me almost boldly:

'Suppose – just suppose, Lydia – that Stephen had fallen in love with me, you believe that I should have been utterly incapable and incompetent as a doctor's wife in his circumstances?'

I said soothingly:

'If I do, darling, it is no reflection whatsoever on you. We cannot all be cast in the same mould; we each have our niche to fill in life and to do so within the framework of our own particular abilities, is to succeed and fulfil our destiny.'

'Meaning that you were intended to minister to others: I, to be ministered to?'

'Exactly; one might say that we are two halves of a circle – each vital to the other.'

She studied me very intently:

'And you will be content to live in Milbury, fight with Stephen so that his ambitions and ideals may be realized – even though, materially, it will be a struggle?'

I felt my heart-beats quicken as I answered:

'Naturally; helping him will be my great

purpose in life. My ambitions for him–'

She interposed.

'Might not those ambitions clash with his conception of success?'

I stared at her; there was something baffling and inscrutable about her as she stood there.

'I hardly think that likely,' I answered very quietly, 'since my ambitions for him are indivisible with those he cherishes for himself.' There was faint challenge in my voice: 'Do you doubt that?'

Instantly, she became apologetic.

'No, Lydia – no! But, somehow, you are so forceful, so dominant, that I can imagine your being capable of inspiring a man to reach out almost beyond his natural destiny – and that isn't always the true fulfilment of the soul.'

Her words vibrated with a certain profound sincerity that shook me; it was as if she had borrowed a depth of thought in no way reflective of her normal powers.

'I hope,' I said lightly, 'that you are not becoming foolishly introspective, darling. You must realize that you don't really know Stephen, I do.'

'How well,' she replied evenly, 'do we any of us know the other person, Lydia? Isn't it rather a question of our liking to think we do?'

'No.' I said with emphasis. 'Not at all.

Obviously, some people just have no under-standing... Are you suggesting, for instance, that I do not know *you?*'

She didn't, as I had expected, immediately give her answer, but pondered the question before saying:

'Not quite; but that there are parts of me of which you are completely unaware. I'm not entirely the Stella you imagine.'

That made me laugh, and I reached out and patted her hand as I murmured:

'Bless you; you are as transparent as cellophane to me, my darling – although you may not think you are.'

She gave me a quick glance that was eloquent of acquiescence which in no way indicated agreement. I could hardly bear to feel that there might be some hidden recesses in her mind that were obscured from me. I asked myself if I could accurately gauge her reactions to Stephen. I dare not question her further on the subject and, thus, give reality to that which I believed to be no more than a dream on her part – an adolescent infatuation typical of her im-pulsive, irresponsible type. Finally, however, I convinced and consoled myself that things were working out very satisfactorily, and I had every reason to be pleased with the results of my efforts: it had been an exacting, delicate and painful business, but it seemed that, at last, I was to be rewarded and allowed to think of my own happiness for a change.

There was but one thought in my mind when Stephen came to the house to see me that evening: to settle the date for our marriage, and make it as speedy as was possible. I trembled to think what would become of him if he were condemned to live in the chaos and discomfort he was now enduring, and had no compunction, since it was so completely in his interests, about tackling the problem boldly and without foolish squeamishness or false pride.

To my surprise, and I had to admit, chagrin, he settled himself in an arm-chair in the sitting-room as though it were his intention to remain there for the remainder of the evening. Every nerve in my body tingled at the irritation of having to talk in front of Stella who, for once, remained in her accustomed place and made no attempt to leave us alone together. I couldn't help being a little hurt by her lack of consideration. And her soft, low voice saying: 'You look awfully tired, Stephen,' made me feel on edge.

I watched him carefully as he studied her and answered:

'The tiredness that comes from hard work is quite pleasant: it is the tiredness resulting from nervous strain that defeats us.'

Her eyes seemed to me to be like veiled

pools of light as they gazed at him and then abruptly glanced away: it was as if a part of her very soul revealed itself in that second and I tingled with indulgent criticism: a man of greater conceit than Stephen would readily have guessed her secret. Fortunately, he knew that Allan was dominating the scene otherwise it might have been exceedingly embarrassing for us both. She said quietly:

'Work must be the most satisfying thing in the world – if one's job is worth while.' She looked at me as she added: 'I envy Lydia her many interests.'

I said with what I hoped was tolerance:

'Interests can sometimes assume the obligations of duties, Stella: you would not like that – you've never had to battle with life and, thank heaven, you never will.'

'No,' said Stella smoothly. 'But battling with oneself can create quite a state of war.'

'With oneself,' Stephen echoed.

'Yes.' Her voice was steady and yet challenging. 'As a doctor you should know that.'

'As a doctor my endeavours should be towards removing the *cause*,' he said abruptly.

Again, she raised her gaze to his:

'If you could control the hearts and emotions of your patients that would be simple.'

I had a curious sense of uneasiness as I sat there. What was it in the atmosphere that was so disconcerting the moment Stephen and Stella began to talk? A tension, a hidden conflict and tumult as of two people speaking in riddles, which brought to me a hateful and disturbing sensation as of being outside their world? I pushed the idea aside as both fantastic and absurd, detesting the weakness that allowed it rein.

Stephen's voice was a little hoarse as he answered:

'It is not as a doctor I would most wish to have that power.'

For a second the tension became electrical and as his gaze fell upon Stella a dull flush mounted her cheeks, making her eyes more starry, and appealing. There was something wholly irresistible about her and a fierce, tormenting pang of jealousy gripped me.

I managed to say evenly:

'Stella darling, I have something I want to discuss with Stephen, would you mind leaving us alone for a few minutes?... And don't be too late to bed to-night, will you? You look very tired and if you are to beat Allan at tennis to-morrow afternoon, you'll need to be very fresh, won't you?'

She started almost guiltily and got immediately to her feet. It was with reserve she said slowly:

'Good night, Stephen; good night Lydia.'

Stephen said impulsively:

'I'm afraid you hurt her, Lydia. I'd hate you to make her feel unwanted – just because of me.'

That stung. It wasn't, I thought, very just.

'Unwanted!' My voice rose faintly. 'Surely, Stephen I have the right to make a simple request; I've devoted my life to Stella but, now, she will have to realize that my duty is to you.'

He took out his cigarette-case, offered me a cigarette which I declined, and lit one for himself. Then:

'I have always felt that the word "duty" was exceedingly ugly and, at times, equally hypocritical.'

'Not,' I countered, 'in the sense that I used it.'

He looked at me very levelly:

'Never feel that I resent Stella's presence, my dear,' he said firmly. 'If I'm to be one of the family then I certainly do not expect everyone to vanish the moment I come to visit you.'

That rankled. I argued that he should want to be alone with me.

'Isn't it,' I said trying to keep my sense of proportion, 'natural for two people in love to prefer to be alone?'

I watched him closely, but it was as if a veil had been drawn between us leaving him remote and inscrutable.

'What was it,' he asked evasively, 'you wished to talk to me about?'

A certain exasperation possessed me.

'There was nothing vital but–'

'I see.' A pause. 'So Stella is playing tennis with Allan to-morrow. Does that mean anything?'

'Should it?' I felt wretched, ill at ease.

'I was thinking of your scheme about Cornwall, and Allan joining Stella there.'

I said hotly.

'My "scheme"? Surely that isn't a very nice way to put it?'

He stared at me.

'But you wanted Stella to go to Cornwall in the hope that Allan might follow her and ask her to – to marry him, didn't you?'

'Is that anything to my discredit?'

'Have I suggested that it was?' He was implacable.

'No, but I have the feeling that you are unsympathetic about my concern for Stella,' I said painfully. 'I thought you would help me, Stephen–'

'I disagree with any kind of interference in other people's lives,' he said firmly.

'Interference!' I could hardly get the word out. 'When my only thought and anxiety is for Stella's happiness. I shouldn't be worthy of the name of a sister unless I tried to help her.'

He looked thoughtful.

'I know you have her interests at heart, Lydia, but take my advice, and don't try to force any issues: it always leads to trouble.'

'And is the very last thing I should dream of doing. Stella has always been absolutely free to make her own decisions... Need we waste our time like this, darling?' I moved closer to him and slipped my hand in his.

He smiled but there was a faraway look in his eyes as though he were thinking beyond me and I said quietly:

'What are you pondering?'

He didn't hesitate.

'The question of Stella and Allan. Do you believe he will go to Cornwall?'

'Yes – I'm sure of it.'

'I'm not so certain she is in love with him, you know.' He spoke slowly.

'I think you can allow me to be the judge of that,' I replied. 'I *am* in Stella's confidence, after all.'

'That isn't always the real test. We can conceal a very great deal from those nearest to us.'

'Stella would have no wish to adopt that attitude to me.' I paused. 'You are very fond of her – aren't you, Stephen?' I added, fearful lest he might misinterpret my words: 'I do appreciate it so very much. I couldn't have endured it otherwise. Neither could I have been happy with any man who failed to understand just what Stella means to me.' I felt better for having expressed the sentiment and ashamed of myself for stooping to jealousy, which I felt wholly unworthy of me.

Stephen gazed at me intently. I leaned forward and pressed my lips to his, sitting on the arm of his chair as I did so while every nerve in my body tingled and ached for his caress. His kiss was strangely unsatisfying, and I drew back a trifle sharply, not daring to complain, or even to comment, and telling myself that only when we were married, and in the silence and sanctuary of our own home, would a man of Stephen's type wholly relax. I realized how desperately unfulfilled his life was; how lacking in emotion and how badly he needed me. Once I was installed to look after him his whole attitude would change; he would be as a man coming into his own and I vowed that, no matter how difficult, or hard, the task that lay ahead of me, I would never flinch and that work, financial anxiety, would be as an altar on which I might lay the offering of my love and devotion and my sacrifice. I said softly:

'Stephen?'

He stubbed out his cigarette.

'Yes.'

'I've been thinking: it is now you need me most and because you are so reticent about asking me to accept what you believe to be very little, and which I know to be the whole world, I am going to dare to suggest that we get married this summer. I could not bear to think of your being alone and uncared for once Winter comes and you are left to the mercy of some incompetent woman.'

He stared and said evasively:

'My dear, I'm all right.'

'Does that mean you are, also, content?'

'Of course not, but–'

'You hate to "impose on me" as you said earlier to-day.'

He answered hastily:

'Yes... And rushing things–' There was a significant pause. 'We'll wait a little while; you want to see Stella settled and if Allan shouldn't–'

I interrupted him.

'There is no question about that phase of things. And, in any case, darling, I think perhaps, after all, that this is one time in my life when I am entitled to study myself just a little.'

He said unevenly:

'It hadn't really occurred to me that you would be willing to marry me until Stella was – was secure.'

Impatience gripped me. The name of Stella seemed like a hammer blow in my head.

'I think,' I said as quietly as was possible, 'that you were right when you took me to task for wanting to protect her too much.' I looked at him fearlessly. 'In any case, she is my responsibility, not yours.'

He got to his feet; there was nothing angry

or irate in his manner, but his voice was firm and decisive as he said:

'We won't make any decisions just yet, my dear... Anywhere you want to go to-morrow? I can give you a lift into Dornford if you like.'

Frustration gripped me in a certain savage disappointment. I felt trapped by an emotion I had never before experienced and which left me vulnerable and quivering against its impact. I could not argue or force the issue: it was as if a door had been shut in my face and I dare not attempt to open it lest it be further barred against me. I managed to say smoothly:

'I am not quite sure what my plans are to-morrow, Stephen, but look in on your way through the village – will you?'

He nodded, then:

'Stella's seeing Allan to-morrow – isn't she? I'm going out to the house and can give her a lift. Afternoon, wasn't it?'

I hated the knowledge that he had thus remembered Stella's actions and my reference to the tennis.

'I'll tell her,' I said smoothly.

He looked down at me and, stooping, kissed me with affection rather than passion, before opening the front door and stepping out into the night.

It was moonlight and the silent streets were dark pools of mystery wherein grotesque shadows etched themselves in sharp relief. The sky was a pale sapphire shot with gold, and here and there clouds, like liquid opal, floated in a splendour that caught at the breath and awakened swift desire.

'I feel as though I'd like to drive back with you – it's so heavenly,' I whispered.

Stephen looked up and, almost as one who found the beauty of it unbearable, said lightly:

'I'd have to bring you back again then.'

I felt my heart quicken its beat rather sickeningly.

'You sound as though that might be an irksome task, Stephen.'

There was faint embarrassment on his face as he exclaimed banteringly:

'Not that; but it could go on all night...' His laugh broke rather harshly upon the stillness. He got into his car and leaned out of the driving window. 'See you in the morning, Lydia. And don't forget to tell Stella I can give her a lift.'

I turned back into the somewhat oppressive silence of the house; a sense of bleak disappointment lay upon me.

A fan of light showed beneath Stella's door as I went to my room. I called to her softly, and she answered and invited me in.

'You should be asleep, darling,' I said anxiously.

'I couldn't sleep.'

'Any special reason?' I felt that I was holding my breath as I spoke.

'You were annoyed with me to-night – weren't you?' she asked solemnly.

'Darling! How ridiculous! Just because I had something important I wanted to say to Stephen? You mustn't take everything so seriously,' I added, the old fear returning as I reflected upon her extreme sensitivity and the dangers that lurked in its wake.

Her face appeared to be in shadow – a dark shadow as of pain. She said gravely:

'Not that, Lydia. I understood and was going in any case. I just felt that always to disappear on Stephen's arrival might seem a trifle odd – that's all. You need never be afraid I shall intrude.'

That awakened within me a certain annoyance. It was tantamount to suggesting that I was petty and mean or, worse still, unreasonable. And after all I had done, it hurt.

'Do you think that quite fair, Stella? Have I ever given you cause to feel neglected or unwanted?'

For once she did not hasten a direct contradiction as she said:

'Never; but you have never been engaged to Stephen before. That makes all the difference.'

I felt myself growing hot with indignation.

'And are you implying that I am jealous?'

She shook her head.

'You used the word – not I, Lydia.'

I stared at her aghast. She seemed almost a stranger.

'This is – is absurd,' I murmured. Then, changing my tone and attitude I added gently: 'This isn't like you, darling; but I understand. I'm hoping that the holiday will do you a world of good – you haven't been fit for some weeks and–'

Her steady scrutiny unnerved me; it made my words seem empty and pointless and threw into relief the fact of her regard for Stephen. Her voice when, finally, she spoke was very calm and had that quality of great stillness:

'I have no need of a holiday, Lydia, and I am perfectly well in the sense that you mean.' She looked at me and added in a matter-of-fact tone: 'When are you and Stephen being married?'

'It isn't decided yet and, in any case, you know my feelings in the matter.' I hurried on: 'Now I must leave you, darling … let me tuck you up.'

She slid down in the bed and I drew the clothes into position as was my custom.

'There we are,' I said triumphantly. 'And don't you dare get any more foolish ideas into your head. All the marriages in the world could never change things between us – you know that, don't you?'

She looked up at me, her eyes wide and so it seemed fascinated, as one under a spell.

'You always win, Lydia; no one can stand up against you – can they?' she said softly and in her old, loving tone.

I bent and kissed her forehead and ruffled her shining hair. She was mine again in those moments and I was at peace.

'Good night, darling,' I murmured gently.

'Good night, Lydia.' It was a tender sound. 'I didn't mean to be horrid.'

'I know ... but I can't bear it; I just couldn't go on with things unless all was well between us, darling.'

Consternation showed in her face and then died in the light of my smile.

'You are so good to me,' she whispered.

I thought of Stephen's offer to take her out to the Westburys' the following afternoon, but decided that it was far better that she should go alone. Stephen's company was only calculated to upset her, and that was the last thing I wanted for her and, equally, the last thing I could explain to him. I could mention it afterwards and was fully justified in appearing to have forgotten, since it was for her good.

It was the evening before Stella and father left for Cornwall that Allan and Stephen arrived at the house simultaneously. Stephen had come primarily to see me and, also, to say good-bye to the others. I was a little uncertain as to why Allan put in an appearance and betrayed my surprise as I admitted him.

'I've come,' he said disarmingly, 'to receive your blessing. Everyone is being good and doing as you wish – aren't they?'

I stared at him, and then saw Stephen's car draw up outside and Stephen move swiftly forward so that he and Allan stood together in the narrow passage-way.

'A party?' Stephen asked in a clipped tone.

'Something of the kind,' Allan retorted, and I knew that it was with the utmost difficulty he concealed his jealousy of Stephen.

We moved into the sitting-room where a certain disorder prevailed and a number of small cases overflowed prior to being shut down. Stella said, by way of greeting:

'How we shall get all this on the train–' She sighed wearily.

Stephen's voice came with a curiously intent inflection.

'If I could get away I'd drive you down – save you all the effort.'

Allan said almost abruptly:

'That is what I am going to do – if I may be allowed. Drive you down.' He glanced first at father and then at Stella. 'The idea came to me to-night.'

Stella gasped:

'*Allan.*' And while I knew that the joy in her voice was eloquent of relief at being spared the journey, I realized that to Stephen it could be a perfect indication of her delight at the prospect of Allan's company. Was it only my over-stimulated imagination that made it seem that Stephen stiffened and the line of his jaw grew firmer and more stubborn.

Father beamed.

'That would be wonderful. Quite frankly, I'm dreading that journey in this heat.'

'Then that's settled.'

'Do you mean you are just going to drive us down and come back immediately?'

Allan shook his head.

'On the contrary, I'm staying down, so that the car will be at your disposal all the time!' He spoke lightly and, even as he did so, turned to me, adding: 'I feel I shall have Lydia's unanimous approval.'

Stephen was looking at Stella in that second with what I should have described, had he been any other man, as hunger; a yearning unmistakable, allied to a certain resistance as if he were fighting the emotion. She allowed her gaze to rest in his for the fraction of a second and, then, abruptly turned away so that her face was in shadow. Was Stephen wishing he could accompany her? Or was it that her foolish infatuation lit an equally foolish flame within his heart. I felt an agony of fear, of overwhelming jealousy and surrendered to both in an effort thus to escape them. Taking myself to task with criticism and condemnation seemed futile against the tumultuous tide now surging through me; it was as if, in my mind, Stephen and Stella were irrevocably linked and, thus, by my own imaginings, I lent reality to that at which reason and sensibility refuted and mocked. I knew Stephen was mine; that it was I whom he loved and wanted for his wife: why then *allow* the fact of Stella's affection for him to pollute my happiness in such a way. A voice whispered within me: 'This will become an obsession unless you kill it now.' I found myself longing for the moment when I might be quite alone in the house even though my anxiety and devotion to Stella remained unimpaired.

I knew that they were watching me, and waiting for my comment and, clicking down the lid of a small suitcase I said lightly:

'You certainly have my approval, Allan.' I added: 'I might even have suggested it had I given it thought!'

Stephen spoke after a long silence:

'You're a lucky devil Allan to be able to move about at will and not be chained to one place.'

Father said blithely:

'Now if you and Lydia could join us that would–'

I interposed hastily:

'It would not be a holiday for any of us;

change of people can be very beneficial and families should part sometimes.'

Allan gave me a faintly mocking smile.

'Quite a new theory for you Lydia. I've always understood that your motto was all together or not at all.'

Stella said quietly:

'Lydia is prompted by what she believes to be best for us.'

'A very worthy motive,' Allan said again.

Stephen might not have heard that.

'Don't be surprised if we pay you a flying visit, nevertheless,' he said firmly.

Stella cried:

'Oh, that would be lovely... Lydia, wouldn't it?'

'Lovely darling; we shall have to see, shan't we, Stephen?'

Stephen nodded almost absent-mindedly as he said:

'If I could put a few patients on ice, you can consider it a foregone conclusion.'

A hateful sickness came upon me once more. Such an innovation would ruin the plans I had so carefully made in Stella's interests. Her thoughts would be obsessed by the prospect of Stephen's visit, rather than concentrated upon Allan and the very real affection she had for him. It annoyed me to think that Stephen had any desire to go; but I had come to know that there was a very great streak of impulsiveness in his nature which, for his own sake, must be curbed; he was apt to make decisions without weighing up possibilities, often regretting them afterwards. Again, I bruised myself on that jagged rock of thought: would that be the case where I was concerned?

Allan stared at me very levelly:

'We shall have the red carpet in readiness,' he said smoothly. 'Somehow, I'm afraid it will not be rolled out.'

Rather foolishly I challenged that.

'Only Stephen can decide that.'

'Then that being so, we shall see you,' Allan retorted.

I could read Stella's thoughts as she stood there in silence. She wanted to believe that we should go down and yet dreaded the proximity to Stephen since he was in love with me. I hastened to assure myself that her feelings would speedily change, and her infatuation die a natural death, if only she were allowed sufficient time alone with Allan. At all costs she must have that and it was, I knew, up to me to secure it and, thus, further safeguard her future happiness.

It was when they had been in Cornwall a week that Stephen rushed into the house one morning and cried:

'Lydia, get ready! We're going to drive down to Cornwall to-night. I can manage thirty-six hours and—' He paused. 'What is it?'

I said, infusing disappointment into my voice:

'Oh, darling, that would have been lovely, but it is quite impossible ... don't you remember?'

He frowned and said sharply:

'Remember – what?'

'That we are going to Lady Hampstead's party to-night?'

He said with emphasis:

'First I've heard about it.'

'Darling,' I said patiently, 'of course it isn't. You agreed and I accepted. You were probably too busy to realize it. We just can't offend her ... too much is at stake.'

'Such as?' he challenged.

I smiled at him indulgently, steering my emotions so that in no way was I vulnerable.

'Her influence in this county and the fact that she is anxious for you to attend the household in future–'

He spoke through half-clenched teeth.

'I couldn't care less. I shall 'phone her and explain. She'll understand, and if she doesn't I'll manage without her.'

I dare not oppose him.

'Of course, if you wish. I had very much looked forward to going, but I'd hate to persuade you. It will be simply wonderful there to-night...' I went on quietly: 'If you can get time off couldn't we just go out quietly together–'

'We both need a complete change,' he persisted. 'Leave her ladyship to me.'

Tiny daggers were jabbing at my heart and mind. I hated the idea that he wanted to go to Cornwall and, above all, that he might so easily jeopardize – by his very presence – Stella's future happiness, after all my carefully made plans and earlier sacrifices. That was unthinkable and must be prevented at all costs. I said sweetly:

'Very well, darling. It's for you to decide. I'll be ready. It will be great fun.'

'Splendid.' He beamed. 'I'll call for you at eight,' he added as he walked to the door.

But at seven-thirty that night I 'phoned him.

'Stephen ... can you come? I must have eaten something that disagreed with me. I feel terrible – terrible.' I added breathlessly: 'I'm afraid the idea of Cornwall is utterly out of the question for me.'

CHAPTER SIX

Stephen reached me some ten minutes later. I was lying on the couch and the nervous strain from which I had suffered during recent weeks – strain due entirely to my anxiety for Stella – produced symptoms which enabled me, with absolutely truth, to say weakly:

'I'm shaking, Stephen, and my head just splits.'

He felt my pulse and made a cursory examination.

'Any sickness?'

'I feel sick,' I explained, 'but that is all.'

He sat beside me and I met his somewhat baffled gaze very steadily as he exclaimed:

'I can find no symptoms likely to account for it ... quick pulse, but that–' He shrugged his shoulders, adding: 'You're in a nervy state–'

Instantly, I cried:

'I've tried not to be, Stephen; fought so terribly hard, but these weeks, almost months, of strain on Stella's account have taken their toll I'm afraid.' I sighed remorsefully: 'I'm so dreadfully sorry to have spoiled things. I was terribly excited about our trip to Cornwall–'

My head rested languidly against the cushions— 'I suppose I couldn't stand that added nervous tension.'

He got up and moved towards the mantelpiece.

'The journey might be advantageous to you, Lydia. Sea air—'

I interposed with a shudder:

'I'm sorry, darling: I'd never stand it—' It seemed that I held my breath as I added: 'But why don't you go without me? I'd be all right and—'

'That,' he said, and I tried to convince myself that there was no impatience in his voice, 'is out of the question.'

'I feel so awful about it,' I murmured painfully.

'You can't help it.'

My gaze met his.

'You're disappointed – aren't you, darling?'

A strange look came into his eyes; a look puzzling and disturbing as he answered:

'Naturally; the break would have been pretty good but—' He made a gesture eloquent of resignation.

'I still wish you'd go.' My heart was racing and I despised myself because the fear lest his desire to visit Cornwall was prompted solely by an inclination to see Stella.

'That,' he said somewhat impatiently, 'is absurd, Lydia. Can you imagine my arriving there and saying that you were not well enough to travel?' His voice deepened: 'A pretty fine doctor I'd appear to be.'

I caught at my breath.

'Would you go if there were no question of your being misunderstood, or thought callous?'

He looked down at me.

'You do not expect me to answer that question...'

'We could, perhaps, go next week-end – return with them all,' I said tentatively.

He sat in a chair facing me.

'Lionel Manning is coming down: I told you.'

I drew my hand wearily across my forehead.

'Of course; I'd forgotten. He's the Wimpole Street man?'

'Yes.'

My heart-beats quickened.

'I shall enjoy meeting him, darling. Has he a practice elsewhere?'

'Yes, at Hampstead; but is confining himself more and more to consultant work.'

'That must be very thrilling.'

He nodded.

'But not in your line?' I waited, tensed, for his answer.

'I believe that my job lies here,' he replied firmly.

'Helping the poor.'

He drew his brows together in inquiry.

'I thought your interests were turned, also, in that direction, Lydia.'

Instantly, I cried:

'But they are, darling. There's so much to be done in a place like this.'

He brightened.

'I want to get a clinic going. I've so many ideas, Lydia that–' He made an expressive gesture with his hands. 'There should be double the hours in a day so that I could do twice as much as now.'

'You'll realize all your dreams,' I spoke soothingly.

He looked down at his hands reflectively as he said:

'I was talking to Stella about my hopes for Milbury; she is very far-seeing you know, Lydia, and very understanding.'

Jealousy flamed to life, but I mastered the weakness as I exclaimed:

'Stella is naturally sympathetic towards anyone's ambitions, darling. It is her nature. But as for being able fully to appreciate the significance of any particular ideal, or to help towards its fruition–' I smiled indulgently. 'Bless her: she would not be the lovable soul she is if she were any different.'

He resisted that stubbornly, I felt.

'I cannot quite agree. Stella's sympathy is born of deep feeling; she is not nearly so irresponsible as you imagine.'

The blood in my veins appeared to chill.

'You, Stephen, have hardly been in a position accurately to judge that. And as for her feeling—' I forced a half-smile. 'Any woman in love is possessed of it and dominated by it. She cannot help herself.' I hastened: 'Her devotion to Allan has certainly matured her, but only I know how adolescent she really is.' I finished: 'It seems inevitable that we end up by discussing Stella – doesn't it?'

He got up rather abruptly from his chair, and then, glancing down at me, said:

'I'd better go back and get you some tablets – although I cannot help feeling that the change away from here for a while would be infinitely better than a mild sedative – which, after all, is all I can prescribe.'

'I think, darling, that I am the best judge of that. I simply could not stand the journey. Don't be unsympathetic, Stephen – it isn't quite fair,' I murmured pleadingly. 'It is my disappointment as well as yours, you know.'

'Sorry, Lydia.' He stooped and kissed my forehead.

Could I reassure myself that his attitude was lover-like or solicitous? I might not be ill, in the accepted sense, and I might, with effort, have been capable of making the journey and while, as a doctor, he might well sense this, nevertheless, he could not gauge accurately the degree of my suffering. My whole nervous system had been impaired through my anxiety for his welfare and Stella's. I had spared no effort in my concern for their future happiness. My own love for Stephen was, after all, purely incidental, and had in no way affected my actions which had been prompted by the very highest and most unselfish of ideals. Even now I was debarring myself the pleasure of the trip to Cornwall so that he might be saved further complications. He would never know, in fact, just how great was the debt he owed me. That fortified me, and made it a little easier to bear injustice and to realize that, since I could not wholly confide in him, I must be prepared for his adverse criticism on occasion. It wasn't an easy position in which to be.

'If you could give me something for my head – it just smashes.'

It was a wretched week-end for me; genuinely I felt far from well and, above all, it was vitally necessary that I should in no way 'recover' with a rapidity likely to arouse Stephen's suspicions or, in any degree, suggest that I had not wanted to go to Cornwall. My mind was seething in conflict and turmoil and I hated every moment of it, especially when Stephen said:

'Since I'd planned to have this time off, Lydia, I shall use it to catch up on my accounts. Not before it is necessary.'

I knew that to protest was useless and I did

my utmost to be understanding. He spent the evenings with me, but it was as though the ghost of Stella sat between us, and I tortured myself with the feeling that his disappointment was out of all proportion.

The following week-end, however, more than atoned. I had wanted to meet Lionel Manning and, to my delight, having done so, found myself alone with him in the lounge of Stephen's house – Stephen having been called out unexpectedly on an urgent case.

He studied me approvingly. And I him, seeing a distinguished looking man in the late forties, with finely drawn features and impressive dark eyes. He said:

'I'm delighted that Stephen has had the good sense to inveigle you into his life, Lydia.'

I liked his use of my Christian name and the manner in which he accepted me into the friendship.

'And I'm equally delighted that you approve of me,' I replied. 'I'm sure that we both have Stephen's welfare very earnestly at heart.'

He looked at me very levelly.

'And just what are your ambitions for him?'

I returned his gaze.

'To further his own,' I said promptly. 'Stephen is an idealist: he needs understanding.'

Lionel Manning smiled knowingly.

'When a woman is wise enough to understand a man she is also clever enough to divert his ambitions into channels most likely ultimately to benefit him.'

I leaned forward; it was as if I suddenly had found an ally.

'Do you think that Stephen should remain in Milbury?'

'He could achieve far greater eminence elsewhere.' He offered me a cigarette, lit it and then his own: 'But as you so rightly say, Stephen is an idealist and heaven knows there is work enough to do here.' His eyes met mine again. 'You don't mind it?'

'Helping humanity can be a very satisfying thing,' I answered quietly. 'And success cannot be judged in terms of the material – after all. I may understand Stephen, but I should never use that understanding – as you suggest' – I smiled as I spoke – 'to persuade him to do anything against his will. I detest the type of person who works by stealth.'

He was watching me closely. Then:

'Most women I meet appear to have no other form of activity.'

'That,' I said indignantly, 'is because they have no desire to help anyone and love only themselves. I meet enough of the type and despise them heartily.'

'So you are a champion of Stephen's ideals?'

'Naturally.'

'Then it isn't any good my trying to get you to persuade him to leave here and take a more fashionable practice?'

My heart-beats quickened, but I knew that I was treading on dangerous ground as I replied:

'I'm afraid not: the decision to leave would have to come freely from Stephen.' I paused before adding carelessly: 'Have you a practice in mind?'

'Not just at the moment, but I've had my eye on one... Still, Lydia, perhaps you're right; never does to interfere with any man's ideals; we each of us must plough a lone furrow up to a point. I would never seek to persuade him.'

'You only just wanted to know my reactions,' I chided.

'Frankly – yes.'

'And now that you do?'

'I congratulate him the more on having found an ally as well as a future wife. He is fortunate indeed.'

'Thank you!' I laughed lightly. 'And I take it that if Stephen ever should want to make a move, he can count on your advice and guidance in selecting the right practice?'

'Most certainly – and he knows it.'

It was when Stephen was driving me home that night that he said:

'Lionel tells me he had a talk with you

about my work here in Milbury.'

I had counted on that.

'Yes. Why.'

'I'm glad you let him know that you were wholly in agreement with my ambitions, Lydia. Thank you; it means everything to me.'

'I know it does, darling,' I said softly. 'And I shouldn't love you as I do if I saw it any other way.'

He picked up my hand and held it for a fraction of a second.

'Bless you,' he murmured. Then, abruptly changing the subject: 'The family will be home to-morrow at this time. Any news of them yesterday? I meant to ask you before.'

I rather dreaded their return, as one hating to be drawn back into that circle with its burdens and responsibilities. I was on edge with suspense because Stella had made scant reference to Allan, and in no way hinted at any engagement. It didn't seem possible that my plans and sacrifices should count for nought: the possibility of failure bore down upon me with depressing significance, and for the first time in my life I experienced a momentary longing to be free from the obligations that had hampered me for so many years. I said smoothly:

'I expect them back for dinner.'

He nodded. I wondered just what he was thinking; was he glad at the prospect of their return, or did he regret that our *tête-à-tête* was over. I murmured:

'It's been wonderful to be alone as we have, darling – hasn't it?'

He gave me a swift glance.

'You are really the best judge of that, after all. The family never intrude upon us.'

'Meaning that you've missed them?' I caught at my breath.

'In a sense – yes.' He added: 'I've a great regard for your father.'

'I know and appreciate it... And Stella?'

He said almost sharply:

'You known I'm very fond of Stella.'

'I shall have to be jealous.' My voice was bantering.

He stiffened.

'If there is one thing I detest on this earth it is a jealous, suspicious woman.' He finished evenly: 'I shall invite myself for dinner to add my welcome to yours. Hadn't you rather expected to hear of an engagement while they've been away?'

Was that elation on his part because no engagement had materialized. I managed to keep my emotions under control as I answered:

'You are fully aware of my feelings in that direction, Stephen. It is quite possible that the results of this holiday may not manifest themselves quite so soon.' I know that I had no desire for Stephen to be with us for dinner and that I resented the intrusion even of those dear to me, but I could hardly tell him so without being misunderstood.

He said gravely:

'I always feel that there is a link missing somewhere in all that, Lydia.'

'Meaning,' I said sharply, 'that I have misrepresented the facts?'

'No, no,' he corrected me. 'Not that; but that some portion of those facts eludes the absolute truth.'

'Facts *are* truth,' I insisted.

'With reservations,' he continued imperturbably. 'You can know all the facts of a case, but if one single element is missing, one word withheld, then even facts can be absolutely distorted and fallacious.'

I said hotly, for I could not help feeling that in all this he was always most difficult.

'Since the only fact in this case is that Stella is in love with Allan and has been praying that he shall love her–' I stopped. It was hateful to me to be forced into a position where lies were necessary and the only means of safeguarding those whose happiness was dearer to me than my own.

Stephen said almost curtly:

'Suppose we leave the matter: Stella would hardly thank us for discussing it. I feel a sense of disloyalty–'

That was almost too much for me after all I had endured for Stella's sake, but I curbed the words that rose angrily to my lips and said gently:

'I'm sorry, Stephen; I hoped that I might talk to you as to myself; that we were sufficiently close for no subject to be barred. I don't think you quite understand my devotion to Stella... Good night, darling ... no, don't get out; I can manage.'

My subdued tone was extremely effectual for, instantly, he apologized.

'I'm apt to see things out of proportion, Lydia. Forgive me. I do understand your concern for Stella, and know how wonderful you have been to her. She has told me many times of your goodness.'

I smiled and leaned towards him, meeting his lips and yielding to the passionate need that consumed me; a need wholly unsatisfied by his affectionate caress that savoured always of reserve.

'Until to-morrow,' he said as he saw me into the house.

'Good night, darling,' I whispered softly and disappeared.

And, as ever, the ghost of frustration walked beside me.

Stephen arrived the following evening before their return.

'Not back?' he asked, looking around him.

'No.'

'Bit late – aren't they?'

Exasperation possessed me.

'An hour actually; but no one can really time a long journey of that description. I've a cold meal and it doesn't matter in the least.'

'Allan,' he said tensely, 'is a most reckless driver.'

A tingling sensation crept down my spine. It was hardly likely that Stephen's anxiety was for father, or for Allan, which brought us automatically to Stella. Was it in accordance with mere affection that such solicitude should manifest itself.

'I'm not in the least worried,' I said coolly.

A faint flush mounted his cheeks.

'It isn't a question of being *worried*–' He broke off rather feebly.

They arrived some half an hour later during which time Stephen had made an unsuccessful attempt to hide his agitation and I had successfully concealed my annoyance at his attitude.

There was the usual noise and bustle as Stella, father and Allan came into the narrow hallway.

I held Stella at arm's length.

'Let me look at you? Ah, that's better! Darling, you're beautifully brown.'

'Sun bathing...' Her voice was lifeless. She gazed beyond me to where Stephen stood framed in the doorway of the sitting-room and, instantly, it was as though I ceased to exist and only he became real to her as she said in a breath:

'Stephen!'

He murmured tensely:

'Welcome home, Stella.'

She moved towards him as one under hypnotic control; their eyes met and she whispered:

'It's good to be here again; how many years has it been?'

He answered hoarsely:

'Many years.' And then, as one drawn back from the brink of a precipice, he added lightly: 'You certainly are brown, but I cannot see any evidence of added weight – you're thinner than when you went away.'

She retorted flippantly as one absorbing his mood:

'I always go in reverse.'

Allan heard that as he put the last suitcase down.

'As contrary as all women... Hello there, Stephen. Is this a civic reception? Lydia, you're looking as well as ever.'

Father insinuated himself into the picture and a few minutes later we all sat down to the meal. Allan said:

'We were terribly disappointed that you didn't join us, Stephen. That flying visit failed to materialize.'

Stephen glanced at me and then back first to Allan, and then to Stella whom I had seated at Allan's side.

'I had made all arrangements to bring

Lydia down last week-end – didn't she tell you? But she was ill on the very evening we were to have left.'

'Ill?' There was consternation in Stella's voice. 'Lydia, you didn't say anything in your letters.'

'I didn't want to worry you, darling,' I said gently. 'In any case it was nothing – just bad enough to prevent my travelling. We were both terribly disappointed.'

Allan looked at me fixedly.

'I'm sure you were.' It was a cryptic sound.

Stella cried:

'I hoped so much that you'd both come.' She stopped awkwardly, adding: 'It was a heavenly spot but I'm afraid father wasn't quite in his element.'

Father broke his customary silence.

'No; I wish I'd gone down to Rottingdean – sounds pretty lazy and all that, but a deck-chair in the garden is my mark.'

Stephen said, and I sensed a certain gravity in his voice:

'Shall have to give you something energizing. What's the good of a doctor if his future relatives cannot be kept in good health!'

I resented strongly the implication that my idea about Cornwall had been wrong and said with what I hoped was smoothness:

'Surely you could rest equally well in Cornwall?'

Stella interposed:

'Daddy found the hills too much for him, Lydia.'

'Then,' I said sweetly, 'you shouldn't have attempted to climb them, Father.' I added: 'And I'm sure that with Allan's car you were well taken care of.'

Allan said a trifle impatiently:

'The most beautiful spots cannot be reached, or even seen, by car.'

Stephen said confidentially to father:

'Next year if you want to go to Rottingdean or Timbuctoo, just you go and take no notice of your daughter. Doesn't do to give in to the womenfolk too much!'

I felt the blood rising in my cheeks. How could Stephen be so unjust. I interposed.

'Since father went to Cornwall of his own free-will that remark is hardly necessary, darling.'

It seemed as I sat there that nothing was going as I had hoped. And depression came down like a great, dark shadow upon me. I longed to talk to Stella and discover just what had happened between her and Allan. Impossible to hazard a guess, for their attitude towards one another was in no way changed, and indicative only of their normal friendship.

It was when the meal was almost over and the silence seemed heavy with suspense that Allan said suddenly:

'I think it is time to ask for your congratulations, Lydia. Stella has promised to marry me.'

Drama, suspense hung in the air and gave to the silence an uncanny power of stillness as though it were listening and recording that second for all time. The elation that swept over me made my spine tingle; my heart thud, my flesh seemed to creep. This was that for which I had waited, striven, prayed; it was my reward; the reward of seeing Stella's future safeguarded, her happiness assured. I said breathlessly:

'Allan!... Stella! Oh, I'm so glad – so thrilled for you both.'

A faint smile touched Stella's lips and then died as though the struggle defeated it. Her eyes were upon Stephen and for a split second it seemed that they exchanged a glance fraught with passionate emotion; a glance betraying the secret of her heart – or so it appeared to my unduly sensitized mind. I watched and held my breath, the room becoming hot and stuffy; the awareness of drama impinging upon every look and sound. I resisted the idea that she was other than perfectly happy; or that Stephen was in any way moved by the announcement. It was so foolishly easy to jump to conclusions and think the wrong thing when so much that was vital was at stake.

Stephen said hoarsely:

'Congratulations.' And to Stella: 'All the happiness, Stella.'

'Thank you,' she said solemnly.

The relief that overwhelmed me denuded me of strength: I felt weak, almost ill with reaction after the long months of strain.

Stephen asked:

'And when is the great event to take place?'

Stella hastened:

'We haven't decided.'

I laughed nervously.

'Why not a double wedding!'

'Heaven forbid,' said Stephen harshly. 'I detest such exhibitionism.'

'And I,' Stella agreed.

Slight annoyance possessed me.

'I was only joking,' I said tersely.

Father looked from face to face:

'It is good to know that both my daughters have been so fortunate,' he said sincerely. 'I am blessed indeed. I cannot wish for you all anything better than I knew. That will give you happiness indeed.'

He got up from the table, smiled, and left the four of us on our own.

But there was no buzz of conversation; no exchange of confidences as might have been normal. A sense of restraint and of strain fell upon us, making us ill at ease. I found it impossible not to intercept every look that passed between Stella and Stephen and, once or twice my eyes met Allan's and it was as if he said: 'Well, I hope you are satisfied.'

Stella said reflectively:

'To lose someone as daddy lost mummie – to lose someone one loves – must be like dying oneself.' Her voice was unsteady.

Stephen said thickly:

'One can die many deaths in this life.'

I infused a note of brightness into the proceedings by saying:

'Then we here should be profoundly thankful that our future promises to be so wonderful. It's so lovely to feel that we are all sharing this same happiness, isn't it? What fun we shall all have, together.'

Stephen didn't speak; his gaze went for a second to Stella who held it and then lowered her eyes.

I got up from the table and the rest followed gratefully.

Stephen said:

'I must be going.'

'Darling,' I protested, 'you said you had the evening off.'

He looked confused.

'I forgot an appointment…'

Allan laughed.

'No romance for a doctor without the shadow of a thermometer – eh?'

'None,' Stephen agreed.

'I'll come back to the house with you,' I said suddenly. 'And walk home again.' I smiled meaningly. 'I'm quite certain that Allan and Stella can bear to be without me for a little while.'

Stella stared at me rather as one unable to fathom my mood. It wasn't a look of reproach so much as what appeared to be amazement. She followed me upstairs when I went to put on my hat and coat. I said:

'Oh, darling! I'm so happy for you. I just knew everything would turn out all right between you and Allan. I knew you'd realize that he was the man you loved. Now I can be happy – completely happy.'

She drew her brows together and gazed at me as one stupefied.

'You know,' she said quietly, 'it isn't like that, Lydia. Please don't let's pretend. I'm engaged to Allan as you wanted me to be; but I'm not in love with him or he with me: there's no pretence between us. Surely you didn't imagine there could possibly be.'

It wasn't what I wanted; it introduced that faintly disturbing element which allowed a margin for perpetual suspense. I said quietly:

'You believe that to be so – you may believe you are not in love, darling – but you will be; you've so much in common that it is inevitable. I'm still happy for you – knowing you as I do; knowing all you need from life. Allan is a very fine person.'

'I agree,' she said gravely. 'That was why I

couldn't attempt to deceive him. Or he me.' She looked at me very steadily. 'It is you with whom he is in love and I whom he loves, Lydia.' She changed the subject swiftly and after the manner of one who wishes the subject to be irrevocably closed; as one who establishes the fact beyond dispute that she had no intention of indulging fantasies any more, or of allowing herself to be influenced, or cajoled, in her opinions. 'I'm sorry you weren't well, dear. Are you quite sure you are better?'

I patted her cheek.

'Quite sure. Don't worry about me, darling... It's wonderful to have you back, Stella. I've missed you terribly. I suppose it is because we've always been together. I shall have to get used to the idea that you are really grown up now – shan't I?'

'Yes; I've been grown up for a long time, Lydia.'

I laughed.

'Bless you, sweetheart: of course you have.'

But as we went down the stairs together I knew that she had gone on ahead of me, and that never again could I hope to mould her ideas or her life. That wasn't important since I had steered her into that harbour for which she was intended, and could, therefore, rest content.

Stephen said as we drove to his house:

'Well, your plan worked, Lydia. Stella's future is settled.'

'I always knew that Allan cared, really,' I said confidently. 'They'll be ideal together. Don't you think so?'

'Certainly – if they are in love.'

'Do you,' I demanded sharply, 'doubt the fact?'

'I didn't say so.'

'I hope we shall be as happy as they,' I said stoutly. 'It won't be for want of trying to make you happy, Stephen – that I promise.'

He didn't answer, but suddenly and almost abruptly he said:

'We were discussing the date of our marriage and the possibility of it being soon, Lydia... Well, I agree with you: there's no reason for us to wait. I'm ready for it to be any time you care to name.'

CHAPTER SEVEN

Stephen's decision came almost in the nature of a shock to me, and the excitement and relief which followed in its wake was the greater for the suspense and fear that had preceded it. I had been prepared for persuasion, of a subtle kind, to achieve my objective, but not for this sudden and complete capitulation.

I looked at him with great tenderness and said simply:

'I'm so thankful you feel like that, darling; I long to help you and make your life smooth.'

He turned to me and there was a note of urgency in his voice as he asked:

'And you do understand my ambitions, Lydia! You *are* absolutely with me about Milbury and all I hope to achieve here?' He added swiftly: 'Not by way of personal achievement, but of really helping these people. It won't be easy and will mean certain privations.' His gaze was very steady. 'There must be no possible misunderstanding about all this, my dear: it would be grossly unfair to you.'

I said firmly:

'I'm with you every step of the way, Stephen; your ambitions are mine and I'll work beside you for the rest of my life in order that you shall realize them. Can I say more?'

He shook his head.

'No, my dear – thank you.'

'At last,' I murmured, 'I have found an ally. I've always been doing something in Milbury; but it was a lonely up-hill job, darling. No one understood my feelings.'

He said instantly:

'Not even Stella?'

I smiled to hide my irritation.

'Least of all Stella. Her interests in that way are purely superficial, darling. You'll realize it one day. She isn't of our world. That is the fairest analysis.'

He was silent for a moment, then:

'Ah well! Allan will certainly be able to give her all that any woman could desire.'

Was that bitterness in his voice? Impossible accurately to gauge his mood. The hateful thought came insidiously: was the reason for his sudden desire to be married based upon the fact that Stella was now irrevocably out of reach? It was as if a branding iron were clamped suddenly upon my heart. Absurd to allow such treacherous ideas to pollute my mind. Stephen loved me; his interest in Stella was purely an off-shoot of that love.

'Allan will carry her about!' I laughed.

'How I should hate that kind of life and yet how right it is for her. She will grace his home, their children will be like pets and she'll be rather like a flower in the sun. I'm singularly fortunate.'

'You?' He gave me a puzzled look.

'Yes; it was always what I hoped Stella would find. The happiness of those we love can be infinitely dearer to us than our own.'

He patted my hand – a gesture I had come to accept as his form of caress.

'You are a most unselfish person, Lydia.'

Elation surged over me. How perfectly things had all worked out, and how right I had been in every step I had taken. Now I could enjoy the full reward of all my efforts and sacrifices and walk into the future steadfastly, without qualm or doubt. I said softly:

'Thank you, darling … you were talking of our marriage. Shall we make it a month from now?'

He exclaimed:

'So soon?' Then: 'I mean can you possibly make all your arrangements?'

'Yes.' My voice was resolute. 'This is our life, darling, and I owe my first duty to you now that Stella is settled.' A laugh. 'Do you want to make it later?'

'No, no,' he hastened. 'A quiet affair, Lydia?'

'Definitely; one carnival wedding will be

quite enough in the family. Although Stella will look wonderful in all the trimmings, won't she?'

'Is that what she wants?' He sounded astonished.

'Of course. The fairy story, bless her.'

It was a week later that Diana Westbury gave a party to celebrate the engagement. I hated every moment of it and felt Diana's antagonism almost as a vital, living force quivering in the atmosphere. She said, when for a few seconds we were alone:

'To-night you see the fruits of your labours.' Her voice was both cutting and mocking.

She could not disturb me. I was even sorry for her in her blindness, her unbalanced inconsistency.

'I see Stella happy,' I said proudly. 'That has been my aim.'

She stared at me, a rather unnerving stare that I met, however, without flinching. Then:

'Happy!' Her tone was quietly, even impressively, derisive. 'You've engineered all this; I might even say blackmailed her into an engagement with Allan because it suited your purpose. You've used your influence upon Allan in precisely the same way.' She caught at her breath. 'But this story isn't ended yet, Lydia; don't deceive yourself into the belief that it is.' Her eyes held an accusing light that flashed sinisterly upon me.

'Human beings are not puppets to dance to your tune forever. And if I have any influence whatsoever I shall use it to prevent this marriage taking place. My time will come.'

Fear assailed me, rather as though a sword flashed in the sun.

'That,' I said with dignity, 'is a matter for yourself, Diana. But when two people are in love they do not take kindly to interference. And there is nothing more despicable than a domineering, scheming mother... By the way, you know that Stephen and I are being married in three weeks?'

'That is your greatest and most diabolical crime,' she cried.

I laughed; it was impossible to do otherwise in the face of her dramatic attitude.

'You always have loved the theatrical, Diana. I can assure you that I neither asked Stephen to marry me, nor did I persuade him to marry me quickly. Do you imagine he has no free will?'

She shook her head.

'I do not doubt the truth of your words because I am confident that you are far too clever to betray your hand by forcing any issue – openly. Yours is the subtle undermining of a person's will; the distortion of facts. You remind me of the dry rot that sets into a house ruining it almost before its presence is realized.'

Anger flamed to life within me. The sheer

injustice and impertinence of her remarks astounded me. Never had I appreciated that she would sink to such depths, or behave in such an unforgivable manner.

'I think this conversation has gone far enough,' I said, and my voice rang with contempt.

'The truth hurts – even you,' she said quietly.

'This is the last time I shall ever come to this house, Diana.'

'I'm glad,' she said stoutly. 'I hate being forced to be insincere.'

I turned and walked away from her.

During the week that had elapsed it had happened – either by coincidence or design on Stella's part – that she and Stephen had not met and, thus, no comment had been made to him by her regarding our speedy marriage. Now, I watched Stephen approaching her and, swiftly, joined them, the anger and upset of my encounter with Diana making my nerves jangling and on edge.

'Quite a stranger,' Stephen began, looking at her and I felt certain, appraising the picture she presented in her soft blue *crêpe* frock, that moulded her perfect figure.

Stella's face was a mask; but I knew the emotion she concealed.

'Conserving,' she said lightly, 'my strength to dance at your wedding.'

He studied her intently.

'I will return the compliment.'

Her eyes were dark, slumberous.

'Thank you, Stephen... How's the work?'

'Too much of it, or too little time in which to do it... And the shortage of nurses is terrible.'

Stella looked interested.

'I ought to have thought of that as a career.'

I interposed:

'Darling! You just couldn't have stood up to it and you'd have hated it.'

Stella's eyes went straight to Stephen.

'Do you agree with that?' Her voice was breathless.

'I'm sure,' Stephen answered with a strange intensity, 'that people would almost welcome being ill if you were to be their nurse.'

'Very tactful,' she retorted.

Why was it, I asked myself, that there was always such tension between these two. Easy to understand Stella's attitude since she still harboured that rather sentimental regard for Stephen... His behaviour was another matter. It shocked me to realize how much I concentrated upon it all, but I argued that once Stephen and I were married everything would fall into the correct perspective and the shadow of Stella be wiped out forever the moment she, in turn, became Allan's wife. Diana's words came back sinisterly: *And if I have any influence whatsoever I shall use it to prevent this marriage taking place. My time will come.'* Their very theatricality negatived their validity. Nothing would prevent the marriage. Certainly Allan would never break the engagement and while I had any influence with Stella for her own good, she would most certainly not do so. To waste even a second of anxiety on Diana's tirade was to insult my own intelligence and sink to her level.

The next weeks passed in a whirl of excitement. Clothes to be bought; changes at Stephen's house to make way for a wife; arrangements where father and Stella were concerned.

'If you'd both move from here,' I insisted; 'go somewhere and–'

Stella said firmly:

'For once, Lydia, I am having my way.'

I looked pained.

'For *once* … don't you always have your own way?'

'That was not what we were discussing,' she said with quiet emphasis.

'I know you don't wish to hurt me, darling, but–' I stopped.

There was something unusually assertive about her just then; an implacability which even I could not break down as she said:

'I shall look after the house and father; we shall be perfectly all right. Give me a month and I'll be a qualified housekeeper.'

'And what,' I suggested, 'when you are married, will father do? Isn't it wiser and better all round that you should solve the problem now once and for all?'

Father looked serious.

'Lydia's right, you know,' he said gently.

I felt strengthened by the encouragement. And, looking at Stella, exclaimed:

'Is there any reason why you and Allan shouldn't marry very soon, darling? You haven't anything to wait for, after all.'

A stubborn look flashed into her eyes.

'We prefer to wait,' she replied.

'But, darling, don't you *see* that–'

'I think,' she said evenly, 'that the question is purely a matter for ourselves, Lydia.'

I knew that it was useless arguing with her. When she liked that rebellious streak could be very disturbing, even irritating. I said with understanding:

'Of course, darling. We'll say no more about it. If you feel that you can carry on here, then do so by all means. I shall at least be at hand if you need me.'

She smiled and was obviously relieved.

'I just known I can surprise you all,' she insisted earnestly.

But I felt it my duty to speak to Allan about it, managing to see him alone a day or so later when he called, at my suggestion, earlier than he was expected by Stella.

'You see,' I told him, 'Stella is quite unfitted to have the reins of a home, Allan; she isn't even physically strong to cope with it. I shall never have a minute's peace about her, and shall feel torn between my own home and this one. Father is quite ready to make his home with very old friends, and it would work perfectly; but if Stella persists in this somewhat selfish attitude then he, too, will be penalized.'

He looked at me very levelly:

'You are suggesting that I persuade Stella to marry me almost at once – is that it?'

'Not suggesting,' I corrected. 'Wondering what you had in mind. After all, it is not for me to intrude but–'

'Your concern for Stella is always touching,' he said gently. 'And you'd persuade me to do almost anything in any case.'

'I should never persuade anybody to do anything unless I genuinely believed it to be for their own good.'

'I know that ... and you know just how I feel.'

I lowered my gaze, then:

'Things will be different when you are married, my dear – believe me.'

'I wonder.' It was a heavy sound. 'Perhaps you are right, and there's no sense in waiting.'

'None, Allan. Stella needs you and I feel very close to you as we both try to protect her.'

His eyes lit up.

'Really, Lydia?'

'Really.'

He was silent for a moment, before continuing:

'I've been offered a rather lovely house some forty miles from here. Take over the entire staff, too. What do you think about it? Somehow, when you're married Milbury won't be the same and—'

A thrill went through my body. Nothing could be better for Stella than such an arrangement. I said with enthusiasm:

'Buy it, Allan. So much better than being too near relatives – no matter how well they get on.' I couldn't resist the pleasure of realizing just how empty Diana's threats had been, and how completely she had been defeated in her evil designs.

'But would Stella be happy away from *you?*'

My expression softened as my eyes met his.

'She will learn to be, Allan – and that is as it should be. Sooner or later she will have to grow up.'

He puckered his brows as though giving full weight to my words.

'You know, she is a very discerning and discriminating person, Lydia. I think we rather underestimate her.'

Again, that irritation swept over me. Why

was it that men were so notoriously blind to facts?

'I think *I* know Stella,' I said quietly, and with confidence. 'Buy that house, Allan. Don't tell her anything about it – make it one of those surprises we women so dearly love.' I hastened: 'After all, forty miles is absolutely nothing. And she is rather tired of Milbury, anyway.'

He said abruptly:

'Very well. I'll take your advice and give the house to her as a wedding present.'

'Does Diana know about it?'

'Actually, no! I intended talking to her about it to-night, as a matter of fact.'

I smiled up at him and knew that he was admiring and loving me in his mind even as he returned my gaze. Gently, I said:

'Then don't tell her – let this just be our secret, Allan. Oh, don't misunderstand me, Diana's the last person in the world to let a secret out of the bag but–' I laughed. 'She'll enjoy the surprise with Stella, I'm certain.'

'You're probably right, bless her. In any case, she never intrudes in my life, or expects me to account for any of my actions. Only one Diana.' His voice was filled with enthusiasm. 'She's a mother in a million.'

Thus, it was all settled.

'I'll persuade Stella to marry me,' he said finally. 'I've lost you, Lydia, and this is the only other way possible for me to build a life. Waiting won't help. I shall take her to Switzerland for our honeymoon and by that time the house will be ready. I can, thank heaven, buy it as it stands – furniture as well. Some pretty good stuff there, too.' He gave me a rueful glance. 'This is all cock-eyed, isn't it?' His laugh served to cover his intense emotion.

'It is sensible and realistic, Allan.'

'Two antagonisms to romance,' he countered.

I said breathlessly:

'You'll come to my wedding?'

'Have I any alternative – engaged to your sister?' A pause. 'I thought it was going to be very quiet.'

'Have I suggested anything to the contrary?'

'Only in the way you used that word "wedding".'

'All women give the word importance,' I explained.

He sighed, gave me a swift glance and said:

'You baffle me; sometimes I look at you and feel that I just don't know you at all; then at other times, when we're alone like this–'

I interrupted him.

'That accounts for your attitude towards me being so odd on occasion.'

He looked shamefaced.

'When I'm jealous I see you as a woman dominating everything, and everyone, and bending them to your will,' he confessed.

'Allan!'

'I know; then, in my sane moments, I appreciate your self-sacrificing nobility of character – even though you have turned me down.'

'Better to have done that than to deceive you and marry you for your position and money,' I said softly. 'As I could have done, after all.'

'True; I haven't overlooked that. Or admired you the more for it.' He paused before saying: 'By the way, you know that Stephen's mother and sister are coming to stay with Diana. I gathered that they are not exactly popular with you, Lydia. Right?'

I knew, of course, about the visit and loathed the idea since, of necessity, it would mean that I might be forced to break my vow never to visit Diana again. What was more, my aversion to Monica, Stephen's sister, had grown even with the thought of seeing her again, as had my feelings of antipathy to Dora, his mother. I classed them all with Diana – undignified, Bohemian and thoroughly unreliable.

'Did Diana tell you that?'

'Not – not exactly but–'

Loyalty to Stephen demanded that I correct the impression.

'On the contrary, having met them only once I cannot possibly pass an opinion. I am looking forward really to getting to know them. I deplore this unfriendliness between "in-laws".' I heard Stella coming into the house and added in a whisper: 'By the way, Allan, don't let her know we've discussed all that we have this evening.'

I must admit that Allan played up to me exceedingly well, as, some little while later, he said:

'Lydia what would your reaction be if I tried to inveigle Stella into marrying me almost immediately?'

I watched Stella's face very closely and her gaze flew to mine. My answer came casually:

'I don't think I have any right even to comment on that possibility. It is entirely a matter for Stella to decide.'

It was all settled before Allan left that night and, just when I was congratulating myself on having won yet another victory in Stella's cause, she began with an impressive calm:

'You put the idea of marrying quickly into Allan's head – didn't you, Lydia?'

The question was direct and inescapable. And I knew that I must go carefully and avoid any conclusive answer.

My eyes met hers very steadily as I said:

'Just what is it, Stella? You seem to have changed so terribly lately. Everything you say to me has an accusing sound, darling, as though I were your enemy instead of someone who has lived for you.' I sighed. 'It is very hard to bear and I don't think I have deserved it.'

She looked uncomfortable.

'It isn't that but it seems as if I'm always doing the things you want me to do – never those that I want to do, Lydia. I cannot explain but–'

I managed to keep very calm; this was a moment when she needed my generosity and my guidance, to help her master an impulsiveness that might well wreck her life if not curbed.

'Since my one anxiety has always been that you have everything you wanted in this world … do you think it fair? There's Stephen, I know… But that wasn't my fault – it wasn't my fault that he chose me, Stella. Heaven forbid that–'

'No, no,' she cried; 'please, Lydia, I wasn't thinking of Stephen; I–'

'But, darling even if you were, I would never have agreed to marry him at all had you not begged me to do so; I would never have grasped my own happiness unless I felt sure that you could be happy too. In all justice, give me an example of anything I have ever prevented your doing, or influenced you in doing – that is unless you have come to me for advice? Why, my every thought and prayer has been for you, Stella; for your happiness and yet, now, suddenly, you accuse me of–' I broke off overcome with emotion.

Instantly, she was beside me, her cheek warm against mine.

'I didn't mean it, Lydia – truly I didn't. I don't quite know what it is, but lately, I've been all mixed up inside.' She added in a strangled tone: 'Unhappiness plays queer tricks on one.'

'Darling!' I was shocked and, as I put my arms around her, I rocked her as one might rock, and soothe, a child. 'Let's forget it all,' I murmured. 'I know you didn't mean to be unfair and unjust–'

She was perfectly calm again as she said in a thin, almost lifeless voice:

'I'm sorry, Lydia. Forgive me.'

There was a moment of silence then she exclaimed sharply:

'Oh, I forgot! Stephen! I saw him while I was in town, and he asked me to tell you that he wouldn't be able to look in after that last case of his: he had to go on from there to the hospital.'

I glanced at the clock. He was due in – according to an earlier arrangement – just about now.

'I might have waited up all night,' I said lightly. 'Were you with him long?'

'He drove me to the Marshalls. Very

enthusiastic about his idea for a clinic. He has some wonderful views about life, hasn't he? Every time I listen to him I admire him more. The world needs millions like him.'

'Stephen is a dreamer.'

She glanced at me almost as though challenging me.

'Are you suggesting that is a fault?'

I forced a smile. I felt that I was talking to an infatuated child. It really was very irritating that she should deliberately continue this hero-worship of Stephen.

'No, darling, no.'

She gave me a penetrating look.

'Good night, Lydia.'

'Good night, darling.' I met her gaze. 'We shall have to talk about the things you will need for your trousseau. Did you decide on a quiet wedding or–'

'Very quiet,' she said and a shadow crossed her face. 'Don't be surprised if we just arrive one evening – married. As for a trousseau... Daddy just cannot afford very much and I would not place him in a position of having to refuse. It will work out,' she added somewhat inscrutably.

Stephen and I were married at St Marks church and although I had tried to keep the wedding as quiet as possible, crowds gathered and friends swarmed around us after the ceremony, many returning to the house until it bulged to overflowing. I was the cynosure of all eyes and could not help knowing that I was looking my best in soft, misty blue georgette with a coat of the same colour in light wool; the two garments could be used either together, or separately, and serve for almost all occasions.

Nothing was as I had imagined it being. Stephen was pale, grave and very subdued, never once relaxing so it seemed, and anything but festive. Stella moved among the guests like a figment of another world; exquisite and never lovelier in her subdued, poignantly wistful sadness. I could not deceive myself about that sadness, even though others might not have noticed it. I heard her say to Stephen:

'This is the end of a chapter, Stephen ... when we all meet again–' Their eyes seemed to leap together, emotion quiver on the breath of their sigh. 'I hope you will be very, very happy.'

'And you.' It was a hoarse sound.

Her voice cracked as she said forcing a laugh:

'I can't believe you are my brother-in-law.'

They stood looking at each other as though words had become meaningless; as though held by a spell which not all the noise around then could break. I felt a tingling sensation creeping over my body; my heart thumped; jealousy flamed to passionate life. Why was it I should be thus hurt by them?

Was it necessary for Stephen to encourage her obvious regard for him? Yet I dare not speak because the last thing I would have him suspect was that ridiculous infatuation. I pulled myself up sharply. What was I thinking; how absurd it all was. This was a day when no cloud should mar the perfection of the horizon. Stephen was mine and I his: I had steered his life safely into the harbour of my keeping and ever would serve and love him. And I had spared Stella from wrecking his life and her own. That was better ... amazing how wrong thinking could shatter and distort one's balance.

I was devoutly thankful when the moment came to say good-bye and escape from it all. Father was serious, without being sad; his attitude dignified and to be admired. I noticed how tired and breathless he seemed; the strain had told on him for it could but revive the memories of his marriage and the happiness he had lost.

'We shall be absolutely all right,' he said cheerfully as he kissed me. 'Stella will look after me.'

I smiled affectionately.

'And in a very little while you won't have any more responsibility with the house and I shall be absolutely happy to see you tucked up with Mr and Mrs Lane and Stella happy with Allan...' I felt suddenly thrilled and elated. How well everything had turned out;

not one of my plans had gone awry and everyone's interests had been perfectly served.

Father laughed. Then said softly:

'You've been wonderful, Lydia. We shall miss you.'

'I hope so!'

Stella stood silently by. She put her arms around me, kissed me and said:

'I'll take care of daddy – don't worry.'

I turned to Allan.

'I shan't worry, with Allan beside you nothing can go wrong.'

Stephen and Stella faced each other. I held my breath. He leaned swiftly forward and brushed her cheek with his lips.

'Good-bye, Stella,' he murmured hoarsely.

She didn't speak and I felt instinctively that he did not expect her to do so. Their eyes met directly – after the manner of two people whose souls might well know that complete fusion and affinity. Then he turned away.

The memory of that moment haunted me long after we left for our honeymoon – all too brief since it was only for five days – in Dorset. The thought wrankled that Stella should thus intrude, dearly though I loved her; it was hard, indeed, that after all my sacrifices on her behalf she should insinuate herself – at least mentally – between Stephen and me. I fought off the depression that settled upon me, inwardly laughing at my own foolishness. Stella would soon be married to Allan and living many miles away. I resisted the idea of my own jealousy because it was foreign to my nature, excusing it since, knowing Stella's foolish infatuation, her very presence, automatically became an issue.

I put out my hand and touched Stephen's.

'All over, darling.'

'Thank heavens,' he said grimly. 'If that was a quiet wedding, heaven preserve me from a big affair.'

My heart missed a beat.

'It wasn't my fault that so many people turned up,' I said aggrievedly, upset by his attitude.

'I wasn't blaming you, Lydia.'

I glanced at him. This wasn't what I wanted. I longed to share his every thought; to have him wholly in my power, not because I wished to dominate him, but because I was woman enough to wish to feel that my charms helped him completely and that he was clay in my hands.

I smiled.

'What are you thinking, Stephen?' I asked a few moments later.

He started, as one made suddenly aware of my presence.

'Many things,' he answered evasively.

'Which is no reply, darling.'

He gave me a swift glance.

'It wasn't meant to be,' came the imperturbable answer.

'Is that a way to talk to your wife,' I asked banteringly.

'It depends on the wife.' He smiled – it seemed a forced smile to me– 'One cannot explain one's thoughts, Lydia.'

'I've always believed that husband and wife should be able to explain anything; live in the very closest communion with each other,' I insisted, aware of a sick sense of frustration.

'I agree; but that communion cannot be forced; it must *exist*,' he said quietly.

'Are you suggesting that you don't feel it with me,' I cried aghast.

He sighed.

'I was not suggesting anything, my dear; you must not jump to conclusions... We shall be in Sherborne just in time for dinner.'

I wasn't interested in dinner. I could not help it; I felt miserable. And I plunged:

'Stella looked very lovely to-day.'

'Very.' There was a strange, faraway look in his eyes as he spoke. I knew that no matter what I might say he would not enlarge on the comment.

But that mood soon passed and as the days flew by I basked in the joy of my position. Nothing, and no one, could take Stephen from me now, I was his wife; he would find that I was indispensable to him; that there was no corner of his life I could not share and, finally, I should possess him wholly. At the moment I had to allow for the transition from his bachelor state to that of a married man. If his caresses were a little lacking in the fire for which I had hoped, I must make allowances and urge him on towards the fulfilment I personally desired so fiercely. He was tender, thoughtful in every way, but as night fell and deepened to dawn, a sense of incompleteness bore down upon me; the dissatisfaction of feeling that he was, at all times, in a world mentally apart from mine, and that his body responded automatically to his will, rather than as an expression of his love or any natural emotion.

They were, I told myself, utterly happy days; we were alone and he was ready to give in to my every whim so far as the places we visited were concerned. I hated the very thought of turning homewards and said as, finally, we did so:

'If only we could have been here a month, darling.'

He looked at me and I knew that he in no way shared my regret at leaving. But he murmured:

'I'm afraid the time has been terribly brief for you, Lydia. But we'll manage a week-end later on.'

'You don't mind going back?'

He laughed evasively, and teasingly.

'So many questions!'

I nerved myself to accept that as I said lightly:

'And so few answers, Stephen.' A pause. 'Are you happy?'

'Naturally.' He laughed. 'Wonder how Stella and father will have managed during your absence?'

'Quite well, no doubt.'

'They'll be glad to have you back.'

We were making conversation and I knew it; but I explained, for my own satisfaction and composure, that these first days were of necessity days of adjustment; that marriage was not entirely an easy state to begin with.

'I shall have a good deal to do to get ready for Stella's wedding – even if it is to be a quiet affair.'

'I look with suspicion on that word "quiet",' he said jerkily. 'They are really being married next week?'

'Of course, Stephen; you know they are. I shall be very very relieved when Stella is settled; it's been quite a struggle to reach this stage in her life, believe me.' I added, anxious lest I might create a wrong impression: 'When a person's happiness is as dear to one as one's own there is always an accompanying fear behind everything.'

Stephen drove on in silence. When he spoke it was as though he were answering his own thoughts as he said reflectively:

'I had a feeling that Stella wasn't too anxious to rush things.'

I laughed.

'Darling you are a very poor psychologist – for a doctor. A woman can hardly appear over anxious, now, can she?'

'That is a very debatable point,' he replied caustically.

I felt slightly on edge as always when Stella was under discussion and tried to avoid perpetuating the mood as I said:

'I'll let you into a secret... Allan's buying her a house for a wedding gift. A lovely place, I believe – just ready to step into.'

'Really?... Where?' His tone was clipped.

'Some forty miles from Milbury.'

He jerked his head around and stared at me.

'Forty miles,' he exclaimed. 'But – but it never occurred to me that they wouldn't remain in Milbury.'

'Why ever should they?'

He seemed to draw back into himself.

'Of course,' he said quietly. 'No reason at all.'

'You sound sorry.' I tried to keep my voice light, steady.

Deliberately he changed the subject and I knew it would be foolish to pursue it.

Stella called to see us almost immediately on our return home and, at the sight of her,

I felt a curious resentment that she should have intruded on our privacy that first evening.

But she began, looking first at Stephen and then at me:

'I hadn't intended to intrude–'

'Intrude,' Stephen echoed. 'You?'

Faint colour stole into her cheeks.

'I've been anxious about daddy. I'm afraid he's far from well and if you could see him, Stephen–'

Instantly, Stephen exclaimed:

'I'll come right away.'

To that I added:

'Of course, Stella; we'll go back with you... Probably just a little reaction, you know,' I said feeling that she could well have waited before worrying us unnecessarily. No one could be more concerned for father than I, but Stella could just not be trusted to understand his symptoms and panicked for no reason whatsoever.

'I don't think so,' she said gravely.

I humoured her and adopted a reassuring attitude. Then:

'Where's Allan?'

For a second there was a heavy, almost electrical silence. Her voice broke into it and for me it was like the sound of silent thunder as she said:

'Allan is in London...' She looked at Stephen for an imperceptible second and then back at me as she added quietly and with a certain implacability: 'I'm not going to marry him, Lydia.'

CHAPTER EIGHT

Stella's words fell upon the silence with all the precision of hammer blows. For a second I was too stunned, too amazed even to comment. My gaze flew to Stephen's and I saw him start almost as one reacting violently to a shock; his expression changed from incredulity to something that it would have been very easy for me to analyse as relief. He looked swiftly at Stella, and for a moment their eyes were as two worlds embracing them both – worlds from which I felt completely and utterly divorced. I managed to say sharply:

'But Stella! You can't be serious? Why, the very idea is absurd.' Confidence returned to me just then. This was no more perhaps than a passing whim; Allan would soon influence her to change her mind.

She stared at me with a cool assertiveness that stung as she said:

'On the contrary, Lydia; it was our engagement that was absurd. Only love ever justifies an engagement.'

I caught at my breath. This was the last thing I had bargained for, and the thought of its effect upon Stephen appalled me. I had, through no fault of my own, been placed in a very delicate situation in which it was almost impossible to justify myself should he choose to raise the issue of all that I had told him about Stella's affections for Allan; it might even appear that I had some ulterior motive other than that designed purely for her and Allan's good. It seemed that I was always condemned to be placed in an invidious position capable of being misunderstood.

I spoke quietly and with emphasis:

'We must talk of all this later, darling, and–'

She interrupted me.

'There is nothing to talk about... Stephen, could you hurry; I hated leaving father alone even to come here.'

Impatience, all the warring elements surged within me. Stella had a very maddening habit of overstatement.

'Father will be perfectly all right,' I insisted calmly. 'After all, Stella, we have hardly got home and–'

She countered:

'I would not, as I said before, have intruded had it not been urgent, Lydia.'

Stephen frowned in my direction.

'If your father is ill I hardly think it necessary to question the degree... I'm ready, Stella.' He glanced at me. 'If you'd prefer to look after things here and feel certain there is no urgency–'

'Of course,' I interrupted, somewhat aggrieved, 'I'll come with you.'

We went out to the car in silence; I had the hateful feeling as of one gazing on the shattered fragments of a relationship that had once been perfect. There was antagonism in Stella's attitude; a silent reproach in her mien, for all the quiet dignity she assumed and which I could not help feeling was designed to impress Stephen.

I never forgot that brief journey, during which time Stephen questioned Stella about father, and I seemed curiously shut off from them both. It was as if they were two people sharing a secret that I should never understand and, although nothing more was said about the broken engagement, the fact of it lay between us almost sinisterly.

Father was lying on the settee in the sitting-room when we reached him, and my heart sank in terror as I saw his ashen face and heard his laboured breathing. Stella gave a little cry and sank down beside him; then for a second she raised her gaze pleadingly to Stephen as one seeking comfort and reassurance.

I knew, then, that far from overstating the seriousness of the situation she had indulged in understatement and I felt slightly uncomfortable to think that I had doubted her.

'Hot water bottles,' Stephen said peremptorily as, swiftly, he plunged a hypodermic into father's chest.

I looked down at Stella.

'You get them, darling,' I said, taking charge. 'I may be needed.'

Stella was holding that limp, blue hand.

Stephen gave the order:

'You go, Lydia.'

I stared at him aghast. Was it that he wanted to be alone with Stella in these moments of drama, or was it that he was studying his patient. If the latter then father would, I know, have leaned towards me in emergency rather than Stella. I said:

'But—'

Father's lips moved and Stella's name came on a gasping breath.

Stella cried:

'Daddy...' Then: 'Oh, *Stephen*—'

It was all over. Stella's head went down upon that inert figure. I stood stunned, shocked into inactivity, incapable of grasping the momentousness of the calamity... I turned to Stephen, thankful for the comfort of his presence; my eyes seeking his, my hand reaching out for that support I so sorely needed. A hollow emptiness struck at the pit of my stomach, and the emotion that churned through my body were conflicting, painful and grievous.

But Stephen bent swiftly and raised Stella to her feet; for an imperceptible second he held her against him with all the tenderness and solicitude of which he was capable and a fierce, stinging jealousy stabbed me as with a dagger. I moved and insinuated myself between them. If Stella needed comforting then I was there to minister to her needs, although her grief, in any case, could not possibly be as great as mine. Father and I had shared responsibilities; Stella, herself, had constituted the larger portion of them; his death would leave a great void in my heart.

At my touch Stella straightened herself and while her eyes were suspiciously bright, no tears fell as she said shakily:

'That was how he always hoped to die... I'm happy for him; he's waited so long to join mummie.' She turned to Stephen urgently: 'Could anything–'

'Nothing could have been done,' he promised her solemnly. 'Nothing.'

'I think I knew when I came to you,' she murmured. 'Thank God you were back in time.'

It was a little later that Stephen said:

'You'd better stay here to-night, Lydia – with Stella. Or, better still, Stella come to us.'

Stella shook her head.

'No; I don't mind being here alone, and I couldn't leave him,' she said softly. 'Lydia's place is with you, Stephen. Please don't make me feel a nuisance.'

I hated the thought of being parted from Stephen even for a night, but my loyalties were torn and it was extremely difficult for me to make a decision.

Stephen said:

'I wouldn't dream of your being here alone, Stella.'

His tone annoyed me; it was both possessive and dictatorial, as though he were in complete command of her life and my views were of no importance. With firmness I exclaimed:

'I will remain here – simpler that way.' I knew that I could not bear the thought of Stella coming to us lest her stay should be unduly prolonged. That, above all, must be avoided for her sake, especially now that the safeguard of Allan was removed. Stella was so unpredictable and irresponsible that it was vitally important I keep hold of the reins upon her.

She protested again, but I was adamant.

'You really must allow Stephen and me to be the judge of what is best for you, darling,' I said quietly. 'It is unthinkable that you should stay here alone.'

'Quite,' Stephen supplemented. 'I shouldn't have a moment's peace.'

It was after the funeral that Stephen broached the subject of Stella's future. He and I were alone almost for the first time in our own home, Stella having gone to stay with Diana for a few days.

'I think,' he began, 'that Stella should make her home here with us until she has decided just what she wants to do – what plans she wishes to make for her future. Since she is not going to marry Allan–'

Amid the turmoil and grief of the past days, no mention had been made of the broken engagement and now that it came once more into prominence, I felt faintly sick at the repercussions it might well have. Also, I had no indication of the attitude Stephen might take and was conscious of a certain trepidation. That he should suggest Stella sharing our home was the very last thing I had anticipated and it shook me. A third person; our privacy gone... Knowing, also, of Stella's regard for him, I realized that I must prevent her being precipitated into further danger. I said quietly:

'I rather imagine she would hate that.'

His gaze challenged me.

'Why should she? And what have you in mind as an alternative?' His tone was faintly critical.

'I still feel that she will marry Allan,' I said imperturbably.

'Don't you think' – his voice was slow and deliberate – 'that you have rather distorted the facts about her relationship with Allan and built up the idea of her affection for him. Obviously had she been in love with him she would not have broken the engagement. I always had my doubts, Lydia, but you were so convincing that–' He broke off sharply and an inscrutable look came into his eyes.

'Are you,' I asked painfully, 'suggesting that I misrepresented the facts?'

He was standing at his desk in his consulting room as we talked, and he flicked over the pages of his diary before raising his gaze penetratingly to mine. Then, impressively, he replied:

'Why should I? Isn't that a rather odd remark to make? What possible reason could you have for wishing to misrepresent anything so far as Stella is concerned?'

The words hung between us dangerously and I drew on every reserve of strength and courage to combat the forces I knew to be ranged against me. Very smoothly and quietly I answered him:

'Listen, Stephen, it would be very easy for us to be at cross purposes over all this and I'd hate that. You know my regard for Stella and my concern for her. She is not an easy person to deal with; emotionally she is quite unstable and her rather fickle affections are not easily described. Genuinely, I believed that Allan would prove the exception, and that marriage to him would be the very finest thing for her. That is why I encouraged the idea and reassured her when she feared that things might go wrong.'

'I can never quite reconcile the idea that Stella is the fickle type,' he commented adamantly.

I forced a smile although my nerves were on edge, and a sensation of sickness gripped me.

'That is because you do not know her,' I protested.

'Are you quite sure that you do?' It was said quietly.

'I?' My voice rose. 'Really, Stephen, isn't this becoming a trifle absurd? Is it necessary to waste our time discussing Stella? She will learn only from experience and gain stability as she grows older. Does it never occur to you that it has been a strain and a responsibility for me always to be on the alert in case she should make a false move? Stella is rather the type whose heart breaks very easily – and very frequently. That I was deceived about the sincerity of her regard for Allan freely I admit – although I do not think I can be blamed for it.'

'But you still think she will marry him?'

'Yes.' I knew that I had no intention of sitting down under this defeat. 'Now that father is dead she will need him–'

'Needing isn't loving.'

'Then suppose we wait and see,' I said testily. 'I am a little weary, Stephen. No matter how one loves a person, or how anxious one is for their welfare, it can be trying always to be confronted by their problems. I want to feel that I have a little right to a life of my own.'

'Naturally; but you've always been so zealous in Stella's cause.'

'I still am.'

Something in my voice must have arrested his attention for he asked sharply:

'What have you in mind for her, assuming that she doesn't turn to Allan again – and I doubt very much that she will.'

'You sound very sure of that?'

I watched him closely; there was something inscrutable in his manner; I felt that I was hitting my head against a brick wall and that never should I have the satisfaction of knowing he shared my views on any given point.

'I am sure.'

'Perhaps you are in her confidence even more than I,' I challenged.

He looked at me.

'Suppose we let the matter rest there, Lydia.'

I couldn't afford to do that. I wanted things settled without the menace of his suggesting before Stella, that she should stay with us. I looked within myself at the thoughts taking shape in my mind. All this was so very much for Stella's good and in her interests. For me to agree to that which would bring her into intimate contact with Stephen – knowing how she imagined she felt for him – would be unforgivable. It was up to me to safeguard her, as always, from herself.

'I see no reason why not,' I replied calmly. 'I have everything arranged in my mind for Stella.'

He smiled, but it lacked humour.

'You are,' he murmured, 'a past master at arranging things – aren't you?'

Anger surged within me.

'Is that a criticism? Really, Stephen, I don't think you are being quite fair.'

'I'm sorry.' He changed the subject abruptly. 'By the way, Diana is very interested in, and sympathetic towards my idea of taking Highfield House and running it as a clinic. It struck me that we might even move there if all goes well and–'

'*Highfield House!*' I echoed the name aghast. 'But this is the first I've heard of it.'

'I have,' he said confidently, 'only just discovered that it is on the market. Naturally, I've not worried you with such things just recently but–'

'And Diana is interested,' I said holding my breath and suppressing the anger that surged upon me. 'Meaning that she would be prepared to assist you financially?'

'Yes.'

I walked to the window and looked out,

playing for time. There must be no false move on my part, no active opposition, but if I truly had Stephen's welfare at heart I knew that, on this occasion, it was up to me to prevent him from taking a step he would always regret afterwards. My voice was low, sympathetic, as I said:

'That would, of course, be wonderful but, somehow, I had thought in terms of our achieving everything off our own bat – together. Business and friendship are not always successful allies, darling, are they?'

'Diana,' he exclaimed, 'is the very rare exception. You don't like the idea?'

There was something disconcerting in the way Stephen spoke; almost as one trying to pierce my armour and I hastened:

'Darling, it isn't a question of that at all – I'd love you to do precisely as you wish. We shall have to see, shan't we? There are so many factors to be considered I suppose... Have you another case to-night?'

'I hope not. Why?'

'I'd like a quiet run out into the country. We seem to have had so little time alone and–'

The 'phone rang at that instant. Stephen answered it. Another confinement, I thought resentfully. But as I listened I realized that such was not the case as he exclaimed:

'Stella!... Yes... Why? Of course. Run over now. Do you have to ask? Bother us? Don't be absurd!'

I edged towards him, wanting to snatch the receiver from his hand, but before I had any such opportunity he had replaced it, saying with what I considered rather elaborate casualness:

'Stella wants to see us; Allan is running her over now.'

Again that prickly sensation came upon me; my heart-beats quickened; there was a strange drumming in my ears.

'I'd wanted to be alone to-night,' I said. 'I wish you could have–'

He frowned.

'I thought the last thing you would want was for Stella to be put off.'

'She's probably coming to tell us that she and Allan are engaged again,' I said somewhat flippantly.

'I don't think so.'

His tone maddened me; never had I experienced such antagonism which, while my love for Stella had in no way lessened, was now fraught with a jealousy I could not curb. Jealousy ... the word offended me and was distasteful. I could not dissipate the ghost of the past, or rid myself of the uncertainty as to the exact nature of Stephen's regard for Stella. Acting in their interests could not wholly dispel the fact that they had been drawn to each other in the beginning. My thoughts ran riot and I curbed them almost violently. I had done all that was humanly possible to protect their individual happiness therefore why, now, should I have a single qualm, or fear in any way their mutual regard. I was Stephen's wife and that was a supreme and indestructible truth, a reality which nothing, and no one, could alter.

Stella arrived alone some half an hour later.

'Allan is visiting some friends and is going to pick me up on his way home,' she explained. 'I'm sorry to worry you, but I have something I'd like to discuss... I couldn't before because daddy's death wiped out all else–' She had a faraway look in her eyes: 'But life goes on–'

Stephen was watching her with that intensity I had come to know so well; as though her every word had both value and significance. I knew that I could not relax my vigil and that I must take the reins of her life again. Allowing her to go to Diana's was a mistake and freely I admitted it, but it might be argued that, in the circumstances, newly married, I was entitled to think of myself and of Stephen a little in whatever plans I had made. I began carefully:

'We've not really had an opportunity of talking since father died, Stella–' I glanced at Stephen hoping that he would leave us alone together since there were matters I could not discuss in front of him. The problem of Allan had to be gone into; a hundred and one things in connection with the old home. Stephen said jerkily:

'I'll leave you and–'

To my surprise Stella cried:

'Please don't, Stephen. What I had to say is not in any way personal and, in any case, I want your advice.'

That was, I felt, a little unnecessary and I resented it.

'We mustn't trespass on Stephen's generosity,' I interposed. 'I–'

Stephen's voice was firm.

'Stella's problems are ours from now on,' he said slowly.

I plunged.

'I've been thinking of your future, in any case, Stella.'

She stared at me; a rather expressionless stare that was slightly unnerving. Then:

'That's kind of you–'

'"Kind" of me,' I echoed. 'Surely, darling, we have got beyond that word.' I knew, even as I spoke, that Diana had not wasted any time and that her influence was both forceful and pernicious. My light laugh took the edge off my words, and I went on: 'It struck me to-day that it would do you all the good in the world to get right away from old associations. At the moment you don't feel that you can marry Allan; but that is most probably because you cannot see the picture in focus. I feel that the very best thing is for you to go up to Cumberland for a month and stay with Aunt Bessie: she–'

Stella's lips parted in the barest smile; but it was a smile of resistance, rather than agreement, and she seemed to have borrowed from Stephen the strength and calm of his implacability, against which even I was powerless.

'It's thoughtful of you, Lydia; but that is the last thing I intend to do. Chasing off to stay with people is merely escapism: I want my life stabilized and purposeful.'

'Darling!' I laughed at her indulgently. 'And just how do you propose to achieve that?'

She looked at Stephen and then back to me as she said:

'I've decided to take up nursing – make it my career.'

I gasped.

'You've – *what!*' Had she said it was her intention to climb Mount Everest I could not have been more shocked.

'I'm perfectly serious, Lydia.' Her tone was measured. 'Stephen will, I feel sure, agree with me and understand my decision.'

Was she, I thought desperately, trying to divorce Stephen from his loyalty to me, by way of enlisting his support in whatever outrageous scheme she might wish to indulge.

Was this to be her way of insinuating herself more closely into his life in order to appease her over-stimulated emotions. I hated myself for the thought ... that I should even think such a thing of Stella for whom I would, if necessary give my life, was appalling. Nevertheless, it might be well to look facts in the face. Consciously, she would never be perfidious; there was nothing vicious in her nature, but I had to confess that she had that child-like *naïveté* which could be equally dangerous, and her attitude to Stephen might well menace the composure and happiness of our home – if allowed free rein. She was, in her irresponsibility, incapable of appreciating the delicacy of any situation, and with all the eagerness of a child would walk towards a given object – blindly and without thought for any issue other than her own desires. That was, I told myself, no criticism; but to ignore all these facets of her character would be as unfair to her as to me.

'And,' I asked gently, 'you are not sure that I shall understand.'

'No; quite sure you will oppose me.'

I smiled tenderly.

'I most certainly shall, darling for you know, don't you, that it is quite out of the question? You are no more fitted to be a nurse than I am qualified to paint a masterpiece.'

'Then,' she said resolutely, 'I shall have to

pursue my course without your approval, Lydia.'

'Stella!'

She looked at me very earnestly:

'You cannot live my life for me any longer,' she said with quiet resolution. 'I must stand on my own two feet from now on, and tread the path of my own choosing.'

'You are,' I said severely, 'in my care. Can you imagine what father would have said to such an outrageous idea? If you were strong or–'

'I am perfectly strong and perfectly capable of doing an honest days work,' she insisted.

I forgot Stephen's presence in that moment as I cried:

'Married to Allan you would have been cared for an protected, and yet you come here and–'

'Married to Allan I should have been a parasite escaping from life; a woman married to a man for whom I had no love in the sense that I regard married love,' she said and faint colour stole into her cheeks. 'No, Lydia … this is what I want and what I mean to have.' She turned to Stephen. 'Can you help me?'

Their eyes met; their glances seeming to dissolve one into the other.

'Stephen,' I exclaimed, 'cannot be expected to help you, and I hardly think it fair you should ask it of him.'

Stephen's voice came very steadily.

'On the contrary, I'm prepared to do all I can to help,' he said gently. 'I admire Stella's courage in wanting to take up what is certainly not an easy profession. I think she is right, Lydia.'

I was astounded at his deliberate support for Stella and his attitude, which suggested a refusal to indulge in any form of compromise, or even to begin to see my point of view. It was as if, suddenly, we had become two people in opposite camps and I was doubly hurt because I felt I had a right to expect that Stella might have consulted me before coming to any final decision. It was very hard to be forced to realize that Stella was fast becoming a great disappointment and that our relationship appeared as a gradually widening gulf. In no way could I reproach myself for her independent attitude; certainly my marriage had not engendered the belief in her mind that my responsibility so far as she was concerned was over; quite the reverse. It struck me, not without bitterness, that her desire to go in for nursing might not be unconnected with an equal desire for proximity to Stephen; the creating of a bond that should unite them at least in friendship from which, conceivably, I was to be precluded. Was that far-fetched? Was I building it all up within the framework of my own disappointment, even disillusionment?

I knew that my voice sounded subdued, lifeless: I felt very still – as though I had suddenly been placed in a sound-proof world where only the beating of my heart appeared audible.

'If that is your opinion,' I said, 'then it would be foolish of me to try to change it.'

Stella said with great conviction:

'I must follow my own hunch, Lydia; find my own niche.'

'But why – why nursing of all things,' I persisted.

For a second it seemed that the air was drained of all oxygen. Stephen moved rather abruptly as one who fears to betray himself even with a look; the atmosphere was heavy; the tension unbearable, and it seemed to me that Stella's love for Stephen took visible shape in those moments – like a ghost that flits through a darkened room to chill the blood and quicken the heart beat.

She looked at me without flinching as she answered:

'Because Stephen's work created for me the inspiration, the desire to help humanity. I've been neither use nor ornament long enough.'

Stephen turned to face her.

'Thank you, Stella; you will go far; for sympathy and understanding are not the lesser qualities in nursing.'

I wanted to shriek. Stella! Stella whom I

had nurtured and guarded, knowing her to be gloriously incapable. Stephen must be mad not to realize the truth and, instead, to judge her now very nearly on her own valuation.

'Then, you'll help me?'

'Certainly. I warn you; it will mean beginning at the bottom.'

'I should hate it any other way,' she told him resolutely. 'If I could begin at the Royal Free Hospital–'

'Here in Milbury?' I spoke in a breath.

She looked surprised.

'Naturally; why not?' She paused; then: 'I could try to start in London–'

'No,' said Stephen. 'We can keep an eye on you here... I was saying to Lydia that you ought to come to us for a while, Stella.'

'Stay here,' she echoed faintly.

'Why not?' It was a clipped sound. 'I hope the idea is not too distasteful?'

'It isn't that,' she hastened, the colour surging into her cheeks. A look at me. 'What do you think, Lydia?'

I could not resist the thrust:

'Are my opinions of any importance to you, darling? I don't see that it really matters what I think.'

'I do.' It was a grave sound. She turned again to Stephen. 'Thank you for asking me; but I've other plans.'

My relief at her refusal made me expansive. I was so thankful that she had been spared the temptations inseparable from such a position should she have accepted; she was too young to meet them in her stride and far too impulsive to avoid them.

'Ah well, you know best ... what plans?'

'Only that Diana wants me to stay with her whenever I've any spare time.' She laughed. 'Which, I rather gather, will not be often.'

'I see.' How dare Diana usurp my place, my authority. 'And does Diana approve of this step?'

'Of course.' She turned to Stephen. 'Are you going to take over Highfield House, Stephen?'

So even that had been discussed: I hated the very thought.

I said instantly:

'I rather think that is Stephen's business, darling. Diana talks too much.'

Stella leaped to her defence.

'She is so zealous in Stephen's cause and so eager that his dreams shall come true.' It was said simply. 'Diana has a lovely character; she just knows people.'

How plain the set-up was. Doubtless, Diana felt this possession and influence of Stella would provide the dagger to be poised at my heart.

'I agree,' said Stephen. 'And I am awfully keen to get that house, actually. It was the only one available in the district and would, in any case, be a good investment and for the purpose I have in mind... Will you join the staff, madam?' he asked lightly, smiling at her.

'Just ask me,' she murmured. 'And I'll even forget the salary!'

'Such magnanimity!' I laughed lightly.

'Don't you,' she challenged me, 'like the idea of the clinic?'

I started; it was as though, suddenly, Stella were doubting and suspicious; as though all my sacrifices and anxieties were as a boomerang striking against me.

'I like,' I said, and knew that my voice sounded curiously stiff, 'anything that furthers Stephen's ambitions; but nothing has been decided and–'

'What,' Stephen asked Stella, 'do you think about it – as a project?'

I laughed lightly.

'Really, darling, how can you expect Stella to answer that since she cannot possibly know the facts?'

Stella's voice was low, tremulous.

'I don't need to know the facts: I know the motive behind Stephen's intentions, and I think it would be the most wonderful thing – the way he would work it and the good he would do.' She forced a little laugh. 'Quite a eulogy for – for one's brother-in-law,' she finished hastily.

I knew even as I stood there that, at all costs, Stephen must be prevented from fulfilling that particular ambition. I could see far deeper into the question, and was not carried away by the philanthropic angle, or even that which was calculated to benefit humanity and provide for them a service sorely needed in Milbury. I could see the dangers attendant upon Diana having a financial hold upon him; I could see the potential dangers of Stella working there, and being forced into constant association with Stephen who, as was his custom, would treat her with the utmost consideration and fan the flame of her infatuation anew. I was his wife and it was my duty to guide his future, not necessarily in the way which gave him most personal satisfaction, but in the way that was best for his welfare.

A thrill shot through me. Diana had thrown down the gauntlet and it was for me to accept her challenge. The very thought of the battle ahead invigorated me; it even dwarfed the problems that had been exercising my mind during the past moments where Stella was concerned. Diana would know that Highfield House would not appeal to me and that I should oppose its purchase – even if not directly. And she was right.

Stephen said, and he was suddenly elated, excited:

'I shall go ahead with the idea. I know it would be a pretty uphill climb but, by heaven, it will be worth it all. What do you think, Lydia?'

I smiled lovingly.

'You know best, darling,' I said gently.

He beamed at me like a man who, fearing opposition, is delighted to find that he has none.

'Splendid! Then we're all set and I'll ask Diana to go ahead...' He breathed deeply. 'Life can be good when the purpose is right... I'll have your moral support – both of you – eh?'

'The whole family backing,' I assured him.

Stella was looking at me very steadily, inquiringly; I lowered my gaze for it was almost as though she could read my thoughts and knew, in advance, my already half-formulated scheme to defeat Diana and prevent Stephen from taking a step I believed would prove to be disastrous.

CHAPTER NINE

It was not an easy task to marshal my thoughts and correlate all the facts impinging upon Stephen's decision regarding the clinic. I knew that many factors had a vital bearing upon the subject which, at first sight, might be abstruse and that a false move on my part would be disastrous. Only the firm conviction that I was acting in Stephen's – to say nothing of Stella's – interests fortified me in the task I had set myself. That Diana, of all people, should buy Highfield House was unthinkable and unless I prevented her doing so, it was probable that Stephen would remain in her clutches for life. Try as I might I could not trust Diana – and this quite without prejudice on account of her unpardonable rudeness and attitude towards me – what was more, I knew that her generosity was primarily designed to anger, even humiliate, me for she, better than anyone, could gauge my reactions to such an arrangement.

It was to Allan I turned; his loyalty was incorruptible and I knew that he could be trusted not only to respect my confidence, but to support me in whatever project I cared to put forward. He had returned from London and I sought him out, having made sure – by vicarious means – that Diana was not at home. To waste so much as an hour was to endanger Stephen's future and I was prepared to go to any lengths to protect him – even from his own folly.

Allan received me in his study. It was our first meeting – apart from the occasion of father's funeral – since the breaking of the engagement, and I was anxious to learn from him the facts which Stella had stubbornly withheld. As he came forward to greet me he said with some gravity:

'I hope I am not altogether in your bad books, Lydia?'

My smile answered him as I said:

'Why ever should you be?'

'Because of Stella and me.'

My eyes met his.

'I am quite certain the fault was not yours.'

'Nor Stella's,' he said swiftly, defensively. 'Things just didn't work out, Lydia; you cannot manufacture human relationships.'

Was that a reproach? I was sensitive to anything in that nature, particularly since my whole life had been devoted to doing what was best for those around me.

'Are you suggesting that I was wrong in my desire to see you both happy?'

'No.' It was a slow, measured sound. 'I

don't think you quite realize how very mature Stella is. Not to be wondered at, of course. But she surprised me, Lydia; she has such hidden depths, such deep understanding as to be unique.'

I felt slightly irritated. How blind men were when it came to judging women. I said meaningly:

'That eulogy might well betoken a far more serious regard than you once knew for her, Allan. Is it so?'

'My affections,' he said quietly, 'have certainly deepened through knowing Stella better; my feelings, nevertheless, will never change, Lydia.'

Content stole upon me. Allan's love was staunch, dependable and, womanlike, I should have been loathe to lose it. All the same, my desires and hopes for his happiness with Stella had been no less sincere on that account. It wasn't easy to analyse my regard for Allan: he was that tower of strength on whom I had come to rely in a strange, indefinable way.

'And I take it that you are fully in agreement with Stella in all this?'

'Yes; it wouldn't have worked. Two people who are not in love with each other *have* been known to make a success of marriage, even to love each other in the end; but two people already in love – and not with the husband or wife as the case may be. Ah, that is another matter.'

I started.

'You mean that Stella told you she was in love with someone else?'

'Yes; can you imagine her being other than perfectly honest?'

I hesitated. Then:

'I hardly think it is a question so much of honesty as of reserve and restraint, Allan... She's a strange little soul; imagines all manner of things and I'm afraid her emotions are most unstable.'

'I couldn't disagree with you more,' he said firmly.

I felt uncomfortable. Had Allan any idea who the man was? Had Stella been foolish enough to take him thus far into her confidence. I had to know this as a safeguard for us all and asked tentatively:

'Did she give you any idea as to whom the man was – I mean–'

He looked at me very levelly; there was something faintly forbidding in his attitude that unnerved me.

'By name – no.' His eyes became more penetrating. 'But there are some things that have no need of words. In the same way that Stella knows where my love lies.'

I hated it all put into cold, unchallengeable sentences; it made the situation far more real and Stella's love for Stephen far more serious than it might otherwise have seemed. And I knew, of course, that it was, in any case, purely transitory and that as soon as she came into contact with other men Stephen would be forgotten. I couldn't explain this to Allan and had to suffer the indignity of his beliefs in silence. It seemed that I was never to know any real peace and that the ghost of Stella shadowed me at every turn. It was a distasteful fact that Allan knew of her love for my husband and it appeared to detract from my position. I resented it – not without cause, and felt a smarting sense of injustice that Stella should have betrayed her feelings so blatantly. But, as ever, my hands were tied and I could but suffer in silence.

'Stella,' I insisted gently, 'romances Allan. I cannot out of loyalty to her, say more than that.'

He studied me intently as one summing me up, and I recalled his words to me when last we had talked together: 'You baffle me; sometimes I look at you and feel that I just don't know you at all–'

He shook his head.

'There are none so blind as those who won't see, Lydia. But you know – you've always known the truth. Sometimes I'm afraid it may be a dagger in your own heart.'

I gasped:

'What *do* you mean?'

'That Stella and Stephen–' He stopped

then: 'I'm sorry,' he said briefly.

I was trembling; a sick sensation struck at the pit of my stomach; the very breath of any suggestion that might involve Stephen's feelings, or couple him with Stella, was anathema. Of course Allan had not that in mind; he was merely following up the thread of conversation regarding Stella's– I could get no further in my thoughts, for a passionate and resentful jealousy tore at me like a turbulent sea tearing and dashing itself against the shore. I managed to smile.

'Strange how most women cherish romantic notions about medical men,' I said lightly. 'Stephen is, of course, amusedly aware of it.'

'And you're not the jealous type.'

'No.' My laughter was spontaneous; just then the knowledge that Stephen was my husband became all sufficing. But the subject has been pursued far enough and I went on: 'Allan, I'm here to ask you a very great favour.'

His eyes held mine with a sudden passionate fervour; his attitude changed as the love he bore me seemed almost to take tangible shape.

'You know,' he said hoarsely, 'you have only to name it.'

For myself I could never have sunk my pride in order to seek his financial aid; now, with Stephen's welfare as the goad, and the goal, of my efforts, I felt no sense of humiliation, or even of inferiority. I had made my plans and nothing must impede them.

'I need three thousand pounds,' I said quietly.

He gave me a rather pointed look of inquiry and, then, as one who has no intention of spoiling a favour by cross examination, exclaimed:

'Then you shall have three thousand pounds, Lydia.'

'Just like that?' My smile came from my heart in gratitude.

'Just like that.'

'You are very dear, Allan. Actually, I shall be able to return the money within a very short while: I will not commit myself as to the exact time, but months – a few months – will cover it. And, of course–'

'You will,' he said decisively, 'repay me when it is convenient and forget the matter between now and then.' He walked to his desk and flicked his cheque book from the top drawer.

I watched him as one fascinated. The idea of any man being able calmly to sit down and draw the sum of three thousand pounds from his bank was a sheer delight to me. The power of it; the complete and absolute sense of superiority it must create, filled me with a great longing, and the determination that, one day, Stephen should be in that same position, for, with money, Stephen would be supreme and I knew that, while he was sincere in his desire to further the cause of humanity, at heart he was a sybarite who would soon tire of poverty and deprivation. He and Stella had that in common, and their somewhat altruistic outlook would never stand fire in the end. I knew them so much better than they knew themselves, and shuddered to reflect just how disastrous their lives might be in the future, without my guiding rein to steer them in their rightful path.

I took the slip of paper from Allan's hand and met his gaze very levelly. He said:

'I hope you are going to benefit from it, Lydia.'

I shook my head.

'Had that been so, Allan, I'd never have had the courage to ask you to lend me such a sum.' A smile. 'I don't think anyone could accuse me of being selfish.'

'Hardly... What do you think of Stella's idea of becoming a nurse?'

'If that is what she really wants then there is nothing for me to say. The unfortunate part of it is that one cannot give advice: if she were stronger–' I sighed. 'I think it will be I who, in the end, will be the nurse: she will never stand the strain and hard work such a career entails.'

'I disagree, you know, Lydia.' He spoke firmly. 'You're so maternal over Stella that you cannot look at her objectively at all.'

'Nonsense,' I protested hotly. 'Responsibility provides all that one needs to see a person truly in focus.'

'Then we'll agree to differ,' he murmured. 'By the way, I understand that Diana and Stephen are becoming financial partners by way of Highfield House... You think it a good project?'

I temporized.

'Frankly, Allan, I don't feel qualified to say much about it, but I'm quite sure that whatever Stephen undertook, he would make it a success.'

'I don't doubt that.'

'And it is most generous of Diana.'

He smiled affectionately as though even the thought of his mother demanded such appreciation.

'Diana thinks the world of Stephen: she's thrilled about it all.'

I felt sudden panic.

'But there's nothing absolutely settled – is there?' Stephen would never keep anything from me I was certain.

'I don't really know.'

I hastened carelessly:

'And Stephen and I have hardly had an opportunity of discussing anything.'

'You've had a very difficult time ... your father's death–'

'I cannot quite believe he *is* dead,' I said

sadly. 'I miss him terribly.'

'I'm sure you do.'

I looked up at him and for a second there was silence between us. Strange that this man who could have given me everything I had ever craved financially, should mean no more to me than a friend. I was prepared to admit that mine was a curious temperament, and that Stephen represented adventure with all the possibilities of fame and renown, quite apart from my love for him. With Allan there could be no planning for the future, no dreams or schemes: the picture of his life was complete, materially, without me. Stephen needed me – and that was life to any woman.

I left a few moments later and went into Dornsford to the solicitors who had acted for my father for many years and whom I knew well. The head of the firm, now approaching sixty-five, greeted me as a friend and was delighted to see me, as he said:

'I hoped you'd come along, my dear; just a few little details about your father's affairs … you're looking well despite your recent ordeal; but, then, you are so pretty that you always do look well!'

I was impatient of such preliminaries and, smiling, began:

'Mr Masters, I want you to act for me in a very important matter. Above all, my name must be kept out of the transaction… You may have heard of a property just outside

Milbury called Highfield House?'

'For sale at five thousand – yes.'

I looked at him very steadily:

'I want you to buy it, Mr Masters.'

He stared at me aghast as one who might well be expected to ask: 'What with?' But he coughed discreetly and said:

'I will attend to it, Miss Drake.'

'You can arrange a mortgage? I want to put down three thousand or that proportion of three thousand which will allow for legal charges to be included. Is that all right?'

'Perfectly.'

I took five hundred pounds in notes from my bag and placed them on his desk.

'That will cover the initial deposit... And I'd be grateful if you'd get on to the agents while I'm here so that I feel the property is mine.' I added again: 'But again, my name must not appear in any shape or form in this transaction: this is a confidence strictly between you and me.'

'As you wish.'

I held my breath while he 'phoned the agents. Suppose Diana had already bought the property? Yet, somehow, I felt that my actions had been too precipitate to allow of that. I knew, from Mr Masters's answers that I was, however, safe; that the property was still in the market and, after a matter of moments, was mine. The receiver was replaced and he said:

'Well, that's that. Sorry I couldn't get them to take less than the five. Other people interested – usual story!'

I smiled at him.

'I didn't want the delay of bargaining, in any case...' I paused carelessly. 'By the way, suppose I should take it into my head to sell the property later on, would it be possible to get more for it?'

'Quite definitely; six-five, I should say.'

'Then why had only five been asked now?'

'Circumstances domestically; a wealthy owner clearing out to South Africa; he wanted a quick sale.'

'I see.' I got up from my chair. 'Thank you, Mr Masters.'

'Thank you, Mrs Ashley.'

My heart was beating fiercely as I left the building. It might have been fear, suspense, or merely excitement at my own daring. Elation came upon me as I realized just what Stephen had been spared. Properties like Highfield House were almost unobtainable and it was, I knew, the only one available in the district, and before anything else was forthcoming many, many changes would have taken place to put Stephen out of Diana's clutches; for once she became his benefactor, he, automatically, would become her slave. Again, I could not hint at such a thing without appearing prejudiced. I well knew how unreasonable men were when it came to hearing one woman disparage another.

So engrossed was I in my own thoughts that it was not until Stephen's car drew up alongside of me that I even noticed its presence. I turned sharply to confront him and Stella who was sitting at his side.

'What are you doing in Dornsford?' he asked lightly.

'What are you?' I replied with equal lightness, adding, 'and Stella?'

But I was far from feeling light-hearted, for I hated to see Stella sitting in my place and to think that I should not be acquainted with their conversation during the journey.

'I picked Stella up at the 'bus stop in Milbury,' he explained, 'and I'm taking her along to the hospital...'

Stella remained smiling silent; it might almost have been likened to passive resistance.

'I'll come with you,' I said firmly. And I looked at Stella as one expecting her to move into the back of the car.

She made a movement to do so but Stephen said swiftly:

'Don't bother; it's only a stone's throw.' He leaned and reached the door at the back and opened it. 'Jump in,' he said easily to me.

I resented having my place usurped, and I felt a sick distrust of the many rides Stella managed to have with Stephen. Also, wasn't it likely that they had arranged this one? She could hardly have 'happened' to be going to the hospital since Stephen was taking her to see the matron.

'Have you an appointment with the matron?' I began, trying not to sound as frigid and withdrawn as I felt.

'No,' she said instantly. 'I hadn't intended going along to the hospital this morning.'

'That was my idea – since I was visiting it anyway,' Stephen supplemented.

I noticed, not without chagrin, that he made no reference to my being in Dornsford when it was conceivable that I might have asked him to give me a lift there. I had, actually, slipped out while he was doing Surgery. His lack of curiosity might be simpler from my point of view, but it was hardly flattering.

'I see.'

Stella gave me a swift, backward glance and then turned in her seat.

'You sound strange, Lydia. Is anything the matter?'

'Nothing,' I said, feeling more incensed by her calm.

'If I can get through at the hospital in time, I'll take you girls out to lunch,' Stephen said airily.

'I thought you were so busy to-day, darling.' I hoped my voice sounded more normal, but jealousy consumed me and there was nothing

I could do to combat it.

'So I am; but I am allowed to eat occasionally,' he replied laughingly, 'and to take my wife out to lunch.'

Would he have thought of that had not Stella been with us?

'Lunch for three,' I exclaimed banteringly.

Stella hastened:

'No; for two.'

I saw the twitching of a muscle just below Stephen's jaw line which always indicated a certain annoyance, and he said briefly:

'Why, Stella?'

'Because I am perfectly certain Lydia doesn't want her relatives to become like the poor – always with one.' She laughed. 'Am I right, Lydia?'

'I think,' I said swiftly, 'that the remark is rather uncalled for, Stella.'

'I'm sorry,' she murmured. 'I'm afraid I'm in your bad books over my choice of a career, aren't I.'

It was, I decided, a subtle way of placing me in the wrong, and I resented it as unfair and unsporting.

'I don't think it will improve matters if I answer that remark, Stella. If my actions over the years do not speak for me then nothing I might say could possibly carry any weight with you. I wish you every luck with your career – you know that. My concern is only lest your health might be impaired through the hardship it involves…'

Stephen said almost sharply:

'If that danger were real, Lydia, I, as a medical man, would be the first to voice it and to do everything within my power to persuade Stella against taking this step.'

Again, I had that hateful feeling as of being the outsider, but I managed to say tartly:

'Sometimes watching over a person for years can teach one more about them than any medical man on earth can ever know… And here we are. I suppose I wait in the car?'

'As you wish,' he said politely. 'You can come inside if you prefer.'

'I'll wait,' I said. 'How long will you be?'

'Not long.'

Stella said quietly:

'Good-bye, Lydia.'

Stephen stared at her.

'But we shall run you back – that is if you won't lunch with us.'

She shook her head.

'Thank you, Stephen, but I'd rather you didn't. I shall probably wander around the town for a bit.'

It was impossible to deal with Stella in her present mood and I grew impatient, particularly as Stephen persisted:

'We'll see about that.'

It was some half an hour later they returned to the car. Stella had enjoyed a pleasant interview and been accepted initially; she was thrilled and eager.

'Wait until you are part of the staff at Highfield House,' Stephen said. 'That will be the day.'

I beamed at them; they really were most irresponsible.

'It certainly will,' I said stoutly.

Stephen hastened:

'Now we must have lunch – to celebrate.'

But Stella remained adamant; we drove her back into the centre of Dornsford and there, to my relief, left her. It wasn't that I minded her company, but that her attitude annoyed me: she had changed so terrifically as to seem almost a stranger to me.

I slipped my arm into Stephen's as we walked into the hotel, but he appeared to be oblivious of my presence and only when we were seated at the table and he had given the order, was the silence broken between us as he said:

'Why is it you are so unpleasant to Stella just lately? Did you have to make it so very obvious that she was unwelcome to-day?'

My mouth opened; I was aghast.

'What are you talking about? I unpleasant to Stella: isn't it the other way round?'

'Just because she has decided upon a career of her choosing and not yours, Lydia.'

'I resent that as being unfair and untrue.'

'It is neither, my dear. You are always so convinced that you are right as to find it impossible ever to see that you are wrong.'

'Stephen!'

'I'm sorry, Lydia. But I cannot pretend. You were both resentful of Stella's presence just now, and antagonistic generally. It isn't what a person *says*, you know...'

'I don't think you can realize what *you* are saying,' I countered hotly. 'And can you tell me why you are always so very much on the defensive these days whenever Stella is involved? You appear to take an inordinate interest in her affairs – an interest, I might even say, that could easily be misconstrued.'

I regretted the words the moment they were uttered, because they could not fail to betray the trend of my own thoughts, and to put words in his mouth, so that I might, in turn, be accused of jealousy.

He said curtly:

'Then so be it, Lydia. Stella's welfare will always be of great concern to me. All I ask is that you show a little more consideration for her feelings in future.'

'This,' I said, 'is absurd.' It had reached a stage when every time Stella's name was mentioned it led to argument and dissension. The atmosphere was tense, antagonistic.

'Then I suggest you stop behaving so

childishly,' he added.

I wanted to shriek in protest, but knew that would be fatal. At all costs I must allay his suspicions, repair the damage I had done by revealing my feelings in the heat of the moment.

My hand slid across the table to his.

'I'm sorry, darling; no one is more appreciative of your solicitude for Stella than I am, because no one in the world could love her more than I. Forgive me; I'm afraid my nerves just aren't too good at the moment, and I've been on edge with worry about this nurse business ... but if you tell me all is well then I won't be anxious any more ... you do think she'll be all right – don't you?'

His attitude changed entirely and I knew that I had adopted the right approach, and that to allow the knowledge of Stella's love for him so to seep and infiltrate into my mind as to distort his every kindly act could mean only ruin to our happiness.

'She'll be fine; she's suited for the work, Lydia; she has that lovable quality which–' He broke off abruptly. 'Anyway, you've no cause to worry: I'll keep an eye on her and matron is a friend of mine; she'll get no quarter on that account, but it won't detract, shall we say... And now what do you fancy for lunch?'

Conversation was fitful after that, until the subject of the clinic was broached:

'Diana's going to see the agents this afternoon,' he confided eagerly. 'Apparently, they want five thousand for the place. Dirt cheap, although the large places are a bit of a drag, but the owner and his wife have separated and he wants to see the back of it... Lydia, what a thrill it will be getting that a going concern. It struck me that we might sell out a good deal of the stuff at home and put the money into Highfield; there are some quite valuable antiques and if we kept enough for us to have a smallish flat in Highfield, I'd be on the spot and–'

'It is an idea,' I said, inwardly appalled at the process of his thought. 'This is, I take it, to be very nearly a philanthropic concern.'

'No profits,' he said grimly. 'No "paying game"; a sanctuary for the poor and middle class alike. I don't want money, Lydia, and I know you don't. With your management we could make it an example, a real godsend to the community and save hundreds of people both physical suffering and financial strain.' His voice trailed away on a note of eager excitement. 'I've so much in mind and it really seems providential that we've found the only house that could, in any way, meet our demands. There just isn't another in all the district.' A broad smile. 'Bless Diana for her faith in us... I think I could raise a couple of thousand on the furniture, and still leave us with all we need, as I said just now.'

It was, of course, madness and I was humbly grateful to think that I was to be instrumental in saving him from it. How like him to contemplate pauperizing himself to benefit those who would in no way whatsoever appreciate, or even understand, the gesture. As for Diana: had she truly been his friend she would have discouraged him, rather than assist him to financial ruin. Projects such as he envisaged were all part of some fantastic Utopia. I said quietly:

'If you think so, darling.'

'I do...' He glanced at his watch. 'Better be getting home; I've a patient at two and Diana's calling to see me just before three – or as soon as ever she's clinched the deal.'

We returned home. I read aloud the name on the white front door:

'Stoneleigh! Did you name it that, Stephen?'

He shook his head.

'Not on your life...'

The first syllable, I thought, was symbolic; for the stone walls seemed to me to give a chill to the whole house, and as we crossed the threshold I shuddered in distaste, hating its sombre shabbiness, its semi-gloom and peeling paintwork. The faint smell of ether offended me; the herds of people who trailed in through the entrance marked: 'Surgery' seemed to leave their depressing presence upon the place and to negative any personality I might have brought to it. This was no setting for a man of Stephen's abilities; it was rather an insult to him. The struggling country doctor ... his brilliance strangled by the bindweed of a poverty-stricken populace, who had neither the courage to help themselves, nor the intelligence to appreciate the waste of his time upon them. And what would Highfield have meant except a larger prison, better equipped. Would he have been content with 'a few rooms'? Wouldn't the strain and struggle of financial insecurity and an ambitious project – squandered in the cause of the poor – kill him in the end and bring his whole world crashing about his head? How he would thank me later on for all I had done ... what immense satisfaction there was in that thought. Stella had encouraged him, of course... How like her with her impulsive short-sightedness. What a tragedy it would have been had they married and plunged recklessly into such craziness. My management... So he had counted on that for his success, and well it might have been so, for only good management could ever have enabled him to reach his goal.

Diana arrived just before three. I had intended not to see her, but realized that might cause unnecessary comment and our friendly antagonism was known only to us, so that Stephen would never suspect that veiled hostility which marked our every word.

Stephen was already in the lounge when she was admitted by the daily woman. He moved forward eagerly, as one walking on air, to greet her and then paused abruptly:

'Diana! What is it?'

'Highfield House,' she cried as she sat down weakly in the chair he offered. 'It's been sold, Stephen – sold. I was a few hours too late – hours,' she added bitterly. 'I could cry.'

Stephen stood very still; his face paled; a shadow crept across his eyes that dissolved into the look he gave me:

'So could I,' he said jerkily. 'I'd counted on it. Not often I do that.' He looked at Diana. 'Any idea who's bought it?'

'No; I tried to find out, but no one could give me any information.'

I held my breath as she spoke and then knew an overwhelming relief. The ordeal was over and I had saved Stephen from ultimate ruin... He would soon recover from his disappointment. Everything had gone according to plan and I felt I was to be congratulated.

CHAPTER TEN

It was both pleasant and uncomfortable to me to sit there in silence while Diana and Stephen commiserated with each other. Gloom descended after the manner of a stifling curtain and I had never known Stephen so upset by a disappointment. Normally, he took everything in his stride, and I felt slightly impatient that he should be so blind to all the disadvantages and follies that would have damned the Highfield House project. At the best it had been ill-conceived and it amazed me how very stupid even a clever man like Stephen could be on occasion. My voice was very steady as I said:

'There may be some very good reason why your plan didn't materialize, Stephen. A new field will open out for you, I'm sure.'

Diana raised her gaze to meet mine; she became alert and, I sensed, suspicious.

'Such as?' she prompted.

I shrugged my shoulders.

'Clairvoyance is not a gift of mine, Diana,' I said lightly. 'But so often in this life things happen for the best.'

Her eyes narrowed.

'So you weren't very enthusiastic about

the venture?'

That angered me.

'On the contrary,' I replied coolly.

Stephen appeared not to hear any of that as he said thoughtfully:

'I wonder if we could trace the buyer whether or not he would take a profit, Diana. Would you be prepared to–'

'It's worth at least six or seven thousand,' Diana said promptly. 'Of course I'd go to almost any figure.' She added seriously: 'I wanted to see you there, Stephen; it would have meant so much to Milbury – to everyone. You're the man for such a scheme.' She sighed in annoyance. 'And I hate being done.'

How maddening it was to hear her talk as though Stephen's future were her personal concern rather than mine. Wasn't it for me to decide just how Stephen should advance, and in what direction? Diana arrogated to herself far too many rights over Stephen. More than ever was it essential that he should be spirited away from the corroding influences of the district, and of people who surrounded him with such apparent affection. They were as weeds hampering him; only I knew the heights to which he was intended to climb and the more I thought about it the more convinced I was that humanity was losing a great saviour by his being buried in Milbury among a class wholly incapable of appreciating his talents. I knew that I had been chosen as the instrument of his delivery, and that I must not weaken because his inclinations would appear to be in direct opposition to my intentions.

'Surely,' I said easily, 'the man who has bought the house can be traced.'

'Not necessarily,' said Stephen ruefully. 'He has every right to remain anonymous.'

'It could be a woman,' said Diana. 'My solicitors are going to do their best; but I've a strange feeling–' she stopped and again her gaze turned upon me as she added: 'that we shall not be successful, Stephen.'

For the first time Stephen's expression changed to a half smile.

'Woman's famous intuition?'

'Perhaps.' Diana paused. 'But this isn't the end; there must be other properties–'

Stephen shook his head.

'There's nothing, Diana,' he said remorsefully. Then: 'But you've been splendid and I shan't forget all you've done; that our hopes haven't materialized is not the point.'

Diana sighed heavily.

'I don't know when I've been more disappointed,' she murmured sadly.

'Neither do I,' he agreed.

She changed the subject abruptly.

'How did Stella get on at the hospital?'

'Very well,' Stephen said, and his voice

seemed to me to hold sudden tenderness. 'Matron took to her, I could tell that.'

'Who wouldn't,' Diana exclaimed. 'Stella is the very loveliest person I've ever met; the more one knows of her, sees of her, the more one loves and admires her.'

Stephen appeared to hang on every word that was uttered and his voice throbbed a little as he said:

'I've come to realize that.'

Jealousy stung me as I listened and I hated it, finding that my heart thudded with almost terrifying swiftness, until I felt physically faint.

'I hope,' I said gently, mastering my turbulent emotions, 'that Stella will stand up to the life she has chosen and really settle to it.'

Diana bristled.

'Stella would never fall down on any job.'

'I'm not,' I retorted, 'implying that she would but–' I smiled – 'you must allow me to know my own sister at least a little better than you do, Diana.'

'I'm afraid,' Diana said shortly, 'it has been my experience that relatives know each other least of all and, if I may say so, I am certain you have many misconceptions about Stella.'

Stella! Stella! It seemed that I was never to escape that name or some discussion or other concerning it. With great effort I remained patient and calm:

'Have I? I don't think so.'

'You must,' said Stephen abruptly, 'have been very sorry Diana that the engagement was broken between Stella and Allan.'

I held my breath; we were on dangerous ground.

'No,' came the steady and emphatic reply; 'I was glad, because Stella had never been in love with Allan, or he with her. Circumstances, shall we say, rather forced that issue, but it was doomed to end as it did. Stella isn't the type of girl to marry one man and' – she looked at me with sudden animosity – 'be in love with another.'

All the air seemed to vanish from the room which became, to me, unbearably hot and stuffy.

Stephen cried:

'But–'

Diana interrupted him.

'I've said too much,' she murmured. 'And Stella would hardly thank us for discussing her affairs.'

I looked at Stephen and felt I could see his thoughts almost as though they were graphs on a chart. His expression was puzzled as he sought to satisfy himself as to the identity of the man to whom Diana had vaguely referred... Was he allowing himself to ask if that man might not be he; were his thoughts racing back to those early days when that same love had looked at him through Stella's eyes... It was agony to watch him and I could find no palliative in argument. Diana had said that deliberately; she was out to wreck my marriage and was the enemy in the camp. I had known her to be unscrupulous, but never had I imagined her going to this diabolical length.

I spoke with sudden forcefulness:

'I agree, Diana. Of one thing I am certain: Stella is not the type to confide her love to anyone other than to me and I know of no such man: a fact easy to prove, since she has no acquaintances, or even contacts, of which I am not aware.'

Diana's smile was slow and warning:

'Nevertheless,' she said smoothly, 'I am quite certain you know where Stella's heart lies – as I do.'

The atmosphere was tense, electrical. I looked at Stephen and saw a dull flush mount his cheeks. Jerkily, he said:

'If you two will excuse me, I've a consultation at three-forty.' And before I could speak he had left us, adding that he hoped Diana would remain for tea.

She sat with a dogged calm in her armchair as the door closed behind him. I looked at her and hated her as I demanded:

'Just what was behind all that nonsense about Stella; what is in your mind, Diana because–'

'Because for once you are not mistress of the situation,' she said with a deadly significance. 'I've lived quite a long while and I know people: as I told you once before: I know you.'

'That is beside the point,' I rapped out. 'Your insinuations–'

'Why should there be anything to insinuate,' she countered maddeningly. 'You condemn yourself.'

I stared at her aghast.

'I don't think you can be quite sane, Diana. Just what is all this? It is you who did the insinuating about their being a man in Stella's life and–'

'Ah,' she said silkily, 'so for once you are at a loss for words. 'I didn't insinuate anything; I spoke the truth. Stella is in love with another man – with Stephen. She has always loved him, and she always will. I don't,' she finished firmly, 'have to tell you that – you know.'

Her words stung me. Just how far could I refute that; just what had Stella confided to her? Stella was so weak and impulsive that she would not stop to think beyond the moment. For me to adopt an attitude of anger or indignation would be fatal in such a crisis. I said quietly:

'You will not hurt me, Diana, by resorting to that kind of thing. If Stella has told you she is in love with my husband–' I paused significantly. 'I hardly feel it is anything of which to be proud and I am more than surprised that she–'

Diana cut in icily:

'Stella would suffer to be torn in pieces rather than discuss the subject with me – and you know that, too. No, Lydia, calm, honeyed words will not help you. I see the whole story: you engineered her engagement to Allan because you knew that, in her, you had a rival for Stephen's affections; in fact you've cheated them both out of each other – deliberately wrecked both their lives.' Her eyes seemed to pierce mine as she added accusingly: 'But your hell will always be the knowledge of the bond between them – not even *you* can destroy that and you'll never know peace of mind; you'll know only a jealousy that in the end will destroy you. There is a poetic justice in these things... You schemed to get Stephen but–'

I was white and trembling; the horror of having such words hurled at me made me almost faint. After all I'd done for Stella, all I'd sacrificed to protect her happiness, to be accused of wrecking it was more than even I could bear.

'You are mad and evil,' I cried vehemently. 'For some unknown reason you dislike me and–'

'Despise and condemn you,' came the implacable comment. 'It is very bitter to see through a person whom one once liked and trusted, Lydia. We'll leave it at that.'

'If you think you can poison Stella against me – allow your wild accusations, your lies–' I paused for breath; every organ in my body seemed to have moved somewhere out of place and I felt sick to the point of collapse.

'Do not judge my standards by your own,' she said sharply. 'I've an idea that Stella is no longer the gullible, trusting and blindly adoring apostle, my dear: she is beginning to see that all your good works and concern for others always have a knack of turning out for the benefit of Lydia Drake and that your pose of unselfishness is just that – a pose – hideously hypocritical and insincere, which enables you to have your own way at the expense of others.'

The woman was, of course, unbalanced. I could have accepted criticism given in the right spirit, even welcomed it; but this tirade, this fantastic condemnation became suddenly incongruous and ridiculous and I felt it beneath my dignity to attempt further to justify myself.

I smiled at her pityingly.

'I don't think you can be quite well, Diana,' I said quietly, 'therefore the venom of your words is lost on me; it is not worth any distress of mine. I must warn you, however, that you will not be welcome in this house. I will not have Stephen's happi-

ness, or mine, jeopardized by your pre-
judices and veiled accusations.'

She stared at me for a second with what
was an unnerving, almost uncanny stare,
then:

'I should very much like to know just what
hand you've had in this Highfield House
business,' she said startlingly.

I kept a tight rein on my emotions and my
voice was steady as I said:

'My dear Diana, your imagination appears
to be running riot to-day, surely. What
possible "hand" could I have in the affair?'

'That is what I'm wondering,' she came
back resolutely. 'It sticks out a mile that you
are not in sympathy with Stephen's ambitions; that being so, you will see to it that
he doesn't fulfil them.'

I laughed.

'I must be a magician as well as a villainess
– according to you. How fortunate for me
that no one else in this world would agree
with your opinions. You really are becoming
childish, now.'

'Perhaps … but one day I shall find out
who bought that house, Lydia.'

She no longer upset me. Only when one's
conscience was weighed down with guilt
could accusations permanently hurt one.

'You're not suggesting that I might be the
unknown buyer?' I spoke with faintly contemptuous laughter.

She answered disarmingly:

'You read my thoughts well.' Her gaze remained steady. 'That would not surprise me.'

'And you imagine that I can conjure five thousand pounds out of the air?'

'No; but you could borrow it,' she retorted.

My impatience was becoming greater.

'This absurdity has gone far enough,' I said, resentful of her intrusion into my secret world; hating the idea that my every plan was suspect, and that she was utterly incapable of giving me credit for any altruistic motives or unselfish thought.

'Not half so far as it will go,' she replied as she got to her feet and walked to the door. 'Good-bye, Lydia. Don't underestimate me – will you? It is time someone declared war against your cunning.'

I sat down weakly after she had gone; the backs of my arms tingled; my nerves were frayed. It was hard enough to have fought as I had for the good of others, to have subjugated my own ideals in their interests, but it was ten times harder to find my motives suspect and the good turned to evil against me. Cruel, indeed, that I should be accused of treachery to Stella and to Stephen whom I loved best in the world, and for whom I would gladly have given my life. I found comfort and consolation in the truth that nobility of purpose and the execution of one's duty invariably imposed heavy burdens, and that giving one's life in the service of others, brought but scant reward – except within the deep recesses of the mind and soul – the supreme satisfaction of having given the utmost in a beloved cause. If being condemned and misunderstood was to be the price I must pay ... so be it. I was convinced, nevertheless, that Diana was becoming unbalanced and that, despite her protests, she had not forgiven me for rejecting Allan as my husband. There could be no other explanation for her extraordinary behaviour since Stephen's advent. I knew, to my sorrow, that I should have a difficult task ahead now that Stella was coming more and more under her influence and domination.

During the weeks that followed I saw little of Stella. Life settled down into the rather dreary rut consistent with Stephen's work in an exacting district. 'Stoneleigh' seemed to me to become more grim and forbidding and although I had, by a certain ingenuity, made it seem more homely, nevertheless its gaunt structure and unsatisfactory accommodation began to pall. It was, I felt, sacrilege that Stephen should thus dissipate his talents in such a place. His Utopian ideas met with my every sympathy but they were, I knew, impossible to put into practise and, while he dreamed of them he was, in effect, missing opportunities of bettering himself.

It was one evening when we had arranged to dine with Sir Malcolm and Lady Scott, and were actually dressed for the occasion, that he said:

'I must just look in at the hospital on our way, Lydia.'

I stared at him aghast.

'But, Stephen! You can't possibly do that: we shall be late and this dinner is important.'

He flicked a handkerchief out of his dressing-chest drawer and thrust it into his pocket. When he spoke it was in a tone of implacable decisiveness that I had came to know so well.

'Nothing is important when a life is at stake – except that life, my dear. You can go on ahead of me; I can walk the short distance from the hospital.'

Tears of mortification filled my eyes. I had planned for, and looked forward to, this evening and the idea of anything being more important to Stephen than accompanying me, filled me with a jealous rage which I felt to be perfectly justifiable. In that moment a vision of Stella came hatefully before me. Hadn't Stephen been visiting the hospital with undue frequency since she joined the staff there? It was as if some demon pursued me as I said:

'Aren't you taking an inordinate interest in hospital patients these days?'

He paused abruptly in his task of taking his wallet and cigarette from his lounge suit; his gaze met mine with cold criticism:

'Meaning precisely what?'

'Asking me another question is no answer, Stephen – merely evasion.'

'Nevertheless, I repeat it,' he said with a deadly calm.

I was tensed, overwrought as I said foolishly:

'I was wondering if your solicitude for Stella might not have something to do with it.'

For a second there was a silence in which my heartbeats appeared to be audible; the emotion surging through my body was so great as to become almost a tangible and visible thing flowing menacingly between us. I knew I had made a mistake, but it was too late to retract the accusation and my suspicions leapt out of the shadows like avenging ghosts. It was torture to me to know that Stella was now close to his work; that he possibly saw her every day, talked to her, and I was not privy to their conversation. The dam of my resentment burst and nothing could stay that flood-tide. But only despair was my reward for he merely looked at me with a cold contempt as he said:

'The insinuation is an insult, Lydia.' He moved to the door, and left me.

I stood there shaken, trembling; it was as if in those seconds my life disintegrated. I had annoyed Stephen, behaved in a manner likely to arouse his suspicion, allowed him to see that Stella had become an issue between us and that I was jealous of his attentions to her – harmless though I knew them to be.

I ran after him; at all costs I must retrieve my position, counteract the damage done. My influence was essential to him for his own good and once my power waned through any false move we should be doomed.

'You misunderstood me,' I began as I reached his side and we stood together in his study. 'I mean that in order to help Stella you had, unselfishly, paid more attention to–'

He looked down at me.

'And do you imagine a doctor can single out one particular nurse,' he said coldly.

'No, but–'

'I suggest we allow the subject to drop ... are you ready?' He glanced at his watch.

'Yes.' I had never felt more miserable. It seemed that Stella's name brought us ever to the verge of an argument, and it was as though she were deliberately trying to come between us.

We drove in silence to the hospital. It loomed up like some giant monster threatening to devour me; for once my sense of proportion failed me, and I allowed myself to wallow in my own wretchedness while jealousy went through my veins like liquid fire. I hated to see Stephen disappear into that mysterious world of which I was not a part; I hated to think that behind those closed doors Stella might be waiting for him – a Stella who had emerged cool and efficient and who was making rapid strides in the career she had chosen, and confounding all my theories. What had they to say to each other? And why had she remained so steadfastly away from 'Stoneleigh'? The thought of Diana obtruded: was she the instrument of my torture? Was she dictating to Stella and seeking to divorce her from me? On, on raced my thoughts, giving me no respite and dragging me deeper into the abyss.

Stephen got out of the car.

'I'll be along as soon as I can,' he said impersonally. 'If I find I can't get away quickly I'll 'phone Sir Malcolm.' And, without a backward glance, he moved in the direction of the building.

I never remember a worse evening than the one that followed. Excitement faded in the gloom of my own bitter reflections, and when, some half an hour later, Stephen 'phoned to say that it was doubtful whether he would be able to get there at all, my unhappiness dragged me down into some bottomless pit of anguish and agony. Both Sir Malcolm and Lady Scott were understanding and charming to me.

'The worst,' said Lady Scott, 'of being a doctor: one's life just isn't one's own.'

The words thrust open yet another door in my mind. Was Stephen's life mine? Or was it Stella's? That faraway look in his eyes; that tender, yet impersonal, attitude of his towards me ... could I, in all truth, say that he was ever passionate, ever truly demonstrative, or that we were two people living in the very closest harmony and communion. Friends, yes. I squirmed as jealousy struck again. I was mad to imagine that Stella meant anything more to him than a sister-in-law... Yet suppose she had so undermined his moral strength by her own love for him ... suppose Diana's words had borne fruit and Stephen now knew just who the man was...

Plans leapt into my mind; was I to be defeated? Was I to degenerate into some flabby creature living in fear and suspicion and even suspense, when action was the thing most needed. For Stella to be thrust into Stephen's company was the very worst possible thing for her; it could only aggravate her condition of mind and feed the flame of her love for him.

The evening dragged to a close – without Stephen. At eleven o'clock I excused myself and drove straight to the hospital. Yes, Dr Ashley was still there … would I wait?

I said inquiringly:

'My sister?'

'I'll tell her you are here.' The bright-eyed, clear complexioned nurse moved away with a smile. I envied her that apparent light-heartedness. My mood was still grey.

Stella came into the small ante-room in which I waited.

'Hello, Lydia,' she said quietly. 'I don't think Stephen will be long.'

I felt strangely tongue-tied and, then, resentment flared.

'You haven't been to see me for over a fortnight,' I said accusingly.

Her gaze met mine very levelly:

'Have you wanted me to do so?'

I drew my brows together in a puzzled frown.

'Isn't it rather a ridiculous question?'

'I don't think so and I much prefer the truth,' she answered. 'You've resented me for a long while, Lydia: we were far too close, once, for me not to have noticed the fact. And to understand it.'

I said in a breath:

'This is Diana's doing. What has she been saying to you?'

'Saying?' Her expression was bewildered. 'About what?'

'Diana has always wanted to get you away from me; it looks as though she has succeeded.' I shook my head. 'It is very hard Stella, after all I tried to do for you; very hard to feel that, now, you turn to, and confide in, a mere acquaintance.'

'Diana isn't just an acquaintance,' came the grave reply. 'And, in the circumstances, it was inevitable that I should see less of you once you were married to Stephen. And if you are honest you know you prefer it that way.'

'How can you talk like that,' I challenged her. 'What have I ever done to deserve it?'

'Oh, Lydia,' she said painfully; 'why is it that we cannot see each other without something like this happening? You don't want me with you and Stephen, and yet you are annoyed if I stay away. I cannot be right for you. It is as though you hate me for loving him,' she said with a sudden access of courage.

Those words smote me; it was torture to hear them when I had so steadfastly told myself that her affections for Stephen were purely transitory. I said hotly:

'That is ridiculous; and you don't know what you are talking about, anyway. This unhealthy concentration on Stephen and your love for him—' I stopped.

She said very impulsively:

'You have a knack of refusing to believe anything you don't want to believe, Lydia – haven't you? But this time you are wrong: I'm not ashamed of my love for Stephen and it will never die because love – real love – never does. You are his wife, but I take nothing from you by loving him.'

'Isn't that for me to decide?'

'No,' she said almost sternly. 'I've done everything within my power to prevent my feelings causing you anxiety and you have now dragged the subject to light. This–' Her voice shook– 'is where we bury it for all time. There is much I could say, but it would serve no purpose… Only don't run away with the idea that my feelings will ever change, or that you can plan my life in any way from now on. Much better that we should understand each other, Lydia – once and for all.'

I said and it was as if pins and needles were tingling into my flesh:

'Feeling as you do, don't you think it would have been wiser to start your career elsewhere – not in continual contact with Stephen?'

'No,' she said adamantly. 'I do no harm by seeing him from afar and I know how he is and–'

'I, apparently, don't come into it.' I added: 'Are you quite sure you haven't it in your

270

mind to attract Stephen in return?' The words rushed out. 'Or,' I finished with vehemence, 'perhaps you think you have already done so.'

The silence of the room deepened; the faint sounds of activity appearing suddenly muted in the face of drama; the smell of ether and disinfectant came sickeningly to my nostrils as Stella's voice rang with sudden challenge:

'Of all the people in the world you are the one best able to judge the exact nature of Stephen's feelings for me, Lydia. Suppose we leave it at that?'

I caught at my breath. Just what was there behind that remark? What poison had Diana poured into that impressionable mind to prompt such a remark that could, on examination, have such far reaching significance? Instantly, my concern intensified. This relationship between Stella and Diana was, even as I had always known, dangerous in the extreme. Yet how could it be smashed; how thwarted in its evil ambition. My maternal instinct flowed back; Stella's welfare being again of paramount importance. No matter what I might feel it was my duty to safeguard her...

In that second Stephen joined us, his gaze going straight to Stella's as he said:

'She'll be all right.'

'And the baby?'

He nodded.

'Fine…'

'You're so tired.' Her voice was low. She glanced at me swiftly and I said possessively, as I put my hand on Stephen's arm:

'Home, darling … and some rest.'

No expression came to his eyes, only a rather lifeless stare. Then he said to Stella:

'I hear excellent reports of you … how's the swotting going?'

'Very well.'

'You know where to come if you're in any difficulties… Yes, Lydia, I'm coming–' This with faint impatience as I interrupted.

Stella smiled; their eyes met for a second and, to me, it was as if he had leaned forward and taken her in his arms, so intimate was the atmosphere surrounding them. Suspense mounted and my nerves became unbearably taut. Something would have to be done about all this: I could not have Stephen's future jeopardized even by my own sister's weakness and folly, for he, unwittingly, might well encourage any attentions she inadvertently bestowed upon him – without realizing they were attentions.

We left some minutes later. It was a strange, unreal sensation to sit in the car with Stephen feeling that the ghost of Stella hovered in the darkness, coming between us rather as though an invisible wall had been built to divide us. I tried to think of something to say but, for once, words failed me. I could not help realizing how unjust Stella's attitude was; how fraught with innuendo... And, even against my better judgment I found myself saying to Stephen:

'I'm worried about Stella; she hardly ever comes to see us now, and I feel that Diana may be influencing her–' I stopped abruptly.

Stephen said almost curtly:

'Diana could only influence anyone for their good. As for Stella not coming to see us' – his voice seemed a trifle unsteady – 'she is working all the hours there are, and, after all, you made it pretty obvious that she wouldn't exactly be welcome when I suggested her staying with us for a while.'

I was shaking; it seemed suddenly that all my ambitions and hopes, all my sacrifices had turned to dust and that every hand was raised against me. Quietly, I said:

'I don't think you are being quite fair, Stephen. Having a person – even one's own sister – living in one's home is a very different proposition from seeing them with normal frequency. I've done a great deal for Stella and, now that she can stand alone, it seems to me that she is behaving most self-ishly and with complete lack of consider-ation. I didn't expect thanks, but I did hope for a little affection and appreciation.'

His answer merely fanned the flame of my suspicion.

'I don't doubt but that Stella has very good reason for behaving as she has. Don't, for heaven's sake, start another discussion to-night.'

It was dawn before I closed my eyes, lying awake in the darkness, trying to formulate some plan that should save both Stephen and Stella from themselves, realizing that this close association must be broken and, realizing too, that for Stephen to remain very much longer in Milbury would be to wreck all his chances of escape from the soul-destroying rut of the country doctor which would end only in a career of mediocrity. Nothing must jeopardize my ambitions for him; I must be the prop on which he could lean and the initiative rest with me. He was not the type to launch out in any scheme to his own advantage and, suddenly, I saw my duty with a dazzling clarity; a clarity that swept away the foolish shadows in which I had allowed myself to dwell that evening. There was one person in this world who would help me to help Stephen... Lionel Manning. He would appreciate how vital it was that Stephen should get out of Milbury and would assist me to that end.

CHAPTER ELEVEN

I went to see Lionel Manning two days later, making my somewhat unexpected trip to London a 'shopping expedition', thus allaying any suspicion and arriving at Wimpole Street just before lunch. There was something very impressive, even dramatic, to me about my being there; the dignity of my surroundings, the seal of success that stamped Lionel Manning himself, was as a symbol: that seal would one day stamp Stephen's career; one day I should see him in just such another house, with its Adams panelling and lofty ceilings, its atmosphere of graciousness. The contrast after 'Stoneleigh' was incongruous and overwhelming, and I squirmed at the very idea of Stephen remaining in Milbury even another day.

Lionel Manning received me in his consulting room – a room eloquent of good taste and unlimited means – and as he came around from his magnificent Chippendale desk to greet me, I felt a sense of power and satisfaction because I was no suppliant, but a woman pleading her husband's cause.

His handshake was friendly and reassuring.

'Not,' he said swiftly, 'a professional visit, I hope?'

I smiled, finding his manner both pleasing and flattering.

'No; but if it were, what better hands could I wish for?' I hastened: 'I came to seek your advice about Stephen.'

'Ah!' He glanced at a pad on his desk. 'How do you feel about talking to me over the luncheon table? I have an hour quite free and–'

'I'd love it,' I said eagerly. 'London is quite a thrill to me, you know. I'm very cut off from social activity in Milbury.' A laugh. 'But I don't have to tell you that!'

He took me to the Hungaria and I had to confess to myself that I belonged in such a world, and that while I had been perfectly sincere in my earlier desire to further Stephen's ambitions in Milbury – to the very limits of my capabilities – I realized how very essential it was for me now to provide the spur that should result in his fulfilling his true *destiny*, rather than merely to pander to his misconceived sense of duty.

I began by saying to Lionel Manning as the first course was served:

'I feel that you understand my motives in coming to you to-day – and that I hardly need to outline my hopes for Stephen.'

He looked at me very levelly:

'I always knew you would get him out of Milbury.'

I drew my brows together in a faint frown:

'It isn't so much a question of my getting him out, Mr Manning, but of doing what I conceive to be in his interests. He is wasting his talents, and while I admire his desire to help the poor, on the other hand I feel that there is a much wider field for him to explore without his degrading his earlier ambitions in the slightest.' I met that still steady scrutiny as I added: 'Don't you agree?'

'Most certainly.'

'But, with reservations?' My heart-beats quickened.

'Only in so far as all this affects Stephen's personal happiness. Can one ever turn the idealist into the materialist?'

'I have no desire to attempt to do so,' I corrected him. 'I rather thought that you shared my views on all this.' A faint irritation possessed me; it was as though Lionel Manning were putting me under the microscope before committing himself in any way.

He said very firmly:

'I do; I'd like to see Stephen here in Wimpole Street. I'd like to see him specialize.' He looked at me with a changing expression that, finally, became gravely inquiring: 'Do you think we could persuade him to break away from Milbury?'

I felt a rush of elation.

'You could – in the right circumstances. It would be fatal for me to do so: a wife is the last person on earth to dictate to her husband; he must have his free will.' I leaned slightly forward. 'I was wondering if the right stepping stone might not be a practice on the outskirts of London – a practice that would bring him into contact with the right people.'

'And enable him to live a more social life?'

I answered carefully:

'That would be up to him. But to see him working as hard as he does now–' I shook my head. 'It hurts me.'

There was a second silence, then:

'It would cost a certain amount of money to buy the kind of practice you have in mind,' he said thoughtfully.

'I'd not overlooked that fact and I could help. The Milbury practice would fetch something.'

He said swiftly:

'I know of just the right thing for Stephen. I hinted at it, you may remember. I've finished with Hampstead these days, but the practice I have in mind is there and it would be an excellent spring-board for Wimpole or Harley Street.'

My heart seemed to stand still in eager anticipation.

'If you could make it seem that his services

are needed – that his good works could go on just as well–' I broke off.

'I could try; but, as I said, the financial aspect cannot be ignored.'

I hastened resolutely:

'I will guarantee to see to that.'

He gave me a studied look.

'A very persistent young woman.'

'Very; in the right cause.'

'Ah!'

'Stephen must have that goad, Mr Manning; I've no desire to influence him, or dominate his life, but there are times when it is essential to work by stealth for his good. He just has no sense of money and is a born philanthropist.'

Lionel Manning smiled.

'I know that; an endearing quality.'

'But not a very comfortable one.'

'I can believe that ... personally, I admire the good works but, also, I am a sybarite and enjoy comfort.'

'Yet,' I hastened, 'you manage to do a tremendous amount of good.'

He sipped his wine.

'Some, perhaps.'

I paused a second before saying.

'You've been very patient with me, Mr Manning, and very kind.'

'Not at all. Stephen means a very great deal to me and I want to help him.'

I said and my voice was very earnest:

'He must never know I came to you, or that I am in any way involved in all this. I hate deception, but in this case it is so vitally necessary for his sake. You do understand that – don't you?'

'Perfectly.'

Was his smile a trifle sardonic, his attitude eloquent of faint cynicism? Again irritation possessed me.

'Can I be quite certain of that?' I asked suddenly.

He turned his gaze upon me and spoke with quiet emphasis.

'You can.'

Relief surged over me; with Lionel Manning on my side nothing could go wrong.

'What do you suggest by way of interesting him in the practice you have in mind?' I asked anxiously.

'I'd better run down to see him – this week-end, if possible and convenient to you.'

'That would be wonderful.' Gratitude welled within me.

It was all arranged and I left him some little while later feeling that my worries were over. He would be able to persuade Stephen, I felt convinced, and my spirits soared as I contemplated the future away from Milbury. A strangely restless sensation came upon me, even as I thought of it, as though its former tranquillity and peace were no more.

True to his word, Lionel Manning came down the following week-end, 'phoning Stephen in advance and soliciting an invitation. He arrived for dinner on Saturday evening and, over coffee, began:

'I'm really here, Stephen, to talk to you of a practice that is going – one that would be ideal for you.'

Stephen started in surprise and I, managing to appear equally astonished, commented laughingly:

'I don't think Stephen would ever be persuaded to leave Milbury – eh, darling?'

To my intense annoyance, it was at that precise moment Stella was admitted. She paused on the threshold almost guiltily as she realized Stephen and I were not alone, then:

'I'm sorry to intrude but–'

Stephen got to his feet swiftly, his expression changing to obvious delight.

'You're just in time to join a family conference ... you have already met Mr Manning?'

Stella smiled her warm, attractive smile as she crossed to his side, and after an imperceptible pause said:

'Yes; I was awed, and not a little afraid of him.' She moved to my side and sat down in the chair Stephen placed in position for her; I saw their eyes meet and my heart con-

281

tracted in painful jealousy. It was as if the emotion that flowed between them encompassed me like a tormenting flame. I said deliberately:

'We will leave the men to talk and–'

Stephen interrupted hastily:

'Don't do that.' He looked again at Stella. 'Lionel has just suggested that I might be interested in another practice.' His tone was faintly ridiculing and I knew that he was resisting even the suggestion that he might be persuaded to leave Milbury.

Stella's expression changed to obvious fear as she cried involuntarily:

'You mean – out of Milbury?'

Stephen nodded.

'I imagine so.' He turned to Lionel. 'Where is it, old man?'

'Hampstead. I thought of you because it needs someone like you to take it over.'

'Why?' It was a querulous sound. 'To cultivate a bed-side manner, treat hang-overs and hypochrondriacs?' A certain banter robbed the words of any ungraciousness.

'On the contrary.' Lionel paused effectively. 'Has it ever struck you, Stephen, that without money no man can help the poor as he would like to do? With it, he can be the philanthropist of his dreams. Success is the gateway through which to dispense charity.' He looked at me. 'Have I an ally in you?'

I hesitated. It was a question to be

answered carefully. I knew that Stephen was watching me and that he would weigh up my every word.

'Only,' I said slowly, 'if you find one in Stephen. Although I must be honest and agree that, without money, one's desires to help humanity must, of necessity, be sterile.'

Stephen asked quietly:

'And what happens to the people here while I make that money?'

Lionel put in with emphasis:

'Precisely that which happened to them before you came, my dear man. Sorry to sound cynical, but only a vast change, a phenomenal improvement in their living conditions, could possibly bring about the Utopian conditions you foresee, or rather hope to create.'

Stephen leaned forward.

'I thought I had the nucleus for that vast change,' he said earnestly. 'A house ideal for a clinic; the home away-from-home hospital, not just for the poor, but for the middle-classes, too. But the house was sold and although I've scoured the district there is no other that is possible – at least not in the market.'

'Then,' said Lionel blandly, 'that is wiped out.' He added. 'As a specialist you could do an inordinate amount of good, Stephen. Wimpole or Harley Street – that is where you belong – your services at the hospitals would be invaluable; you've all the degrees and are the finest gynæcologist I've struck – and that no idle flattery.' He leaned forward. 'Will you think it over?'

'I belong here,' said Stephen simply.

Stella's gaze flew to his and seemed to melt into his. Fury possessed me then; her flagrant betrayal of her emotions appalled me; I realized that it was an urgent necessity for me to cut off all contact between them, lest she undermine even his loyalty.

Lionel turned to me.

'Then you are my only hope.'

'I?'

'Persuade him; knock some sense into his head for heaven's sake.'

Stephen looked faintly grim.

'And just – supposing for one moment I were interested in your proposition – how do you suppose I should be able to purchase such a practice, Lionel?'

I held my breath, tensed lest Lionel might not present this aspect of the case in quite the detail we had previously agreed upon. But he said easily:

'You can buy it from me in your own time. I'll attend to all that.'

Stella caught my eye as Lionel Manning spoke and, once more, I felt the impact of her suspicion, as though she were silently accusing without in any way being able to justify her reactions.

Stephen said jerkily:

'That's awfully decent of you but–'

Lionel Manning and I exchanged glances, both knowing that the moment was not propitious to pursue the conversation.

'We'll have another chat about it,' Lionel Manning said airily, 'before I go back. Meanwhile, talk it over with Lydia.'

Stella asked suddenly, and it seemed to me a trifle aggressively:

'Are you in favour of Stephen leaving Milbury?' Her gaze was steady and a trifle unnerving.

I answered with emphasis:

'I'm in favour of anything that means Stephen's happiness – just that, Stella. You should know that by now,' I added almost involuntarily.

'The perfect wife,' commented Lionel Manning smoothly. 'Stephen, you're a lucky man.'

'Very,' Stephen agreed, but his voice lacked expression and I felt he could have added a word of praise to the assent.

There was something strangely disconcerting about Stephen's attitude; the violent opposition I had expected appeared to be completely lacking, and an uneasiness possessed me as I tried to fathom the reason. Perhaps it was purely my own imagination and yet the hateful feeling persisted and it was as though I were completely shut out of his innermost thoughts, and as one gazing upon a screen completely blank of film.

It annoyed me as he and Stella began a conversation about affairs at the hospital. Lionel Manning, immediately interested, said, looking at Stella:

'Nursing?'

She smiled and her loveliness smote me, for it was inexpressibly tender and holding a radiance which was as a lamp turned on within her soul.

'Yes; just beginning.'

'Hard work.'

'Satisfying work,' she exclaimed with enthusiasm.

'How about coming to a London hospital when you're qualified? Or even before?'

Stella shook her head.

'No; I shall stay here, Mr Manning; there's so much in Milbury that cries out to be done, and nurses are pitifully short in the district so that even a "rabbit" is worth something. I'm afraid I'm really the country bumpkin, in any case. London makes no appeal to me whatsoever.'

My heart was racing in anger. Stella seemed to me so pious and smug in her attitude; this love of good works was beginning to pall on me for, although I had devoted my entire life to others, and to ministering to those less fortunate than I, there could be no denying that such a pattern of living could be entirely wrong when carried to extremes. I had indulged those extremes with Stella and, now, it was as though I had made a rod for my own back: certainly she was by no means grateful and at times wholly unappreciative of my efforts. A sense of frustration bore down upon me; Stella's influence was becoming insidious and I shuddered as I reflected upon its possible effect upon Stephen, whom it was obvious she was seeking to persuade to remain in Milbury. The disloyalty of that stunned me. It was hard to know that my own sister was so utterly insensible to my happiness and so unscrupulous when pursuing her own.

'I think,' I said banteringly, 'that my sister fancies herself in the rôle of Florence Nightingale, Mr Manning.'

Stephen cut in sharply:

'And what finer ideal could there possibly be?' His eyes met hers for a fraction of a second, then he added almost aggressively: 'I have the very highest praise for Stella's ambitions; good nurses are the very salt of the earth and, without them, even the cleverest of doctors would be miserable failures.'

Lionel Manning stoutly agreed with that.

I said, trying to keep my voice smooth and steady:

'A born nurse is very noble.'

Stella challenged me lightly as she said

with a low chuckle, addressing Lionel Manning as well as me:

'My sister has a very poor opinion of my capabilities, or chances of success in the profession I've chosen: I'm certain she pictures me as eventually being thoroughly incompetent and my patients lamentably neglected.'

I laughed to convey my annoyance.

'Hardly, darling; the regulations of the hospital would prevent that, surely.'

Stephen's voice came with sudden gentleness:

'Never mind, Stella; if I'm ever in need of a nurse I'll send for you and feel quite safe in your hands.'

Lionel Manning grinned.

'Doctors always choose the pretty ones, Stella, and on the whole there are more pretty women in the nursing profession than in any other. I often wonder why.'

Stephen took that up.

'Couldn't it be because they must have something within themselves likely to radiate beauty, otherwise they would never choose so badly a paid task, or so exacting a one?'

Stella's cheeks grew a becoming pink; she smiled warmly and shook her head.

'I didn't ask for bouquets, you know.'

'Just hoped for them,' I said teasingly. 'What time have you to be back to-night?'

I wanted her to leave; she crashed into the atmosphere rather after the manner of thunder crackling through silence; she had become a disturbing element and I hated, remorsefully, the fact that I could no longer trust her: the old, loving, and frank Stella was dead, and in her place had come a woman subtly scheming whose obsession for Stephen was something I must fight tenaciously – bitter though it was that such an invidious task should be imposed upon me.

Stella winced, and I knew I had hurt her, even though she deserved it, I hated the idea.

'Not until ten,' she said quietly, 'but I must be going now.'

Stephen flashed a critical glance in my direction. He was annoyed, and a desperate misery settled upon me making my resentment of Stella all the greater: had I devoted my life to her in order that she might, eventually, ruin it and shatter all my hard-earned happiness?

'It is only nine, now,' he said to her pointedly. 'Must you leave so soon?' He looked at me as one who expects a supporting comment, and I knew it would be foolish to ignore that silent plea.

I said with banter:

'Of course she has no need to go yet, Stephen. You should know by now that

Stella is always just about to go – aren't you, darling?' I added sweetly: 'Such a pity you cannot stay the night; they certainly keep you on a lead. Ah well, perhaps that is as well; you young things can so easily get into mischief.'

Stella's smile was inscrutable; but her body was tensed and I knew that nothing would have induced her to remain as she got slowly to her feet.

'Good night, Mr Manning,' she said quietly, ignoring my remarks.

Stephen exclaimed:

'I'll run you back, Stella.'

Instantly she protested.

'No; I wouldn't dream of dragging you out again–'

'You won't be,' he said firmly. 'I'd like to do so – if you'll excuse me, old man,' he added glancing in Lionel's direction.

I seethed. Had Stella deliberately angled for that? Swiftly I interposed:

'A run would be rather nice: why don't we all go?' I turned to Lionel Manning as I spoke.

He said implacably:

'If you don't mind, I'm more than comfortable where I am; but don't let me deprive you out of a run, Lydia.'

Stephen's voice was faintly cynical as he said:

'I hardly think that Lydia will suffer any

great hardship by remaining here, old man... Ready, Stella?'

Stella looked wretched and embarrassed.

'I wish you wouldn't do this, Stephen,' she cried.

For a second there was a tense silence before Stephen murmured:

'Don't deprive me of the pleasure.'

They left and I turned away from the front door – having seen them off – with a sensation of sickness in the pit of my stomach. For at least ten minutes they would be alone ... and I should never know what passed between them in that time. It was a hateful feeling and one which, no matter how generous I might try to be towards Stella, could not fail to fill me with jealousy.

That night, alone in our room as we prepared for bed, I began tentatively:

'Lionel Manning seems very anxious for you to take over that practice, darling; he was talking to me about it while you were out with Stella.'

Stephen flicked off his tie and undid his collar.

'You'd like to get away from here, wouldn't you?' he said suddenly.

I stared at him.

'I?' It was necessary for me to dissimulate, much as I loathed having to do so. More than ever I realized the urgency of completing my plans in order that Stephen might be spared the dangers attendant upon his remaining in Milbury. Looking at him, appreciating anew his attractiveness and my own overwhelming love for him, it struck me more forcibly than ever just how his talents and charms were wasted in the slums he frequented with such amazing sympathy. I added: 'What possible reason have you for saying that? Haven't I always been with you in all your ambitions for Milbury?'

He spoke as one who was both doubtful and uncertain.

'I wish I knew, Lydia. Sometimes I wonder.'

'Stephen! Is that fair?'

He sighed.

'Perhaps not; but it is, nevertheless, how I feel.'

'You have,' I protested hotly, 'no reason for making such an assertion. I've done everything within my power to help you and–'

He interrupted me.

'I'm sorry,' he said apologetically. 'And since you *are* with me and my fears are unfounded, then it is quite easy for me to tell you that I have no desire to accept Lionel's offer. My place is here among people who need me.'

I avoided his gaze as I sat down at the dressing-table. Disappointment tore at my heart like claws cutting deeply. Failure stared at me grimly, for there was nothing, so it seemed, I could do to force his hand.

'Then,' I commented with what I knew to be discretion, 'there is nothing more to be said. The decision obviously rests with you.' I changed the subject swiftly: 'What did Stella have to say about it?'

'Very little.' He flung himself into bed. 'Stella never needs to *say* very much; she just understands.'

'And always agrees with you most conveniently – eh, darling?' I forced a light laugh. 'You certainly have a very soft spot for my sister – haven't you?'

His gaze was steady and critical.

'Which is more than you appear to have for her these days.' He dug his head into the pillow as one who has no intention of indulging further discussion.

I challenged that.

'I have been mother and sister to Stella,' I protested. 'You have no justification for making such a remark. Why is it you are so touchy the moment her name is mentioned?'

'It is you who are touchy,' he exclaimed. 'Your anxiety to get her out of the house tonight was positively rude.'

'Nonsense; I merely asked her what time she had to be back.'

'True; it was what you implied and how you looked, my dear, that betrayed you … good night; I'm far too weary to argue.'

Misery washed over me; a bleak sensation of failure added to that misery.

I spoke to Lionel Manning the following morning while Stephen was out on his rounds.

'Has Stephen told you of his decision about leaving here?'

'Yes; he seemed quite adamant. I'm sorry, Lydia; I did my best.'

Emotion churned within me; the bitter reflections of the night came back to haunt me; it seemed that I was defeated and yet I knew that, no matter how great the obstacles, somehow I would have my way and save Stephen from the mediocrity of his life in Milbury.

'I appreciate it to the full.'

'But you are not beaten yet?'

'No.' I looked at him boldly. 'When does the practice in Hampstead become available and the house ready for occupation?'

'In four months.'

'Would you be prepared to negotiate for it.' I outlined my financial position and the profit likely to be made in the event of my selling Highfield House. 'I could make it over to you, protect you against any loss and, in the meantime–'

'Persuade Stephen?'

'Yes.' I smiled. 'Sooner or later he is bound to realize that he is throwing away his talents here and, should that not be so, then I can resell – can't I?'

'Most assuredly.'

'Would you be prepared to help me?'

'I'd be delighted.'

'Then I shall sell out here,' I said stoutly, at the same time making a mental note to take all precautions against the house being placed in the open market so that Diana might bid for it again.

Lionel Manning looked at me.

'You are an amazing woman, Lydia,' he said slowly.

'I'd go to any lengths, make any sacrifice to help my husband,' I said earnestly, 'and feel justified.'

'A pretty piece of feminine philosophy,' he said blandly. 'For all that, in this case, I think you are wise.'

Faint colour stole into my cheeks. Just what was behind that remark? He was, I knew, an excellent psychologist and, as such, had he sensed Stella's foolish idealism towards Stephen? I always recoiled at even thinking of the word 'love' in connection with her regard.

'Meaning?' I prompted.

'Suppose we say no more,' he suggested with a faintly subtle smile.

The next three months did nothing to increase my happiness. A state of tension hung over 'Stoneleigh' and my nerves were strung to breaking point. Adroitly, I managed to take less and less interest in public affairs, and subtly to deprecate the waste of time involved. Financially, Stephen was getting into deep water; my economies were discounted by his foolish generosity; every moment of his days and half of his nights were devoted to people who rarely paid the full fees. 'Stoneleigh' itself was crying out for repairs and, for Stephen's ultimate good, I refrained from making it appear better than it actually was. By innuendo I suggested its dismal, atrocious state. And I in no way made light of the work, or the fact that we could not afford servants. Stephen must be made to realize that the situation was impossible and only hardship and difficulties could be expected to force home the truth. It was one night when, tired almost to the point of utter exhaustion, he said:

'When I think of what might have been could we have got hold of Highfield House, it just defeats me. All my hopes and dreams went with the loss of that place. Here,' he glanced around him, 'there is no chance of launching out; no room and–' He sighed as a man weary unto death.

I said gently:

'I know, dear; but do you seriously think there is any sense in going on as you are now? I'm not complaining, but no one woman can hope to do all that there is to do here. I'd hoped to manage–' I shook my head, then as

I thrust a hand in a much darned sock, I added without emphasis: 'I sometimes wonder if you don't regret turning down Lionel Manning's offer. I've often thought of his words about not being able to dispense charity without money. However ... I expect he has disposed of the practice by now.'

Stephen said grimly:

'I'd plans for Milbury – you know I had. But everything lately seems to have disintegrated...'

'Without money that is inevitable.'

'But I've not earned any less,' he said.

I said painfully:

'Are you suggesting, Stephen, that I am a bad manager?'

'No; no; but that, somehow, I haven't felt your support morally, Lydia; it's like that brake all the time ... oh, I'm not blaming you; I probably asked for far too much.'

'This place is killing you,' I said sorrowfully; 'and it isn't making me feel any younger. Not,' I hastened, 'that I am important ... have you thought of a holiday, by the way?'

I knew that we couldn't possibly afford one, but to emphasize the fact upon his mind would not, I felt, do any harm. Somehow, I must save him; I must get him away and now was the time to strike.

'No,' he answered dully. 'That isn't possible financially, I'm afraid.'

I sighed and deliberately made no comment.

Stella looked in later that evening and when Stephen was out of the room, she said earnestly:

'He looks so worn out, Lydia.'

'He is worn out,' I replied. 'This place is ruining him financially and physically.'

Her eyes narrowed and a light of battle gleamed in them.

'You always intended that he should leave Milbury – didn't you?' She caught at her breath. 'That's why you've not lifted a finger really to help him... Oh, Lydia, how could you – you, whom I once thought so noble, so self-sacrificing. Stephen's dreams could all have come true with your help. This house ... you could transform it if you cared... But, no! You've been undermining his position here ever since you married him, hoping that, in the end he would be forced to accept defeat.'

I stared at her, stunned and aghast.

'Are you quite *mad?*'

It was impossible to describe the effect of her words; they seemed to strike with the force of hammer blows, making me so faint that I leaned back in my chair almost on the verge of fainting.

Stephen came slowly into the room in that second and never shall I forget the expression on his face as looking first at Stella and then at me, he said heavily:

'I've decided to leave Milbury and accept Lionel's offer – if it is still available.'

CHAPTER TWELVE

Stephen's announcement came to me as a reward for all my efforts. At last I should see him progressing in that world in which, rightly, he belonged. The relief was almost overwhelming and every nerve in my body tingled, my pulse quickening as a thrill of happiness surged over me. But I knew that I must be guarded in my comments; that to betray undue delight would arouse his suspicions and negative my earlier insistence that I was absolutely in sympathy with his ambitions for Milbury. I said swiftly:

'Why, Stephen! What a sudden change of heart. Are you serious?'

'Perfectly.' His tone was faintly grim.

I found myself wondering suddenly, and uneasily, just what was responsible for this reversal of his decision and a little of my triumph vanished, because I could deduce nothing from his attitude suggestive of enthusiasm, or likely to engender the belief that his leaving Milbury meant that he genuinely wanted to get away from the district and all it embraced. I watched Stella carefully in those seconds, intercepting the glance she gave him, aware of an almost unbearable tension between them and of Stephen's withdrawn inscrutability. He might have been a man resigning himself to a situation he could no longer fight against.

Stella's voice trembled with emotion as she murmured:

'Oh, *Stephen!*' There was regret and incredulity in the utterance.

He said, after the manner of a man labouring under great strain, 'Let's not hold any post-mortem. Things here are getting quite beyond me and' – he paused before adding– 'and Lydia.'

Stella's momentary silence challenged me; her eyes met mine accusingly, bitterly.

'They could very easily be changed,' she insisted.

I interposed.

'Suppose you allow Stephen to be the judge of that, darling. If I may say so, this really is no possible concern of yours.'

The timid child had vanished; now, she was a woman fighting the cause of the man she loved.

'As a member of the family, I claim the right to speak,' she said urgently. 'Stephen's work here is only just beginning and to leave now–' Her eyes were suspiciously bright.

It was, I considered, in the very worst possible taste for her thus to impose her views and I said sharply:

'I rather think, Stella, that you are looking

at this purely selfishly: *you* just don't happen to want us to leave here.'

Firmly, resolutely she answered:

'I was thinking only of Stephen: my feelings are not in the least important; his life's work is all that matters–'

'And,' said Stephen gravely, 'you think, Stella, that my real life's work is in Milbury, don't you?'

'Yes,' she said unhesitatingly, 'I do.'

He looked at her and my heart seemed to stand still: was it possible that she could sway him, that victory was to be snatched from within my grasp. I exclaimed sharply.

'You don't really know what you are talking about, Stella. And since Stephen has made his decision of his own free will, I hardly think your comments in good taste.'

'Stephen asked me a question,' she replied simply. 'I answered it, Lydia.'

Warring elements gathered around us in the silence that followed. Stephen looked worn and grave; Stella was pale, deeply concerned. I, for my part, felt rebellious and angry. How dare she adopt the attitude she did, almost as though claiming some special dispensation, and suggesting tacitly, that there was a secret understanding between her and Stephen.

He looked at me coldly:

'I think, Lydia, that it is you who offend the canons of good taste. Suppose we say no more about it?'

'And you really are serious,' Stella said desolately.

'Yes.' He hesitated, then: 'For very many more reasons that may appear obvious.'

She glanced up at him swiftly; a glance that seemed to dissolve into a long, lingering gaze; a gaze that might have been the fusion of heart, soul and thought, and I knew, again, that dagger thrust of jealousy. Why shut my eyes to the fact? Stella was deliberately trying to steal him from me, and for that I both hated and despised her. It was cruel beyond description after all she owed me over the years.

She got to her feet very slowly as one beaten, almost dejected. Stephen cried involuntarily:

'One day, perhaps, you will understand.'

It was after she had gone that I said:

'Just what made you change your mind so suddenly about all this, darling?'

He looked at me very steadily:

'I don't think you need an answer to that question, Lydia.'

'What do you mean?'

'You know perfectly well, my dear; nothing has quite worked out – has it? Your heart hasn't really been here in my work, to begin with and–'

I recoiled from his unfairness as I countered:

'Well, really, Stephen! I hardly think that is the attitude to adopt. I've done everything humanly possible to help you since our marriage, been in sympathy with your every ideal and ambition and now – now because you have grown weary of the struggle and poverty of it all, you want to shelve the blame on me and suggest that I'm responsible for your decision.'

The grim lines around his mouth tightened; in that second he seemed a stranger as he said with quiet dignity:

'You hardly expect me to lower myself by challenging such remarks, Lydia – do you? The discussion had better end.'

It was unthinkable that I should be placed in the wrong.

'That is because you cannot possibly have an adequate reply,' I said smarting under the injustice. 'I don't expect any gratitude for all I've tried to do, Stephen, but I think I am entitled to be given credit for it and not be made the scapegoat.'

He stared at me, rather ruefully:

'You are a very strange woman, Lydia; you have the supreme knack of always being right – in your own opinion. It must be a very satisfying state of mind.'

I said, aggrieved:

'How can you be so utterly unfair?'

He gave an impatient grunt.

'Oh, for heaven's sake let's have done with

the wretched discussion. I'm sick to death of the whole business. Impossible to talk sanely to you these days.'

'Well!' I was outraged and wounded, and my anger against Stella increased a thousandfold. Driven to desperation, I cried: 'And suppose you stop asking Stella's opinion about everything. She always causes friction whenever she comes here.'

'Because you make it,' he answered.

'You always defend her – don't you?' My voice was suddenly calm and I knew that my words had significance for him. His attitude changed to a quiet gravity as he said solemnly:

'I think it would be as well if we didn't discuss Stella again. You will not be annoyed with her presence much longer.'

I gasped.

'Do you realize that Stella is my sister?'

'I realize it,' he said cuttingly, 'but I thought *you* had forgotten the fact long ago – judging by your attitude.'

And with that he turned and went from the room.

The next few weeks passed in a whirl of activity. Lionel Manning rose to the occasion magnificently; arrangements were made without the slightest hitch and without engendering suspicion of any kind in Stephen's mind. From his point of view Lionel Manning had purchased the practice as an investment and he, Stephen, was taking it over, paying interest on the capital but with the privilege of buying it by instalments as, and when, his finances allowed.

I sold the Highfield House advantageously and discreetly to the London Syndicate, who intended converting it into a Preparatory School for boys. And on completion of the purchase, I went to see Allan and, coming straight to the point, said:

'May I pay you back two thousand of the three I owe you, Allan? I need that thousand pounds for decorations, furniture, where we're going – to be quite honest.'

He looked at me with a strangely intent expression:

'There are many things about all this that just don't add up, Lydia.'

I didn't intend confiding in him, not because I didn't trust him, but because I knew that, for Stephen's sake, I must have regard to all potentialities, and allow for Diana's cunning in wheedling facts out of Allan: that which he did not know he could not repeat – even inadvertently.

'Do they need to add up, Allan?' I smiled at him. 'Of course I shall understand perfectly if you don't feel inclined to trust me further but–'

He said almost sharply:

'Don't be ridiculous! Obviously the money, as such, doesn't come into it and I couldn't care less if you never paid it back. Keep the whole amount if you wish. I was just curious to know–'

'How I made the two thousand with which now to repay you?' I spoke slowly and with a certain provocative air.

He said honestly:

'Frankly – yes.'

'I had what might well be termed a gamble – and won. Simple.'

'Very; it could cover a multitude of sins.'

'Such as?'

He eyed me steadily:

'Highfield House,' he said tensely.

'Don't be ridiculous,' I said sharply.

'I don't think, my dear, that I am.' He added: 'Perhaps I am just beginning to know you – the real you, Lydia.'

I laughed.

'Does any man know a woman?' I teased. 'You've always been very undecided about my character, Allan – haven't you?'

He studied me gravely:

'Has it ever struck you that Stephen might strongly object to your schemes?'

I frowned; this wasn't like Allan. My voice was subdued as I answered him:

'Since you know that only the highest motives prompt my actions where Stephen is concerned, I don't think the question at all necessary.'

He changed his attitude completely. How

easy it was to play on his emotions and, if I so chose, bend him to my will. Allan would never fail me.

'I'm sorry, Lydia; but it isn't easy for me, you know, and I hate the thought of your leaving Milbury.'

'You speak as though London were part of another world.' My smile met his steady gaze. 'I shall expect you to come to stay with us, then. Probably see more of you than we do now.'

'The "we", Lydia, makes that quite impossible... How is Stella taking your going?'

'Quite well.'

'You don't see much of her, in any case – do you?'

I started. Had Stella been talking – talking disloyally?

'As much as is possible – why?'

'No reason.'

I left him a little later with an uneasy feeling as of something lost in our relationship; the shadow of Stella loomed almost sinisterly, and now it was as if the very mention of her name cast a gloom upon me. Perhaps, I argued, I had expected too much of her, but all I knew was that she had disillusioned me to a point of acute distress and I had reached that stage where I was happier not to see her at all, than to do so only to have salt rubbed into what was still an open wound.

We moved to Hampstead early in October. Our going was a depressing business with all Stephen's patients calling continually, until I felt that the entire place was in mourning – so consistent were their laments.

'I feel I'm deserting them,' he said almost harshly as he came in from the Surgery on that last night.

I said gently:

'Well, darling, since it was your own choice–' I changed my tone. 'By the way, I've chosen sapphire blue for the hangings in your consulting room at Hampstead – you like blue, don't you?'

He eyed me with a certain anxiety. Then:

'Just where is the money to come from with which to pay for all that is being done?' he asked abruptly. 'I've wanted to talk to you of it before but–' His tone was that of a man who hasn't the heart to start an argument.

I had, of course, been waiting for that question and had my answer. This was no time to be squeamish: if Stephen was to be given the opportunity of lifting himself out of the rut into which he had sunk in Milbury, then it was essential that neither effort, nor expense, should be spared in order to provide the right setting for his new venture. I felt strongly that the atmosphere within the Hampstead house would be of great import; that it must be a home I could grace rather than inhabit and, in the process, set the seal on his success. My voice was steady and firm as I replied:

'I've wanted to mention it to you, too, darling, but the right opportunity hadn't presented itself.' I paused before adding: 'Actually, the money is that which father gave me two years before he died. It was a gift – something for an emergency – and a secret just between the two of us.'

Stephen's expression was incredulous.

'But what about Stella – surely she had a right to share it?'

I bristled at that. Stella again. I said icily:

'I rather think father was the best judge of that, after all. And don't forget I took mother's place in the home while Stella was, after all, merely decorative. Possibly father took that into account.' There was faint sarcasm in my voice and I resented the idea that, instantly, Stephen should leap to Stella's defence and plead her cause.

'Even so, I hate the thought of your using it as you are. The money was left to you and should be spent–'

I hastened, interrupting him:

'As I choose, darling; in a manner calculated to give me most pleasure. Well, helping to make your home as you would have it ... that is my pleasure. Need we say more?'

'No, but–'

'Don't be difficult, Stephen. One day you

will smile at the thought of a thousand pounds representing anything.'

'A thousand pounds!' He spoke as though it were a million.

'Don't make it sound such a fortune,' I protested, laughingly. It struck me that he might wonder just how father – on his salary – had managed to save so much, and I added: 'The money was left to father by his great-uncle.'

'That,' came the stubborn rejoinder, 'in no way makes me like your spending it in the manner you are doing, Lydia.'

I resented his tone which suggested a certain adamant disapproval.

'Please,' I exclaimed, realizing that he was not the type to listen to persuasion and that to prolong the discussion would get us nowhere. 'Don't spoil my enjoyment, Stephen; it doesn't hurt you after all and, no matter what you may say, we do need the purchases I'm making.'

That hardly left him a loophole for further argument. He looked at me very levelly, appeared about to say something and then lapsed into silence.

At that moment the 'phone rang and when he replaced the receiver, he said swiftly:

'Timothy.'

'The asthma boy?'

'Yes.' He moved to the door. 'Don't wait up for me, Lydia.'

Annoyance gripped me. Couldn't these people let him have even his last evening in Milbury to himself. In any case he was no longer the Milbury doctor and I said:

'But, darling, surely you don't have to turn out now… I mean–'

He interrupted me.

'If I were at the other end of England and I was needed for that little chap, I should go, Lydia. He trusts me and I can do more with him than anyone else – children are like that.'

'But,' I protested fearfully, 'what will you do when you are in Hampstead?'

'Come down here,' he said without hesitation, 'in any emergency. I've promised them that.'

The old sickness returned as I listened to him. I had not bargained for anything of the kind, but I consoled myself that as time went on and he tasted the thrill of real success, he would cease to foster such ideas and all would be well. If only he were a little less idealistic how much simpler everything would be. No one appreciated ideals more than I, but Stephen carried his to ridiculous lengths of sacrifice.

There was something very strange about 'Stoneleigh' that night; practically all the furniture had already gone and that which was left was no more than essential for our needs over the remaining twenty-four hours.

While Stephen was out I did the last minute packing, my footsteps echoing hollowly along the draughty corridors, and emphasizing the dreariness of the place which I had come to regard as a morgue. Stephen was not back until midnight; he was grave and preoccupied. I looked at him inquiringly and he said:

'God, it's damnable to see a kid like that.'

'It must be.' I had cut some sandwiches which I placed before him. 'You must eat those, darling.'

'No thanks... You shouldn't have waited up.'

Don't I always?'

'Yes, but–'

I put out my hand and touched his.

'It will mean so much to me when you no longer have to work so hard, darling.'

A rather cynical smile touched his lips as he said:

'No doctor interested in his work counts the hours, Lydia. I've enjoyed every moment of my life here – in the professional sense.'

My heart lurched painfully:

'And not in the personal? Hardly a compliment to me.'

A faint flush touched his cheeks.

'We were talking of work,' he suggested.

I wasn't satisfied.

'And you spoke, also,' I said regretfully, 'as though you hated leaving Milbury. That

313

being so, why are you going?'

His expression became withdrawn and inscrutable. His voice was uncompromising, almost stern as he answered:

'We need not go into that problem again, Lydia.'

I dare not pursue the subject, knowing in any case that it would avail me nothing informative; Stephen's feelings seemed as a closed book to me and my only comfort lay in the fact that once out of Milbury, everything would change.

The following morning Stella called to say good-bye.

'I don't suppose Milbury will be seeing you again,' she said, and her voice deepened almost to criticism as she added: 'It will seem far too insignificant and unimportant after your fashionable Hampstead practice.'

Stephen winced.

'My feelings for Milbury, and the people in it,' he said gravely, 'will never change, Stella. And I am not going to any "fashionable practice" as you call it. Lionel Manning assured me there was real work to be done.'

Stella's gaze turned first to me and then back to him.

'I imagine that will rather depend on what you mean by work,' she said quietly.

There was a suggestion of pained reproach, not altogether divorced from disillusionment, in her attitude and a certain hesitant pleading in Stephen's, almost as though he wanted to convince her that his going was not of his own volition. That incensed me for, in all fairness, his decision had been made entirely of his own free will.

I changed the trend of the conversation by saying:

'I am going to be secretary-cum-receptionist – I shall love the job.'

Her expression changed. She was as one resolved not to say more lest she betray herself completely. She came over to me and brushed my cheek.

'Good-bye, Lydia,' she murmured.

I could not help thinking how very different it was from the old days when she had appreciated, or seemed to, my devotion and all I had done for her. Now we were as polite strangers and it cut me to the very depths that she should be so insensible to the facts of our relationship and of all the efforts I had made in her behalf.

I waited, almost rigid, as she turned to Stephen. Would he kiss her; I felt it was more than I could bear to watch him if he did and yet, when he said gently, but with infinite tenderness: 'Good-bye, Stella,' and made no effort to touch her cheek with his lips, I knew an anguish almost greater than any his caress might have caused me. Was it that he dare not trust himself to give her the impersonal kiss of a brother-in-law? Was it that his regard for her was so strong as to make casual affection quite impossible. She appeared to be oblivious of the omission, but I knew that she was trembling for all that, and her pain in some measure acted as a palliative for my own.

'Good-bye, Stephen,' she murmured solemnly. The next second she was gone.

Stephen stood as one transfixed, staring after her. I spoke to him, but the sound evoked no response; he was as a man rendered suddenly oblivious of his surroundings, to whom nothing was real except his unspoken thoughts.

Thankfully I found myself a little later gazing for the last time on 'Stoneleigh'. It held no particularly joyous memories, but it had been the stepping stone to greater things and, as such, I gave it honour. To it I had gone as Stephen's bride – that fact emerged to set it high in my recollections – but even in that the ghost of Stella obtruded. What suffering her attitude had caused me, and how hard it had been to live with the shadow of her reckless infatuation for Stephen.

Stephen had not seen our new home, 'Gable's End', since his first visit of approval, and therefore the hangings and decorations were new to him on his arrival. I had spared no expense as far as my means allowed, and the spectacle that met his eyes evoked his cry of amazement. A London firm had executed the order and rich velvets glowed against delicately tinted walls, falling finally to honey-shaded parquet.

'You like it?' I was eager, anxious for his praise.

'Very much,' he answered me, but there was a certain reservation in his mien.

'But – what?' The words fell rather impatiently from my lips.

'Isn't it a little more the Salon for an actor, than a doctor's home, Lydia?'

I could have cried with disappointment.

'Do you think that – fair?' I managed to keep my voice steady. 'I've tried to give you a beautiful home, Stephen, and I thought I'd succeeded. It isn't for myself I want it – only you count.'

He gave me a steady, inquiring glance.

'*My* tastes are far simpler, Lydia.'

'But in a place like this,' I began and stopped. Fatal to stress the fashionable angle or he would retreat even further.

'Suppose we don't say any more?' he suggested. 'It is what you wanted, and, since it is also your money, you are fully entitled to have it so.'

It wasn't anything for which I'd hoped. And after all I had done it seemed the height of injustice that I should, thus, be tacitly accused of furthering my own ambitions rather than his.

'That's not fair,' I protested.

He sighed.

'I do not mean it unfairly...'

'Some men would–'

'I am not "some men",' he corrected me. 'But since we are here–'

'I suppose you prefer the dinginess of "Stoneleigh"?'

'In many respects – yes. I feel that, at least, there I shared much with my patients and that they were my friends.'

'This practice will yield you more friends than ever you want, darling,' I said soothingly. 'You're tired; oh, I shall be so thankful to see you having a little leisure.'

He stared at me.

'You are quite insensible to my point of view over all this – aren't you?' he said quietly. 'Quite incapable of realizing that the things *you* want people to have are mostly those things *for* which they have no desire.'

It was a bitter blow and I recoiled from it. To seek to justify myself would be lowering; far better to turn the other cheek and win his admiration for my tolerance.

'I don't think you expect me to comment on that, Stephen. It is too fantastic.'

The next weeks brought some semblance of normality to our lives; the practice was reorganized and I took charge of all the essentials, so that everything ran on oiled wheels. Stephen was left to attend to his patients, among whom were numbered many elegant young women who found him decidedly attractive.

'They positively nauseate me,' he said fiercely. 'Idle, rich and wanting nothing more than a doctor to dance attendance upon them and hold their useless hands. Lionel must have been mad to suggest there was work to do here.'

'You cannot,' I said swiftly, 'form a true opinion in this short while.'

'I can and I have,' he retorted.

'You've made more money in this three months than you would have made in Milbury probably in years – you worked there almost for nothing,' I said hotly.

'But I was doing some good,' he persisted. 'And I thought money meant so little to you?'

'It means nothing to me, personally,' I snapped. Really, one required infinite patience to deal with Stephen. 'But you – *for* you–'

He shook his head.

'I can just imagine all that Stella would have to say about this crowd here.' His voice was low, its expression eloquent of deep feeling.

'And what has she to do with it?'

'Nothing, Lydia.' He sighed. 'And what is the programme for to-night?'

'We're giving our first dinner party,' I

added swiftly as I saw his expression change. 'You know we are, darling. Lionel Manning is coming and bringing Sir Gordon and Lady Markly.'

'This,' said Stephen, 'is news to me. That Lionel was to have dinner with us – yes; but a dinner party–' He stopped abruptly. 'Just what have you at the back of your mind, Lydia? What is all this? You know how I detest this social business.'

I managed to keep very calm as I answered him:

'Of course you do, Stephen, and so do I, but my dear, we can't isolate ourselves completely you know. My whole objective is to do what is best for you and Lionel Manning wanted you to meet Sir Gordon and–'

'You took it upon yourself to arrange it as though I didn't exist,' he said sternly. 'I will not have my life run for me, Lydia.'

'Stephen! How can you?'

'I can and I will,' he exclaimed raising his voice. 'This is just an insidiously progressive journey into a world I cannot tolerate. If you'd had half the zeal in the running of "Stoneleigh" that you have shown in the managing of this place, things might have been different. I should be very blind if I didn't make comparisons.'

'I refuse to talk to you while you are so unreasonable,' I said. Then: 'Oh, Stephen … this isn't like you; we can't quarrel and–'

'For people who cannot quarrel we seem to do a very great deal of it, nevertheless,' he countered.

'That isn't my fault,' I said hotly.

He shook his head.

'We just don't speak the same language,' he murmured.

In that second it was as if a vision of Stella insinuated itself between us; as if her shadow had fallen across his heart – and mine. Useless my denying that I had experienced at every turn a jealousy that was growing alarmingly, and that his every remark appeared to me as having a double meaning.

'Is there anyone with whom you do speak the same language?' I demanded fiercely.

For a second there was a deadly silence; a silence that throbbed to a degree of unbearability as it beat about us, destroying harmony, understanding, and mocking at our failure.

'You don't expect me to answer that question,' he said icily.

Panic gripped me then; my love for him was a torment that seemed to tear at my body and sear my soul. I moved closer to him and whispered his name; my hand reaching out to him. I must change this mood, placate him... But his eyes met mine coldly; his hand remained inert; I might have been a stranger as he walked away from me and so from the room.

With great effort I managed, however, to rise above what, after all, was a quarrel such as hundreds of married couples indulged. The guests arrived and I knew the thrill of receiving them with Stephen at my side; knew the sensation as of having brought him to that point of success he so richly deserved. And yet, somehow, I was on edge lest anything might happen to mar the smooth perfection of the evening. There must be no interruptions, no 'emergencies', and I had given special instructions that on no account was 'the doctor' available no matter who might call, and that I was to be approached should anyone ask for him.

It was just before dinner that Betty, the housekeeper, called me aside to tell me that a gentleman from Milbury was urgently asking for Stephen.

I hastened to the consulting room where a haggard-looking man, at the sound of my footsteps, almost flung himself forward in greeting as he cried:

'My name's Wade... I'm Timothy's father. He's worse – much worse, and Doctor Stephen said he'd always come – always... I–'

My heart was beating wildly; this was a crisis that I must face alone. Stephen's whole future depended on how this situation was handled. It was unthinkable that he should be dragged away from a dinner party that might mean his future career being sealed, his social success assured – and all for a child whose life, in any case, was almost forfeit. I said as quietly as I could:

'I'm terribly sorry, but it is quite impossible for my husband to come to your son; he is–'

'But if he knew – if he knew he'd insist on coming,' the man said, raising his voice in his frantic agitation.

'Then,' I said gently, 'I will fetch him–'

I knew that it was the only way, and with that I went from the room, waited a second, and returned. No one was going to spoil my triumph on that night. I had earned every second of it and for Stephen to be taken from my side, back to Milbury, would be symbolic of my failure.

The man moved forward and gripped my hand:

'Well! What did he say–' He looked at the door as though half expecting to see Stephen standing there.

I kept a steady rein on my emotions as I said:

'I'm very sorry, but my husband says that it is absolutely impossible, for him to do as you suggest. And that the doctor who took his place in Milbury is more than capable of looking after your son.' As I spoke I opened the door, anxious, fearful lest Stephen, missing me, might seek me out.

The man looked at me as one dazed, stunned.

'I – I don't believe it,' he murmured. 'He said he'd come – at any time. You don't understand. If I could talk to him–'

'That is quite out of the question,' I said firmly. 'And now, I really must ask you to go. Your son will be perfectly all right in other hands... I'm sorry.'

The man straightened his shoulders and a grim light came into his eyes as he said, glancing around him:

'It isn't far from Milbury here, but from this house and the doctor's old home–' He shook his head. And then, almost stumbling, he turned and went swiftly from the room and so out of the front door. It was at that moment Stephen appeared in the hall, a look of inquiry on his face.

'Who was that?'

'No one,' I said lightly. 'Just a message for me, darling.'

CHAPTER THIRTEEN

Stephen glanced at the front door almost as though he was hoping for the caller to reappear. There was something curious, even suspicious, in his attitude as he asked:

'From whom?'

I stared at him with a smile of faintly amused tolerance as one who suggests, or implies, that the question was superfluous. Then I answered him:

'Merely from my dressmaker, darling.'

'At this hour?'

I became impatient.

'Really, Stephen, is this a cross-examination?'

'Sorry; I thought I heard a man's voice...'

I hastened:

'Darling, we can't both be away from our guests.'

'Guests,' he said disgustedly. 'I'm bored to death before the evening is a fraction of the way through.'

He was, I decided, a most annoying and irritating man.

'They are all influential people, Stephen and–'

'Can be *used*,' he finished for me.

'Well–' I hesitated unsure of my ground. Then, playing for safety, exclaimed: 'You have no need of any such help.'

'Thanks; and no desire for it – remember that, in future, Lydia.'

It was not the evening I had planned and hoped for. Stephen was polite, courteous, but he made no attempt to create an atmosphere of warmth or friendliness, or in any way to suggest the charming, successful man on the threshold of a brilliant career – as I had fervently hoped he would do. A stubborn resistance lurked behind his every word as though he were on the defensive against any possible patronization.

Sir Gordon and Lady Markly, great friends of Lionel Manning, went out of their way to inspire him with confidence. Sir Gordon was a Harley Street physician and I knew that his approval would be invaluable to Stephen. Sir Gordon said:

'This practice must seem a trifle different to you, my boy, after Milbury. Lionel tells me you're going a very long way.'

I held my breath as I waited for Stephen's answer:

'I hope,' Stephen said quietly, 'that I am travelling in the right direction, Sir Gordon. In Milbury I felt that I had a mission; here, I am not so sure, while being fully appreciative of Lionel's confidence in me.'

Lady Markly said evenly:

'I know Milbury – a dreadful place.' She turned to me. 'How grateful you must be to have escaped from it, Mrs Ashley.'

'I am,' I said swiftly, adding as I saw the expression on Stephen's face: 'although I had many happy days there that colour it for me.'

'Of course.' It was a gentle comment accompanied by a warm smile.

Stephen said with emphasis:

'It was the prospect of improving Milbury that appealed to me.' A faintly ironical laugh. 'The folly of the idealist, perhaps.'

Sir Gordon chuckled.

'I began with just such pipe dreams, my boy. But I soon learned that they didn't pay the bills.' A pause. 'Ah, well, if there's ever anything I can do for you, just let me know. Shan't be satisfied until you move into Harley Street.'

I said breathlessly:

'You are very encouraging, Sir Gordon.'

He smiled at me.

'And you, Mrs Ashley, are very inspiring to your husband, I'm sure.'

Stephen made no attempt to comment upon, or enlarge on, the remark, much to my chagrin; it was the perfect opening for a pretty compliment had he wished to make one.

Dinner was a very successful meal, but, again, Stephen's attitude was apathetic; I had the irritating feeling that he was contemptuous of those around him, and that all my efforts in his behalf were wasted, and he regarded every second of it as a bore.

Lionel Manning said to me a little later, when we were able to talk without fear of being overheard, because the rest of the gathering was clustered about Sir Gordon and Lady Markly:

'You've a long way to go, Lydia, before Stephen accepts all this.'

I feigned surprise.

'What makes you think so?'

'His attitude generally.'

Resentment flared within me.

'Stephen is never enthusiastic.'

Lionel Manning smiled.

'I couldn't quite agree with that, you know... In fact I'm a little worried lest any part I have played may not be against his happiness and, after all, happiness is success – no matter how we may differ in our conception of it.'

'Stephen is perfectly happy,' I replied. 'He came here of his own free will, so I really don't see that you have anything with which to reproach yourself – even if he shouldn't care for the actual practice. Time is the only thing: getting used to the abrupt change.'

'I suppose so. I admire him, Lydia; he's one of the very few incorruptibles.'

'How true,' I agreed, beamingly and

wishing in my heart that he was, also, a little less stubborn.

The hours passed and I knew that, despite Stephen, it had been a success in the end because, realizing that Stephen was not going out of his way to make it so, I redoubled my efforts, and allowed my own personality to emerge instead of remaining discreetly in the background so that Stephen might shine the more brightly. Conversation sparkled and I initiated it. I overheard Sir Gordon say to Stephen on leaving:

'You're a lucky man – a charming home and an exceptionally charming wife. How about dining with us on Friday next? I've a proposition I'd like to put to you.'

Stephen's face was mask-like as he said:

'I'm sorry, Sir Gordon; Friday is impossible. I promised to go down to Milbury to look at a hospital case there.'

I interrupted, emotion surging wildly within me:

'But, Stephen, haven't you forgotten that the appointment was altered and–?'

'No,' he said firmly; 'it still stands for Friday: it is you who have forgotten, my dear.' And with that he turned to Sir Gordon and Lady Markly, made his apologies once more, said good-night to them and the last guest and, with the house suddenly quiet, flung himself down wearily in the nearest armchair.

'Thank God that invasion is over. What a waste of my time.'

I said hotly:

'You were anything but gracious; in fact you behaved abominably.'

'Splendid; let that be a warning to you,' he added. 'I did not come here to lead a social life, Lydia. I detest it, what is more I will not have my house filled with people whom I hardly know, and like not at all. The leisure I have–'

I interrupted him:

'Don't you realize that it was an honour for Sir Gordon and Lady Markly to come here?'

'I am not unmindful of the fact, Lydia; neither am I unduly elated. All this is just not what I wanted. Let it go at that, please.'

I looked at him, anger descending upon me with a violence I had never quite experienced before – not at least to such an overwhelming degree. The thought of Milbury came to me ... always Milbury and that, of course, meant Stella.

'I take it,' I said, trying to keep my voice as steady as possible, 'that now you wish you were back in Milbury – is that it?'

He rested his head against the cushion of his chair; there was unutterable weariness in the gesture, but I felt far too dispirited to be sympathetic. I had fought so hard for him, studied him to the very last degree, that now

I found myself dwelling upon the situation purely from my own standpoint; I had been unselfish long enough, surely I was entitled to a little respite.

He drew a hand across his forehead and sighed; then, glancing at me, he heaved himself out of the chair rather as one who finds his body heavier than his strength to combat it.

'You know the answer to that question, Lydia.'

'Then why did you ever come here – you did so entirely of your own volition.'

'You have,' he said coldly, 'reminded me of that fact on several occasions; truth, you know, Lydia can be so twisted and distorted as to be even a greater untruth than a lie … who's that?' He was instantly alert as the front door-bell rang and he heard the maid's footsteps hurrying to answer it. 'An emergency surely at this hour.'

But to my horror, it was Stella who came slowly into the room; a Stella deathly pale and so calm as to be alarming, as she stared first at Stephen and then at me.

'Stella!' Stephen's voice broke upon her name even as he uttered it, rather after the manner of a thirsty man who sees water after many long days.

I cried:

'What on earth are you doing here at this house?' Then, testily: 'Don't stand there looking like the edge of doom – what is it?'

'I hope,' she said, 'that now you are satisfied, Lydia.' She turned to Stephen and it was as though her very gaze was a comment in itself upon his evening clothes, as she went on, and now there was a fire and spirited attractiveness in her fast growing scorn and anger as she rapped out: 'And you, Stephen; you who were so full of concern for humanity; you who left Milbury promising that if ever you were needed you would return ... well, you were tested tonight, weren't you? And found wanting.' She glanced around her, taking in the artistic furnishings, aware of the atmosphere still redolent of the party which had so recently been held. And in that second my flesh began to creep; in that second I remembered Timothy's father ... was all this linked up with his visit. If so–'

I cried frantically:

'Come into another room, Stella; Stephen's tired and–'

Stephen cut in authoratively:

'Go on, Stella, you were saying–' His eyes were upon her hungrily, desperately; as he spoke he took a few paces forward as one yearning to reach out and draw her into his arms. Never had I seen him so tensed with emotion, so obvious in his reactions.

'I was speaking of Timothy Wade,' she said, and her voice cracked. 'He's dead,

Stephen – dead. And you could have saved him...' A sob crept into her voice. 'Oh, how could you be so callous as to refuse even to see his father – how *could* you.' She finished scornfully: 'Or were your social activities so much more important?'

Stephen gasped:

'For God's sake what is all this?... I didn't know, Stella; I wasn't told anyone had called ... when did all this happen?'

Stella's gaze leapt to mine in a look of swift, almost incredulous accusation.

'Lydia,' she whispered, horrified.

I said, fighting for control, realized that I must still protect Stephen from her distortions:

'Isn't this a trifle melodramatic? The child is dead and this ridiculous conversation will get us nowhere. Obviously there was some mistake and Stephen wasn't informed that the father had called; it's unfortunate but–'

Stephen's words came like silent thunder:

'Did Mr Wade tell you whom he saw when he came here, Stella?'

It was curious, but as I stood there it was as if all emotion died within me. These two were in conspiracy against me, that was obvious; just as it was obvious that throughout my married life with Stephen, Stella had tried systematically to undermine our happiness. I said, and now, some semblance of life crept back into limbs which, a second before, had appeared almost paralysed; my brain ceased to be stupefied by the disaster imminent and I found myself saying:

'Obviously, Stephen, the servants; isn't the question rather an insult to me?'

'Not,' he said with almost terrifying anger, 'if you are innocent.' He looked again at Stella whom I knew was torn between natural loyalty to me and her love for Stephen.

She said, shaking her head.

'I–I–'

He cut in fiercely:

'You don't have to answer; I know.' He swung around to face me. 'It was Mr Wade whom you described as "a message from your dressmaker" – that's it, isn't it?' His voice rose. 'You deliberately kept me away from him because of this wretched party... Oh, how clearly I can see it all ... and what a fool I've been.'

I dare not relax; dare not become the suppliant; dare not betray the sheer panic that gripped me in that second. Slowly, carefully, I said:

'Anything I may, or may not, have done, Stephen, was in your interests. I acted for the best; your going down there to-night would not have made any difference – and you know it. The boy was doomed, in any case. I'm afraid I was far more concerned with your welfare; you were tired and–'

His voice lashed me with its scorn:

'But not too tired to remain here and be bored to death; not too tired to conform to your plans like some damned marionette on a string – a string in your hand. You know how deep my affection was for that boy ... and to think I wasn't even with him... By God, Lydia, that's something I could never forgive you for.' He stared at me. Then: 'It's a terrible thing really to see a person for the first time – as I am seeing you now.'

'Listen, Stephen,' I said, and there was a frantic note in my voice which I could not conceal, 'you must understand, see it from my point of view–'

'I both understand and see it from your point of view,' he said accusingly. 'What was the dying child to you? Or a father's grief? Nothing beside a dinner party designed to further your social ambitions. Oh, it is all so plain to me now. Every cunning move of yours; every motive ... well, now I know.'

Stella said:

'I–'

In that second I loathed her. She was responsible for all this; she had jeopardized my happiness and was now in the process of completely destroying it.

'How dare you,' I cried, 'come here like this – trying to make trouble? I've spent my life in devotion to you and this – this is how you repay me.'

Stella said very slowly and now she was calm as one strong in the knowledge of her own sincerity:

'I'm sorry, Lydia; but even I would not have dreamed of your sinking to the level you have to-night. I regret, more than I can say, that it was I who, inadvertently, betrayed you, but perhaps that is poetic justice, after all. The real tragedy is that nothing can bring Timothy back to life and nothing will ever deaden the sound of his piteous gasps for Stephen – Stephen who could have saved him because–' She broke off too overcome with emotion to continue. 'I, too, cannot forgive you for all this.'

Stephen was pacing the room.

'I gave my word that I'd be there in any emergency,' he said with a desperate bitterness. His gaze sought Stella's: 'What did the father say – what must he think of me–'

Stella shook her head.

'He'll understand, Stephen. I'll make him understand.'

I hated the intimacy between them; hated the gentleness of their voices which made me feel an outsider, and a despised one at that.

Stephen looked at me with a cold mercilessness:

'And just where does this lying begin and end, Lydia?'

I started.

'Meaning precisely what?'

'What other facts have you kept from me "for my good",' he added cynically. 'Somehow I've a feeling that all this doesn't end here.'

I stood stunned and bewildered by the impact of all that was happening; almost incapable of assimilating it; of realizing that I – I was being accused.

'This is beyond me,' I said, and suddenly I knew that my best method of defence was attack. Why should I take all and say nothing? If Stephen would not accept a perfectly reasonable explanation of my conduct, then he could hardly expect any quarter from me.

'I'm sure it is,' he answered deliberately. 'But that doesn't answer my question of a moment ago ... there are many things that occur to me now as in need of explanation and I propose to demand that same explanation.'

'This,' I said sharply, 'is the kind of discussion to settle when we are alone.'

Stephen looked at Stella, gently, as one who caresses with a look.

'Stella, I'm sure, could tell me all I want to know, but she is far too loyal to do so.'

'And do you,' I began, and there was a scathing denunciation in my tone, 'imagine that I am so blind I can't see through all this? Realize just why you are trying to discredit me?'

For a second the silence beat around us like revengeful wings; the room became stifling and while my heart was pounding madly, so it seemed, at the base of my throat, almost choking me, I knew that they were moved no less than I, as Stephen's gaze held Stella's and she stood there, helpless, as one from whom all strength had been drained.

'Suppose,' said Stephen icily, with a merciless calm of manner, 'you tell us... As for discrediting you, that is impossible since you have already discredited yourself.'

'Whatever I have, or have not done, has been in love of you,' I stormed; 'my every thought and act has been prompted by my unselfish desire for your happiness... Can you say the same? Have your instincts been as loyal or as worthy...?'

Stella cried:

'Lydia ... stop all this; it's horrible – horrible.'

'Oh no,' I said, and now I was beyond control or caring, wounded, bitter in my hurt. 'I'm not going to stop, I'm going to speak the truth you are so anxious to hear ... or are you? You and Stephen are in love with each other – deny that if you can! You've plotted and schemed behind my back and now you want to put me in the wrong to justify yourselves.'

I watched their faces as I spoke, saw them

both start and appear to move involuntarily nearer to one another as the tension mounted and emotion sprang to quivering life, flowing between them as from some magnetic ray. For a second the silence was heavy and dramatic. Stephen broke it and my heart seemed to stop beating as he said:

'I have no wish to deny the truth that I love Stella; that in fact I have always loved her, and should have asked her to marry me had you not convinced me that she was in love with another man who could give her far, far more than I.' He looked at Stella as he finished, his expression passionately earnest, his voice hoarse in its emotional sincerity.

I knew, then, that I had made my one fatal mistake; I had put words into his mouth that could never be retracted; undone all the good work I had striven so hard to do for his benefit. Nothing, nothing would ever convince me that for him to have married Stella would not have spelt disaster for them both, and that my actions had not been fully justified.

Stella took a step forward, her eyes wide with both love and bewilderment as she cried:

'That I was in love with another man... Stephen you can't, oh you can't mean that Lydia told you *that*–'

I cried out:

'I will not stand here and be pilloried; I am accusing you, both of you; I am not under cross-examination. I challenge you both that you've lied and deceived me, that you've indulged some clandestine affair behind my back and betrayed my trust in you. I–'

Stella whipped round on me, and now there was spirit and courage in her bearing; courage that, even in that second, forced home upon me the utter loveliness of her pale, sweet face ... and I saw her, then, for a fleeting second, as the child I had loved and nurtured and a pang shot through my heart.

'Betrayed your trust,' she echoed. 'Oh, Lydia!' She allowed her hand to stray over her forehead as one incapable fully of grasping the significance of all that was taking place. 'That you – you of all people should have been capable of such lies when you knew – knew how I felt–'

Stephen's defences were down then; I might not have existed as he covered the distance between himself and Stella and gripped her shoulders, looking down at her with a passionate and demanding possessiveness:

'How you felt ... are you saying that you were never in love with Allan?'

'Allan!' It was a gasp.

I put in frantically:

'Stella doesn't know from one moment to the next how she feels she–'

'I was not,' said Stephen curtly, 'talking to you, Lydia. Suppose you allow Stella to speak for herself for once.' He added hoarsely: 'Stella, tell me – please. Oh, my dear, don't you realize that I must know–'

For a second she hesitated, looked at me as one weighing up the rights and wrongs of the situation then, firmly, resolutely, yet with great tenderness, she murmured:

'I was never in love with Allan – never; I've never been in love with anyone, Stephen' – she caught at her breath as she finished – 'except you.'

A sharp exclamation passed Stephen's lips; he stood there, shaken and yet as a man who suddenly is re-born, while his expression of drawn and unutterable weariness gave place to an ecstatic worship and blinding happiness while, for a moment, he absorbed the wonder of loving and being loved. How well I could read his mind; how terribly well I could understand all that was now flowing silently between them. I wanted to speak but no words came; it was as though my lips refused to move, my brain became deadened by its own suffering as I heard him whisper tensely:

'You love me – *me.*'

Stella turned her gaze to mine.

'I owe you no further loyalty, Lydia,' she said quietly, remorsefully. 'You deliberately wrecked our happiness, parted us; you are

Stephen's wife, I know ... but–'

'Get out of my house,' I said, coming to life and feeling anger surge murderously upon me. 'Get out.'

Stephen said gently:

'I will see you to an hotel for the night. There's one quite near which is open at all hours, I believe.' He added, his eyes caressing in their tenderness: 'We can talk in the morning.'

I interposed sharply:

'Stella can return to Milbury; there's a train at midnight.'

He answered implacably:

'Stella will do as I ask.'

'I demand,' I retorted swiftly, 'that my wishes be carried out. I am your wife, after all.'

He gave me a steady gaze as he said gravely:

'You *were* my wife, Lydia.'

Stella's voice was rather like a whimper. And although I hated her I knew that she was suffering because hers was not the nature to inflict pain; and upheaval of any kind seared her sensitive soul. But I steeled my heart against any such sentiment: she had wrecked my plans by her visit to-night. An hour ago, or less, I had been secure, strong in the belief that, ultimately, I should reach my goal and see Stephen working among the most brilliant names in medicine.

I groaned inwardly: what a fool I'd been not to realize the dangers of such a situation. In my zeal for him, my concern for his welfare, I had been driven to retaliate... It was hard indeed that I who had spent my life in the service of others, was not allowed even one mistake.

I managed to master my emotions sufficiently to say:

'Is that quite fair – after all I've done.'

'It is all you have done that makes the statement true,' he countered.

And with that he put his hand beneath Stella's elbow and led her to the door of the room.

'I hope,' I said fiercely, 'you are satisfied, Stella. I've heard of ingratitude, but never anything so diabolical as this.'

She turned and looked at me and her expression was infinitely sad as she answered:

'I'm sorry for you, Lydia; one day you will see yourself as you really are... I pity you with all my heart; you cannot realize what you've done; the misery and harm you've caused – that is a punishment yet to come... Good-bye.'

I squirmed.

'I've devoted my life to you,' I cried; 'that's what I've done. And you repay me by trying to steal my husband – you, my own sister.'

'That,' said Stephen contemptuously, 'needs no comment; don't make me despise you more than I do now.'

His face was pale, granite-like as he looked at me; but all the time, beneath the surface of drama and hostility, I was aware of the excitement of a love newly declared; of two people having found each other after months of weary denial. I tried to deaden my senses to this awareness of their emotions, but it was impossible: they were in love and no power on earth could touch them – no power on earth... How that knowledge stung. No longer could I sway their destinies; no longer guide or warn them; it seemed that they had already passed out of my orbit and that I was left with no more than the agony of reflection, of thwarted aims.

Panic assailed me as Stephen and she passed from the room into the hall. I went swiftly to the door:

'You'll be back?' I asked him.

He glanced at me.

'Oh, yes, I'll be back,' he answered grimly. 'I haven't finished yet, Lydia, or said half of all I intend to say.'

That was better: breathing space to correlate all the facts and formulate some definite plan. How best to meet the situation? No longer could I emphasize the weaknesses which I rightly knew to be Stella's; no longer could I pursue a course of solicitude for his welfare; or plead for his ambitions. At that moment he was ignorant of many things and

I felt sick as I remembered Highfield House, the money that had been borrowed from Allan, and the arrangement with Lionel Manning. Yet it was all so tragic because he would never understand my nobility of purpose, or the high ideals by which I was moved; any more than he would give me credit for my unselfish devotion. All he would read into it would be deceit – the very last thing in my mind or heart and the one thing I deplored above all else. How terribly easy, I reflected, it was to be misunderstood when one rose above the material. No, there was but one weapon left to me – a feminine one. I must implore his forgiveness, place him in that position where to deny it would seem harsh, even unctuous. Stephen, I knew, never presumed to judge anyone. Well, I must take advantage of that characteristic and put it to the test. Impossible to argue my way out of the situation, but at least I must attempt to stem the tide that was fast threatening to engulf me.

There still, however, remained the fact of his love for Stella ... that love which had gleamed as a sword between us throughout our married life; a love that had kept from me that final surrender of his body as well as his mind... No, no ... I would not accept such ignominious defeat. Stella was immature, she would soon pall upon him ... this love declared, and in the declaring borrowing something of fulfilment, would die a natural death if I remained passive ... passive. A superhuman task ... but the alternative of life without him was not to be considered even for a second.

I heard his key in the lock of the front door, listened to the familiar movements and, finally, watched him come into the room. Never, even in my emotional stress, had he appeared more attractive to me than in that second. His serious expression had nevertheless a light I had never seen there before and a wild and fierce jealousy gripped me. He was thinking of her; loving her; I didn't count. Rage surged back murderously and I wanted to kill them both for the torture I was enduring.

He looked down at me as he took up a position on the hearthrug and rested one elbow on the mantelpiece.

'Now, Lydia,' he said very quietly, 'I want to hear what you have to say; or rather, I want the truth – you understand? The truth,' he added fiercely.

I played for time as I said tremulously:

'Don't you think I have a right to some explanation, too, Stephen? It isn't a pleasant thing for a woman to hear her husband confess his love for her own sister–'

'And it isn't,' he answered grimly, 'a pleasant thing for a man to realize that his wife tricked him into marrying her while being fully aware of that other love. You knew Stella loved me and I did everything but put my love for her into words during those early days. But how cleverly you put me off; how damnably you built up the picture of her character and her love for Allan ... just as damnably as you lied to me to-night about Mr Wade's visit–'

I said, determined not to allow emotion or anger to ruin my chances:

'I know I was wrong about Mr Wade, Stephen; I'm sorry; surely you'll be human enough–'

He cut in icily:

'I can be human enough to know that you are responsible for that boy's death; he died, Lydia, and I believe I could have saved him...' He shook his head. 'You can't bring the child back to life and nothing you could say will mitigate your crime. Nothing; you had a sacred trust... And just as you have wrecked Stella's life and mine, in your maniacal desire to have your own way, so you have brought misery to others– God knows to how many others.'

I cried:

'You don't understand ... please Stephen be reasonable. I can explain–'

'With more lies,' he flung at me contemptuously.

'No, no; only don't look at me like that,' I said, and my voice broke. 'I love you; whatever I may have done has been only because of that love ... forgive me, darling; you can't in all fairness deny me that... I'm your wife; we can start again and–'

He shook his head.

'I may find it in my heart to forgive you, Lydia, but I shall never live with you again. This is the end.'

CHAPTER FOURTEEN

I heard Stephen's words as one might hear the sentence of death. And, even as I listened, an agony of longing came to me to have them retracted. Somehow I must make him understand; I must extricate myself from this damnable and invidious position which had tainted me as a liar and a cheat, and wiped out all my sacrifices. It was inconceivable that a few sentences could end a marriage and condemn me to life-long misery. I said feverishly:

'Listen, Stephen; all this looks black, but if you could see into my heart–'

He stared at me.

'That would pile tragedy upon tragedy,' he said solemnly. 'Are you utterly incapable of appreciating what you've done?'

'I'm incapable of accepting as evidence against me the motives you impute to me,' I countered. 'You say that I parted you from Stella? You had your own free will and–'

'Free will,' he echoed scornfully. 'How many times since our marriage have I heard you use those words; words which subtly concealed your domination of Stella's life, mine, your father's...? How blind I was;

how sickeningly blind,' he added disgustedly. 'Looking back there is so much I
can see now... Your skilful handling of the
situation when Stella broke her engagement
to Allan; the clever suggestion that she was
fickle; the general atmosphere you created
about her and Allan. How convincing you
were in your solicitude for her and all the
time – all the *time*,' he cried and his voice
rose, 'you knew that she was in love with
me. That any woman could sink so low–' He
stopped.

It was almost as though I could see his
mind working as a film of flash backs, and I
dreaded the impact of memory.

'Little things,' he went on, his brows
knitted in reflective bewilderment; 'the visit
to Cornwall ... how cleverly you avoided
our going down there; the general trend of
things at "Stoneleigh". Here, you manage
everything to perfection; there, it was chaos
and dismal incompetence.' He drew in his
breath sharply and I rushed in with:

'That's not fair; here, everything is different; we've more money, the whole place is
easy to run; the work pleasant and–'

'You were never in sympathy with my ambitions,' he said with a deadly calm. 'Now I
realize it all ... you never intended that I
should stay in Milbury and achieve my
aims, yet you posed as the wife concerned
only with her husband's happiness... The

Highfield House project–'

I caught at my breath; fear descended upon me almost paralysing; he must not know the truth, but there was a sudden suspicious gleam in his eyes as he rapped out:

'And just what had you to do with all that … just how far *have* you gone, Lydia?'

I knew that I must keep calm; that pleading or appealing to him was futile and degrading. If he couldn't know by instinct that my motives were worthy – I stopped that trend of thought. I wanted him; I wanted to keep him in my life at all costs; I must keep him and I said shakenly:

'Listen to me, Stephen – you must listen. What does all this amount to, after all? Admittedly, I was wrong to-night and I'm sorry; but even in that I was acting for your own good–'

'My good,' he scoffed. 'According to you everything you do in life is for somebody's else's good – never your own.'

'And,' I insisted, 'that is so. All my life I've sacrificed for others; all my life–'

His gaze met mine levelly:

'All your life, Lydia, you've lied and cheated,' he said with a terrible calm and denunciation. 'You've deliberately and systematically arranged the pattern of things so that your desires, your happiness, your ambitions, were fulfilled, while all the time acting under the cloak of self-sacrifice… You began with

Stella and me... I can see through you as clearly as I can see to read a book – a very unpleasant and distasteful book–'

'And you,' I hurled at him; 'what about you ... in love with my own sister. I suppose that is commendable and right – you, my husband–'

'You knew,' he said icily, 'of my feelings for Stella when you married me; you knew that I fell in love with her almost at first sight, as she fell in love with me... To her you built up the idea that I was in love with you; to me you created the impression that she was in love with Allan ... that she was a rather naïve child who would never be prepared to face up to life, or hardship, and must be guarded at all costs.' He laughed a hollow, mirthless laugh. 'And so good were you at dissembling and lying that I believed you; in one evening you convinced me that to make love to Stella, even try to win her love, would be very nearly caddish since I had so little to offer her... It was a damnable and deadly piece of work,' he added vehemently.

For a moment I lost control of myself; I couldn't bear to see the studied contempt in his eyes, or to feel that every second I was losing ground. I cried sharply:

'It was all true. Stella was in love with Allan and she needed someone to–'

'Don't,' he cut in mercilessly, 'add insult to injury. Stella was never in love with Allan and she was always capable of looking after herself. But, to you, human beings were mere puppets to dance to your tune... Stella mustn't work, she was too delicate. Stella must marry into security... Why? Because, firstly, you wanted to dominate her life just as you managed to dominate your father's life and as you hoped and intended to dominate mine... And, secondly, because you made up your mind to marry me yourself.'

I felt the burning colour rising in my cheeks.

'That's insufferable,' I murmured.

'No; merely just,' he came back at me remorselessly.

'But, of course, even in that you were marrying me for my own good–'

'It was for your own good,' I protested. 'Can you imagine what a mess you and Stella would have made of things?' Scorn added to the fury of my words.

'I pity you,' came the heavy, tense reply. 'You are an obsessionist, Lydia; a woman possessed, unbalanced; you cannot even see the wrong you have done to us both. Yet, heaven knows, the truth is plain enough.'

'Stella,' I insisted, 'would have ruined you; she–'

'I don't propose,' he interrupted firmly, 'to discuss Stella with you. What I do propose is to get to the bottom of every rotten trick you've played on me, Lydia.' He glanced around him as he spoke. 'Just how much truth was there in the story about your father's money paying for all this ... how much truth is there in anything you've ever told me?' His voice held a warning note. 'I promise you that I mean to learn the facts, or by heaven I'll know the reason why.' He looked at me with a cold, almost paralysing, stare. 'Do you propose to tell me, or must I find out for myself?'

My heart seemed permanently to be beating inches lower than was normal; my legs refused to support me and I sank down in the nearest chair. I was desperate, cornered, bewildered by the injustice of all that had befallen me. It wasn't possible that this was happening to me – I who had devoted my entire life to others. I began frantically:

'There's nothing more to tell, Stephen. What else could there be?'

It was as though some instinct were prompting him; some power against which I was helpless, as he said:

'Highfield House for instance... You never wanted me to have it... Just what part did you play in all that? Diana was always suspicious about the whole thing and–'

That was almost more than I could bear and I shrieked:

'Diana! That scheming, evil woman who has always hated me. You'd listen to her?'

'Yes,' said Stephen calmly. 'And believe

every word she uttered. And unless I am very much mistaken she could enlighten me.' He crossed to the 'phone as he spoke and I cried:

'What are you going to do?'

'Find out the facts,' he retorted quietly, implacably. 'And if she cannot supply them, then I'll go to the solicitors; I'll go to Highfield House, if needs be … but I'll find out, Lydia. Rest assured of that. And–' He shook his head.

I was trapped and I knew it. Sooner or later he would find out; my only hope was to throw myself on his mercy. Plead with him as an erring human being. He was so high-principled that he could not escape from me if I put the responsibility of my redemption upon his shoulders. Later he would thank me for it; it was impossible that our lives could be split asunder; this must weld us closer together; I must sacrifice my pride and my dignity and beg where I had always, before in my life, demanded and … given.

I said slowly, trying to keep my voice low, even tragic:

'You don't have to find out, Stephen. I've no wish to lie to you, or keep anything from you. I did buy Highfield House – but not because I wanted to keep it from you, but because I wanted to use the money towards your betterment. This practice was in the market and from the sale of Highfield House

– and the profit I made – I was able to lift you to the heights you have reached now. Everything I did was for your own good.'

'I see.' Those two words held neither mercy nor hint of compromise; they fell almost sinisterly upon the silence that hung between us; silence heavy with tragedy and dramatic suspense, as I waited, tensed, quivering, for him to continue and, then, able to bear the strain no longer, cried:

'That's just it, Stephen, you don't see; you don't see because' – I gained courage as I went on – 'you don't want to see. You want to discredit me because only by doing so can you excuse your own conduct, but that isn't fair,' I added, fighting back the vituperation that came readily to my lips as I realized it was dangerously far removed from my resolve to throw myself upon his mercy. Whatever happened I must be consistent. I stopped and added: 'Oh, I know, Stephen; I know how it must look to you, but please, please put yourself in my place: I wanted so much for you; believed in you so absolutely – in your abilities. It wasn't hardship that I minded for myself, I swear it–'

He might not have heard me as he asked incisively:

'And just where did you get the money with which to buy Highfield House?' He hurried on contemptuously: 'And don't give yourself time to think up another lie.'

I groaned inwardly. 'Another lie'. I, who loved truth above all else, yet had been forced to indulge subterfuge for his sake. Could he be so indifferent to my ambitions for him; could he be so blind as to condemn me for helping him – as I had. But for me he would still have been grovelling in Milbury and living in a house that was fast crumbling around him. Was there anything so hard to bear as a man's ingratitude.

'I'm waiting,' he said in a deadly tone. 'Where did you get the money, Lydia?'

If only there were some way in which I could extricate myself from this debacle, I thought desperately; but what hope had I of doing other than tell him the truth – and be misunderstood. Could I guarantee that he would not learn all the facts eventually, no matter how I tried to protect myself? There was Diana and, now, Stella: between them I had no chance – no chance at all – I reflected bitterly. I said quietly:

'Allan lent me the money.'

He started, surprised.

'But he knew that Diana wanted to buy the place–'

'And he didn't ask me what I wanted it for,' I said sharply. 'Allan happens to trust me.'

Stephen puckered his brows.

'It just doesn't seem possible ... that you, *you* would smash my ambition so wantonly, plot and plan behind my back. It's horrible,' he finished desperately.

'Please,' I cried feverishly, 'don't look at me like that, Stephen. I did it for you – because I loved you so much... Everything was for you. I knew that once you started that clinic you'd never make any headway and when Lionel Manning–' I stopped.

Instantly he came back with:

'What has Lionel to do with all this?' His eyes blazed into mine. 'Don't tell me he connived with you – that–'

'No, no,' I insisted. 'It wasn't that. I went to him and–'

'I'm sure you did.' He laughed mockingly. 'How well I can reconstruct it all, and I've no doubt, whatsoever, that you fooled Lionel as you fooled me, with your solicitude and air of self-sacrifice.'

'That's not fair,' I said desperately. 'Oh, Stephen, you must understand; whatever I may have done my motives were right. I loved you and–'

'Love,' he cried derisively. 'You don't even know the meaning of the word, Lydia. All you know is the obsession of self; I was merely a pawn in your game... Well, I'm that no longer. And I'll get the facts of all this business from Lionel himself.' He drew a hand across his forehead. 'I'm far too weary, too disgusted, to talk more to-night.'

I said sorrowfully:

'One day you will know the wrong you do me, Stephen. I've sunk my pride, borrowed money, everything – all for you. I had no ulterior motive, after all, beyond your success and–' I watched him closely, aware of every shade of expression on his face and conscious of an imperceptible change in his demeanour that brought renewed hope to me: was it possible that I had, after all, touched the right chord. I played up what I believed to be my advantage: 'Don't you see, darling ... that I was wrong over Timothy; wrong over everything, doesn't alter that – really it doesn't... Oh, Stephen, I'm your wife; I love you ... you mean the world to me ... forgive me, please forgive me. I can see now that, from your point of view, I was trying to dictate your life ... but I didn't mean it that way. I'll do anything – anything,' I cried desperately, 'to prove how sorry I am and to redeem your opinion of me–' My voice broke and I felt the thrill as of having, at last, made an impression as I waited, breathlessly, every nerve in my body taut, for his answer. It came very slowly and deliberately:

'Very well, Lydia, I'll accept that and I'll give you the opportunity of proving your sincerity–'

Light pierced the gloom of my misery; triumph flowed back; I had wrested victory from ignominious defeat. Foolish ever to imagine that I shouldn't win in the end...

Stephen could never be so unjust as to condemn me for studying his interests.

'Oh, Stephen,' I murmured. 'Thank God you understand… I'll do anything – anything; I couldn't bear things to be wrong between us or for you to think ill of me–'

'Then,' he said firmly and with great determination, 'that being so, and in proof of your sorrow, give me my freedom in order that I may find happiness – the happiness of which you cheated me.'

I stared at him aghast while a sensation of sheer panic gripped me. The word 'freedom' hung between us with a terrible significance and I echoed it almost stupidly, adding:

'What do you mean by – by freedom?'

He held my gaze masterfully; there was no escape from his merciless scrutiny, under which I found myself squirming, the blood seeming to burn in my veins and my heart swelling as though it had become twice its normal size.

'I mean precisely what I say; don't let's waste words, Lydia,' he added curtly. 'If you are sincere–'

'Are you,' I gasped, 'suggesting that I should give you your freedom in order that you can marry Stella?' My voice cracked; I couldn't believe the words even though I uttered them.

'I am,' he said implacably. 'You wished me to believe, just now, that you would do anything to redeem yourself... I am taking you at your word.'

I found myself shrieking:

'You must be mad – mad. For you to marry Stella after all I've done–'

'To smash our lives,' he put in icily. His eyes were like points of steel as he said heavily: 'I might have known that your sorrow was as false as you, yourself, have been.'

'That's not fair–'

'Fair?' Scorn made his voice quiver. 'A strange word on your tongue; you haven't even the faintest conception of its meaning.'

I said desperately:

'I love you; you are my husband; I've fought and slaved in order that you might get where you have and–'

'For pity's sake spare me that unctuous hypocrisy,' he rapped out. 'For the last time: are you prepared to do as I say, or aren't you?'

'You can't possibly expect it of me,' I insisted. 'It is too cruel – too cruel, Stephen.'

'I do expect it,' he replied firmly. 'As for my being cruel.' A bitter laugh escaped him. 'Could anything be more diabolically cruel than the way in which you have cheated me not only of Stella, but of my ambitions, ideals; you've impeded me in everything I set out to do–'

'Impeded you!' Anger whipped me to fury. 'When, but for me, you would still have been grovelling in Milbury.' I added feeling a surge of triumph as I realized how strong my position still was: 'Oh, no, Stephen; you are my husband and I intend that you shall remain so.'

He looked at me with a withering contempt.

'Legally that may be so; but in all other respects I cease to be your husband from this moment. I've told you before: I shall never live with you again, Lydia. I'm leaving you just as soon as the arrangements can be made. Better you should understand that once and for all.'

I lost control, so great was my fear and my anguish.

'I'll ruin you ... you, a doctor ... do you hear me: I'll ruin you.'

He laughed; laughter that was a scornful ridicule.

'From my point of view you have done that already,' he said cuttingly. 'Go ahead. In any case I've no intention of remaining in this practice.'

I could hardly breathe as I sat there; my lungs felt that they had collapsed and that no air could penetrate my shaking body. For the first time I was incapable of dealing with the situation; inspiration failed me.

'And what do you propose to do?' I managed to gasp.

'That,' he replied briefly, as one who

dismisses me, 'is my business.'

Hatred surged like a burning flame upon me; emotion churned violently within me, making me sick to the point of faintness.

'This,' I cried, 'is Stella's doing; she's responsible for everything... A nice little plot; her coming here to-night to betray me so that you could justify yourself with impunity... Well, you won't get away with it, Stephen – do you hear. I'll make you both pay for this – this ingratitude.'

He stood there staring at me as one who might disbelieve his own ears. Then he said, more in a professional, than a personal tone:

'You just have no moral sense at all, have you? You have deluded yourself for so long, Lydia, that you believe your own lies.'

'Lies,' I cried desperately; 'I hate lies; everything – everything I do is to help others, not for myself and–'

'You believe that, too,' he said gravely, 'don't you? Perhaps there lies the tragedy – the very root of all the evil.'

'I've said I'm sorry,' I went on frantically; 'I've asked your forgiveness; what more can I do?'

'Nothing,' he said quietly; 'I've given you my answer.'

'I'll never divorce you – never.'

'So be it,' he said curtly, and with that he strode swiftly to the door.

I called his name, wildly, pleadingly, feverishly; but he might not have heard me. The front door opened and closed; the house became a morgue, chill forbidding ... and through the silence I heard again the chink of glasses, the echo of laughter – sounds of but a few hours before... Was it possible that a life could be wrecked in the space of seconds, that one could come within reach of triumph only to have it dashed from one's grasp? The name of Stella came slowly, on the breath of my own hatred; a hatred which, as I stood there, mounted homicidally. She was responsible for all this: she it was who had smashed my life, for I knew Stephen and I knew that he would never come back to me. I glanced at the clock; the hands pointed almost to midnight. Too late to go to her hotel ... I must wait until the morning... If Stephen thought it was all going to be simple, then he was very much mistaken; the punishment should fall where it belonged. If I must suffer then so should they for their base ingratitude.

Mechanically I went upstairs to my room; the room that had such a brief while before, been Stephen's and mine; now it seemed quite empty, as if even the furniture had shrunk into the walls which leaned forward as I entered as though mocking and derisive... My head felt curiously heavy and then strangely light; I shivered as with a fever; my stomach might have been deprived of food for many days, and my legs appeared to be made of cotton wool. I pressed a hand against my heart as a pain shot through it and to still its wild beating. I was hardly conscious of undressing while yet, subconsciously, aware of the beauty of my discarded evening frock, rather as though it lay in a heap upon the bed as a symbol of all I had lost; a symbol of that world of which Stella had deprived me, and which I had fought so desperately to bring within Stephen's grasp.

It was folly to try to sleep and I sat huddled over the gas-fire in my housecoat, thinking until my brain almost snapped. The stillness of night accentuated the heavy silence and I listened for any sound that might herald Stephen's footfall... Where had he gone? If he came back might I not try just once more to swerve him from his harsh, embittered attitude. It was just as dawn was flicking banners of light across the windows, and shadows were stealing upon the carpet, that I heard his key in the lock.

He'd come back! He'd come back!

I held my breath as I went to the door of the room and opened it; I saw him mount the stairs as though his legs were leaden, his body sagging with tiredness. I called softly:

'Stephen ... oh, Stephen; thank God you've come back.'

He glanced at me as he reached the

landing; it was the stare of a man who gazed upon that which, to him, was dead and whom, above all, he wished to forget.

He didn't speak; merely turned from me and went into a spare room at the end of the corridor.

I stumbled back and fell, half fainting, on the bed. I knew, then, beyond all doubting, that hope and all possibility of reconciliation was gone.

One thought obsessed me as morning came and I left the house early and made my way to Stella's hotel. There was no one in the reception desk and I glanced at the register: Stella's name was the last to be written there and beside it, Room No.12. I made myself known to a manageress, who appeared seemingly from nowhere, and went upstairs.

Stella answered my knock and stood back for me to enter – closing the door behind me as I said:

'I want to talk to you.'

She looked very young as she stood there, clad only in her nightdress and filmy négligé; even in those seconds of drama I noticed the exquisite curves of her slender body, the air of delicacy about her and the fact that, without make-up she, nevertheless, had that bloom which not all the powder and rouge in the world could achieve. I remembered, suddenly and sharply, and almost poignantly, all that I had done for her in an earlier day. It seemed incredible that, now, we faced each other as enemies.

'Is there anything left to be said, Lydia?'

'I think so.' My voice was stern. 'I'm here to tell you that if you imagine you are going to take Stephen away from me you're very much mistaken, and to warn you that any friendship or contact with him that you may imagine yourself indulging from now on, will mean his ruin.' I added triumphantly: 'A doctor cannot afford to be talked about and–'

Her steady stare unnerved me; it seemed that she was trying to fathom my mood; trying to understand all that was passing through my mind and, at last, completely bewildered, baffled, she cried:

'Oh, Lydia–' Her voice rang with regret; 'that things should come to this; that you, of all people, should behave as you have. I just can't believe it.'

I rapped out:

'That *I* should behave – it is not I who am at fault; but you – you. Everything I've done, everything I hoped for was for Stephen's good – and yours; but you wouldn't listen to me; all you thought about was getting him for yourself and that was why you came here last night – to wreck our marriage, implant suspicion and evil in his mind so that he would turn to you.'

She shivered; her lips parted and closed again as though the power of speech failed her.

'Ah,' I said bitterly, 'you cannot deny it: you hated me because Stephen loved me and not you, and this has been your revenge.'

It seemed that she drew from some invisible power as she said with a compelling calm:

'In your heart you know all that to be lies, Lydia; you know that I became suspicious weeks – weeks ago and when the Highfield House project fell through–'

Faint colour mounted my cheeks. I took the fight to her, however:

'Why drag that up? It won't help you now.'

'Because had I been guilty of the foul motives of which you accuse me, I had every opportunity of betraying you then. You see I knew that you'd bought Highfield.'

I gasped, taken off my guard:

'How?'

'Diana found out; but it was too late to do anything. I begged her not to tell Stephen.'

The very thought of being at Diana's mercy made me writhe and I snapped:

'I'm not impressed by your noble efforts on my behalf.'

Her eyes flashed with the light of battle.

'None of my efforts was in your behalf; my thoughts and concern were for Stephen and I knew that it wouldn't help him to damn you in his eyes – merely cause him further suffering.'

'Your solicitude for him is disgusting.' I was too angry to know what I was saying; the words tumbled out in my rage and blind, homicidal jealousy. To look at her and know that Stephen loved her made me hate her with a hatred that was as some terrible disease. I could hardly bear the pain of it; the stabbing, sickening torture of looking ahead and realizing that, from now on, I was debarred from his life. 'Or have you forgotten that he is my husband.'

She looked at me sorrowfully:

'I have forgotten nothing, Lydia; most of all do I regret the fact that a sister of mine could stoop so low. I watched you at "Stoneleigh" impeding Stephen's progress at every turn; piling worry upon worry for him until he knew he couldn't carry on there. You've undermined every ambition he cherished and you dare to pretend that you love him.'

It was in that second Stephen's voice was heard outside the door. Stella rushed to admit him and he came into the room, his gaze meeting mine in bitter accusation as he said:

'I thought I should find you here.'

A desperate longing possessed me as I stood there; a terrible anguish of fear as I thought of the future without him. I said weakly:

'You – you want me?'

'I want to make quite sure that you don't upset Stella,' he replied coolly. 'You can hardly expect me to trust you in the circumstances.'

I looked from face to face and it was as though they suddenly became conspirators against me; deadly, cunning enemies. The longing dissolved into a terrible rage even as I watched the glance they exchanged; sensed the flow of love that passed between them, even without a word being uttered; love that tormented and seared me, rousing me to wild and desperate fury against which I was helpless.

'You'll never get away with it,' I said, and my voice was cold, unlike my own. 'I'll–' My brain seemed incapable of holding a thought for long and I added: 'May I not visit my own sister without you–'

'No,' he said firmly; 'you've done her enough harm.'

Stella cried:

'Oh, Stephen, what are you going to do?'

He looked at her with great tenderness.

'Don't worry, my darling, I'm going back to Milbury... I'm going to begin again and–'

'You're mad,' I cried; 'mad; now, now, when you are on the very threshold of success; when fame is yours for the asking... I won't have it; I won't stand by and see you–'

'You haven't a further say in the matter,' he retorted.

'Milbury – the two of you. A nice little arrangement. Well, go back and see what happens,' I said viciously. 'I'll create such a scandal that you'll be glad to leave... Do you think I'm going to be dismissed like this?'

Stella gave a shuddering cry and Stephen said to her again:

'Don't worry ... I'm not afraid; we've right on our side, Stella, and even though you may be able to help me only from afar' – his gaze caressed her – 'that will give me more of life and happiness than I've thus far known–'

Her eyes answered him in their shining radiance; they were as two people transfigured; two people whom nothing could destroy, nothing taint, and I knew it even as I stood there; they were incorruptible and would rise above any gossip that I might feebly start, just as they made it seem the very idea was pathetic and melodramatic...

How then to be revenged; how then to make them pay for all they had made me suffer...?

And suddenly I knew what I must do; they should never find happiness together – never. I would stop at nothing to prevent it ... nothing...

I stared at Stephen almost fascinated as I

realized the power that was still mine to wield ... and as my plan took shape in my seething, overwrought brain. How plainly I could see him projected into the future, giving evidence at the inquest ... the inquest on my death; my suicide... I could see him, white and shaken, as the letter I should leave was read aloud; the letter in which I established the fact, beyond all shadow of doubt, that he was my sister's lover and that their relationship had driven me almost insane with unhappiness...

How simple it was; what was life to me without him? I moved to the door and looked back at them and now they were staring at me half-fascinated, and it was as though my mind were a photograph on which they were gazing without *seeing*...

My voice seemed to come from a great distance as I said slowly:

'Good-bye Stella ... I hope you never regret this day; or the part you've played in wrecking my life.' I added tensely: 'We shall see who wins...'

CHAPTER FIFTEEN

I wasn't conscious of making the journey from the hotel back to the house. My brain was in a state of complete turmoil and, emotionally, I was tensed almost to breaking point. A great sickness was upon me as I dragged myself along the almost deserted streets, staring at, but not actually seeing, the objects around me which became as grim, dark shadows upon the blurred screen of my mind.

Suicide... The word echoed sinisterly in my ears. How Stephen would hate and shrink from the publicity; how pathetic and innocent Stella would try to appear, and how utterly impossible it would be for them to disprove my indictment against them. It was, I decided, a very subtle and clever move, damning their chances of happiness for ever; ruining Stephen as a medical man and creating a scandal never wholly to be lived down. I could hear – rather after the manner of echoes tearing through the corridors of my mind – people saying: 'That's Stephen Ashley ... oh, *you* know, Dr Ashley ... his wife committed suicide because he'd been unfaithful to her – and with her own sister, too. A terrible thing.'

Yes; it was as easy as that. And what value did I place on my life at this stage since Stella had robbed me of all that made it worth living. To lose Stephen ... never; death was infinitely preferable. I wasn't in the least afraid of it: my conscience was clear; I'd done my best for humanity and those whom I was leaving behind; that I'd been misunderstood, placed in the invidious position in which I now found myself, was no criterion whatsoever of my actual worth. The idea began to fascinate me as I dwelt upon it... But how to accomplish the task. What drugs to use. I marvelled at my cold-blooded approach to the matter, but I was fast reaching that stage where my feelings were becoming completely absorbed by the desire for revenge; revenge that burned within me inducing a choking, almost fiendish rage... To make Stephen and Stella suffer for all the misery they had caused me. Strange, I had loved Stephen so desperately, and still did, yet I could, in this mood of overwhelming bitterness, contemplate that which would encompass his ruin.

The home to which we had come only a brief while before loomed up suddenly out of the morning shadows; a chill, bleak December wind cut through me and my impressions, for a second, became as an etching in grey. I inserted my key in the lock of the front door and stepped over the threshold. Betty came forward and stared at me as one who, while having discovered I was not in my room, nevertheless was completely baffled by my presence in such circumstances. I could almost hear her thoughts buzzing… So much the better. I must act the part I was determined to play and I said wearily:

'You must have been startled when Hilda – the general maid – told you that Doctor and I were out.' I knew that Hilda would have taken the early tea up some twenty minutes before and learned that we were not in our room.

'I was,' came the anxious reply. 'I hope there's nothing wrong, Madam?'

I drew a hand wearily across my forehead.

'I've had a great shock, Betty … but I shall be all right.'

'I'm sorry,' she said respectfully. 'Shall I have breakfast served and–' she hesitated, then: 'Will the Doctor be in?'

'No breakfast for me… I'm not sure about Doctor; *he* will give you instructions in any case. I think I'll lie down, Betty. Don't disturb me for a few hours.'

She looked at me with great intensity as one trying to weigh up a situation she could neither understand, nor question.

'Very good, Madam … but are you sure you wouldn't like some tea sent up or coffee–'

'Nothing,' I said gently. 'Thank you all the same, Betty; you've been most kind.'

I saw her through the haze of a coroner's court; heard her voice as she gave evidence: 'There was something strange about the way she spoke to me, thanking me and–'

'Would you tell Doctor I don't wish to be disturbed, if he should come in,' I added as I paused half way up the rather imposing staircase, which swept from the wide hall in a semi-circle to the floor above.

'Yes, Madam... You're sure you're all right?'

Her face was upturned and I glanced down at her as she stood before me, seeing her through the baluster railings. I knew she was agitated and a little thrill of triumph surged over me. Her evidence would be invaluable...

I forced a sad smile, sighed and said:

'I'm all right, Betty.'

Upstairs, I went into Stephen's equipment room where all emergency supplies of drugs, etc., were kept. The name Phenobarbitone began to drum in my ears. A common enough drug, heaven knew, with radio appeals for tablets lost or mislaid, coming over the air with monotonous frequency... Or Luminal; or Nebutal... I wasn't very certain as to the effect of the others. What had Stephen said ... that it all depended on the person as to what constituted a dose calculated to kill them... Better to stick to Phenobarbitone ... they were small, easily swallowed...

My heart thumped madly as I clasped a box of them in my hand. Stephen should have no trouble in discovering the exact nature of the drug I had taken... I began to shiver... I felt almost like my own ghost.

A sound arrested my attention in the hall below and, again, Betty's voice came, this time urgently:

'I'm afraid you're not well, Madam ... are you sure–'

'Quite sure; don't worry, Betty...' And with that I went into my own room, shut and locked the door.

The thought of Stella came back dangerously; the burning hatred surging and swelling within me as though some evil spirit were inhabiting my body without resistance from me. My own sister stealthily seeking to wreck my marriage because she was in love with my husband; it was a dastardly crime for which due punishment should be enacted. A tiny gimlet seemed to be boring into my brain. Stephen had not been blameless, but he was a man, and men were malleable clay in the hands of any scheming women... Stella a scheming woman when I had thought of her as a lovable, naïve child...

I must think coherently; I must do those

things which would appear, after my death, to be natural for a woman of my character and temperament even while the balance of my mind was affected. Nothing must be *too* perfect for, normally, a suicide was in no state to weigh up the situation to a fine degree of judgement and I, as a woman distraught, anguished, must remember that. And I was that woman, after all, I thought rather wildly ... a woman whose world had been torn down by ruthless hands; the picture was both dramatic and tragic, and a certain self-pity overwhelmed me as I dwelt upon it. Tears stung my eyes... My mind raced like a giant wheel turning, turning... To die here, in this room and for Stephen to find me and destroy the note I had left behind... To write that note and post it to him, or to some other person who would convey its contents to the police? Wasn't that rather too studied... No; it was dangerous to remain here; Betty would, most assuredly, tell Stephen that I was not well and it might be that he would discover me before the tablets had achieved their purpose. An uncanny silence filled the room as I sat huddled on the edge of the bed. Had any other woman been in this position, planned her own death with such meticulous care as I... Yet what did life hold for me? The torment of knowing that, even though denied the fulfilment of their love, Stephen and Stella would have that spiritual bond which nothing could ever destroy. The torment of being ostracized by them both, of knowing that Stephen despised me and looked upon me as the woman who had wrecked his life. Never. I felt my lips tightening and, catching sight of myself in the dressing-table mirror, I recoiled from the tensed, strained expression on my face which seemed as pale as death. Unjustly, he believed I had smashed his happiness when all I had fought to do was to preserve it; very well, then, I would give him cause for his beliefs and smash it in reality. My ghost would forever stand between Stella and him; the memory of me would haunt them, as well it might.

I thought of Diana ... this would answer her; it would shatter her illusions about both Stella and Stephen... Lionel Manning would not be surprised: hadn't he suspected something weeks before... I couldn't quite recall his words to me but... Difficult to indulge a perfectly coherent analysis when one's heart seemed to be heaving upwards in one's body which was cold and sick with suffering. Allan would mourn me ... he loved me; of that there was no doubt. Poor Allan; I should have married him; quite probably I could have moulded him to my will and converted him to my ways. Ah, well, it was too late now...

The clock struck nine... I went to my

writing-desk and began to write. The words flowed as though some other impulse and not mine were writing them...

Stephen,
I'm sorry; I just cannot go on any longer. Your relationship with Stella has wrecked our marriage and my life; your callousness and indifference to my feelings, even though I was prepared to forgive your infidelity, is more than I can stand. I have done my best and kept faith. Good-bye...

Lydia.

And, now, to Stella ... that must be found with my body. I began feverishly, and a great sickness crept upon me:

Stella,
I trusted you so implicitly and all the time you were betraying me and trying to take Stephen from me. Your association with him has ruined my happiness and I'm so desperate that I cannot go on any longer. I can't write more...

Lydia.

My signature trailed away impressively, and I stared at it in fascination... for was it not the last time I should write it? Few people were able calmly to sit and contemplate their last moments of life. Who would be the first to read these words and to find me? And where was I going?

I dragged myself from the bed, put the Phenobarbitone tablets in my handbag, together with Stella's letter, and, hatless, made my way from the room.

At the sound of my footsteps, Betty appeared seemingly from nowhere, her gaze meeting mine in startled, anxious inquiry.

I said, rather agitatedly:

'I can't rest, Betty, and my head splits ... a little air might help. I'm going for a walk.'

She said earnestly:

'Do you think you should, Madam? I mean, won't you wait until the master comes in?'

'No... I'm perfectly all right,' I said wanly, and rather haltingly made my way down the stairs, across the hall and passed out of the door which she held open for me.

'Good-bye, Betty,' I said quietly. (Funny, those would be recorded as my 'last words').

Once outside, the damp, faintly foggy air, enveloped me like a wet blanket. I shivered, not only with cold but with an excitement impossible to describe. I had defeated them after all. I could see Diana's face when she heard the news... And I felt myself gloating over her sorrow at the thought of Stephen's suffering, to say nothing of Stella's. She had always detested me and accused me of the wrong motives... This was the one time when I should triumph.

I wasn't conscious of making my way to the round pond at the top of Hampstead Heath, but I reached there and gazed at the panoramic view that stretched before my eyes ... it had a curious beauty in that grey December light, like a misty painting quivering in shadow and sombre half tones. The trees were stark and taut against a leaden sky; a few dead leaves, clinging tenaciously to the branches, fluttered and dropped and were swept along the pavements, rather as a requiem.

I saw down on a deserted seat... And now my heart was thumping madly... Was it fear, the sudden shrinking from death... Swiftly, as one who defeats a threatening impulse, I began to take the tablets, swallowing them with water from a small phial I had remembered to bring. And, at last, the box was empty.

How long would it take? My head was still clear, my vision in unimpaired... No, the scene around me was beginning to become slightly out of focus; my eyelids drooped; my body became heavy. The thought registered: I'm going to die; every second that ticks by means... Suppose I hadn't taken enough; suppose I had miscalculated the correct number necessary for my particular constitution: I could be sent to prison for attempted suicide... My head was curiously light in that second; the effect was becoming grotesque, almost as though my appearance must be changing to bear testimony to the imminence of my death ... death... The cold wind stung my cheeks; the winter scene held a sudden poignant nostalgia ... was I not gazing upon it for the last time. And I was young; too young... The thought of Stephen came to me suddenly, sharply... I was going to ruin him; he would be ostracized and condemned and, most probably struck off the Register. That was what my death meant to him ... and Stella would suffer no less than he since she would suffer for him... What a perfect revenge ... revenge... Did I want revenge...? For what... Strange, I was floating now in a curious haze, seeing my life; remembering this and that... Stella, sitting at my knee while we sipped our tea... Stella confiding her love for Stephen to me... 'I think he'll love me, Lydia'... How hot it was; stiflingly hot... Yes, Stella had always loved him and he her ... they would have married ... married... I prevented all that – so cleverly. It didn't seem so clever as it flashed through my mind just then... I was wrecking their lives twice over, when I had no justification for doing so even once. Now Diana's voice came stridently like a voice echoing through a long corridor: 'You are probably the most dangerous hypocrite I've ever had the misfortune to meet, because everything you do, while appearing to be self-sacrificing and for the good of others, nevertheless always turns out to your own advantage and as you wish it. One of these days life will catch up with you and you will be forced to pay your debts.' There was something horrible about those words as they tormented me... Had I been like that? And if I had... Suddenly panic gripped me; I didn't want to die; it was as if in my semi-moribund state the pattern of my life wove itself into my fevered brain like bind-weed, clogging, destroying and yet betraying for me the weaknesses of the structure to which it clung... Of course, I could see it now; Diana was right; I was that vile, evil person. I'd wrecked Stella and Stephen's happiness deliberately, under the cloak of virtue of my concern for them. I groaned ... and, now, if I died ... if I *died*... I gasped for breath ... mustn't die; leave behind a trail of misery, wreckage... But how to fight this sleepiness... And suddenly I remembered the note I'd left behind in the bedroom; a note to Stephen, but purposely unsealed so that Betty, or anyone who might find it, could read the contents... I must get back; Stephen mustn't see it; mustn't know the depths to which I'd sunk... I knew, then, in that moment, just how much I loved him; just how I loved Stella... How tired I was ... could I walk? I must walk ... not far down the hill to the house ... the walk would do me good ... must keep awake; strong coffee; get Betty to make me some ... how far down the road could I see... I began to shuffle off the seat; my legs shaking, weak; the longing to lie down and sleep almost overpowering me. I must get back; I must live ... this time to pay my debts ... must make amends; must be forgiven. Stephen would forgive; and Stella; must make them understand... I was almost upright now, but staggering slightly as I began to walk...

Someone said:

'Can I help you?'

Help ... must lean on someone; couldn't manage alone. My speech was blurred as I heard myself – rather like listening to a strange voice – say:

'Would ... you ... don't feel very well...'

And their reply:

'If you could manage to get down the hill; there's a doctor's house–'

'I ... want to get ... there ... please...'

The man half supported me and I dragged beside him... The air rushed into my lungs, seeming to reach them through a vacuum. I shook my head, closing my eyes for a fraction of a second and opening them as one striving to see more clearly as a result...

I said uncertainly, aware that my condition could but give rise to suspicion:

'I must have – fainted, or something.'

The man didn't speak; I could see his features but dimly as I glanced up at him; everything was so blurred, almost distorted... Could I walk the remaining distance... How far to go ... was that the corner, over there, or was it miles away... No; just over there... I was terrified, now; it seemed that a cold sweat broke over me, but it might have been the wind tearing at my body. Suppose Betty opened that note first... I'd not written any name upon it... And Stephen, pray God he might not have returned to read it; to read it and thus know of my vindictiveness, my unforgivable intentions; my deliberate attempt to smash his life. I didn't want to die; I wasn't fit to die... I felt unclean, hideous... If only I could lie down and sleep ... mustn't sleep; but how weighted my eyelids seemed; how intolerably heavy my body was to drag along.

'A few more steps,' said the voice beside me.

'I'm ... I'm giving you so ... much trouble.'

I didn't hear his reply... We were there; home. I wanted to cry, but even that power was lost to me, dissolving into the tiredness that followed in its wake.

'I'll be ... all right, now,' I said, as I stood leaning against the railings by the front door. It registered in my bemused brain that I didn't want Betty to see anyone bringing me home, or for the man, himself, to realise it was my home... I didn't quite know why but ... Timothy Wade; I'd killed him... Funny, how clearly I saw the father's stricken face – almost as though it were a screen suddenly projected into space – space that absorbed all the span of my vision... And the clinic... Highfield House; I'd cheated Stephen of that, too...

The door opened, and before I could speak to a suddenly alarmed Betty the man said:

'This lady is ill and–'

I was swaying as I managed with superhuman effort to say:

'Is doctor in?'

'No, Madam, but–' She stopped and cried: 'Oh, Madam; I knew you ought not to have gone out alone; I said so–' She took command as she added: 'It's all right, sir; madam lives here; it is her home–'

Their voices seemed to be lost to me after that. I stumbled into the hall, reached the staircase, and holding the balusters dragged myself up each stair while aching to drop and ... sleep. To get to the bedroom; to get that note...

'Black coffee, Betty,' I cried. 'Please – hurry ... black coffee; I think I must have taken ... the wrong tablets for my headache; I–' Was that being indiscreet? I couldn't think coherently or hold any thought for more than a matter of seconds; the longing to lie down and sleep was an agony indescribable. I heard Betty's anxious cries as from a great distance; they were of no importance to me.

'Black coffee,' I said again. 'I'm quite all right...' My tongue seemed to stick to my mouth as I tried to add: 'Please don't ... tell doctor ... perfectly all right, Betty.'

Only a few more steps... Stephen mustn't come in before I reached that note; he mustn't know me for the evil creature I was; I must be given just this one chance to redeem myself and atone for the misery I'd caused... I mustn't give way to the slow paralysis that seemed to be creeping upon me; I must fight to keep awake; note or no note, my death would involve him in publicity and gossip he in no way deserved...

Where was he now? Suppose he were not to come back at all? No; that wasn't Stephen: he'd carry on with his work until arrangements could be made for it to be transferred to another doctor. He was probably with Lionel Manning now; finding out the last minute details, hating and despising me the more – as he had every right to do. I shivered in a desperate wretchedness; even in my drugged state the knife of remorse turned in my heart...

And it was then that I heard Stella's voice in the hall below ... followed by Stephen's. They were here; here; and Stephen would know; I'd never drag myself to the bedroom in time ... never... My heart was pounding and I crouched against the wall so that they might not see me; every nerve was quivering as though suddenly exposed... But they weren't staying... I heard Stephen say:

'I'll just get my bag; one second – and if you want to see Lydia–'

Stella stood hesitantly. Her face was visible to me through the rails, although blurred and indistinct. She cried in a low, pained voice:

'On second thoughts ... there's nothing more to be said, Stephen. I'll go out to the car.'

And with that she hurried away.

Stephen fetched his medical bag and Betty, hearing footsteps, emerged hurriedly from the kitchen.

'Oh, sir, I'm glad you're back... Madam isn't at all well and–'

I could imagine, rather than see, the cold contempt that flashed into Stephen's eyes as, remembering my previous faked 'illness' which prevented our Cornwall trip, he said:

'You'll find that she will be all right, Betty... I've an urgent case.'

And with that he turned ... and the front door closed behind him.

I shuffled the last few yards to the bed-room; dazed, giddy, sick with the knowledge of just how vile and treacherous I must be to

Stephen... How ironical it was and what poetic justice that never had I needed his ministrations so urgently as now...

I could not have told anyone just how the next few hours passed; they might have been weeks or years as I struggled, fought to stave off the effect of the drug I had taken. I drank black coffee until the very taste of it was sickening, and at last I knew that the battle was won... I should live. In those moments, it was rather like coming round from an anæsthetic, with life gradually moving into focus and perspective. I should *live* ... and the terror that had lain upon me was no more; horror and fear vanished... The dim, grey light of a now drizzling December afternoon seemed to hold for me a curious luminosity as though my eyes were suddenly capable of seeing in its very greyness some great and new significance. A part of me had, I knew, died during that nightmare experience and, in a crucible of suffering, a more worthy human being had taken partial shape. The test lay ahead – I didn't deceive myself on that score... The carrying out of resolutions was not the lesser part of their nobility; the conceiving of them was simple. To relinquish all claim to Stephen ... to become to him barely a memory... Better, by far, I told myself swiftly, to be a fragrant memory than a harsh reality.

I slept a little before dinner and, then,

bathed, dressed but still shaky and feeling desperately ill, I went downstairs to await Stephen's return. He must return if only to acquaint me with his arrangements about the practice.

He came in after eight. I thought he had aged as I saw him walking slowly towards me in the lounge and yet, despite that fact, there was a new strength and composure about him as of a man resolved; a man who had settled, once and for all, those matters vitally affecting his personal life.

He glanced at me swiftly, lit a cigarette and said firmly, decisively:

'There are things to be discussed, Lydia. I want every detail settled.' He paused as one arrested by something about my appearance then: 'Betty told me you weren't well: certainly you look extremely pale. What is it?' His manner was instantly professional.

'Nothing,' I said quietly. 'I'm better now, thank you. And it is I who want to talk to you, Stephen.'

He flung out his hands in a gesture of appeal.

'Please, Lydia–'

'I'm not,' I said, 'going to start any discussion. All I ask is that you sit down and listen to me.'

'Very well.' There was a tolerant reasonableness in his attitude, typical of him. A pang shot through me as I realized how completely I had lost him, and how completely I deserved to do so; but that didn't make it any the easier to bear.

'You asked me to prove my sincerity by setting you free,' I began, striving to keep my voice steady. 'I am ready to do just that, Stephen; not merely as a gesture, but as one who realizes all you've been denied by me and all you've suffered through me.'

He stared, aghast and incredulous.

'Lydia,' he murmured, and again: 'Lydia.'

It was as though the very gentleness of his inflection released all the pent up emotions within me and I cried:

'Oh, Stephen, I've been so wrong; so terribly wrong. Everything you said about me was right. Everything. I've used my influence in every evil way possible; I deliberately prevented your marrying Stella – oh, let me speak, my dear, please. Mine has been a deceit and a cunning that appals me as I look back on it.' I managed to draw in my breath and keep back the sobs that were threatening me. 'I don't want to be mawkish or sentimental, but if you could find it in your heart to understand and forgive me–'

'You don't,' he said, obviously moved, 'have to ask–'

I rushed on:

'I want you to be happy, Stephen – you and Stella. She's right for you; I always knew it, really; but I was so jealous – so terribly jealous as to be blind to every worthy emotion. She will never fail you and together you will achieve all your ambitions for Milbury.'

'I can't,' he murmured, 'think of anything to say. I've been so bewildered and bitter that–'

'I know,' I said remorsefully. 'Oh, Stephen, I must have been mad.'

He stared at me as one seeking to fathom that which was wholly inexplicable to him.

'What – what has brought you to this–'

'What has brought me to my senses, do you mean?' I was silent for a second, then I added: 'I've looked on many pictures today, Stephen – pictures in focus. And I knew that my only hope of redemption – if that doesn't sound too dramatic – lies in atoning to you and to Stella.'

'What are you going to do?' He spoke gravely.

'I've not yet decided; but very definitely, work of some kind.'

He was staring at me, still incredulously. I said:

'You must almost wonder whether or not this is an "act" and find yourself waiting for some ulterior motive to emerge.'

He shook his head.

'No, Lydia; no.' His eyes met mine. 'To say that you don't baffle me would be wrong, for you do. The change is so complete, so final as to be convincing beyond all shadow of doubt. You might have died and returned to life – a different person.'

I twisted my wedding ring as I answered:

'Perhaps I almost have...'

'What do you mean?' It was a sharp inquiry.

I forced a half laugh.

'Nothing – I just feel your description to be an apt one, that's all.'

It was typical of Stephen that he used no flowery language, indulged no sentiment other than that strictly compatible with sincerity. He was in love with Stella and had declared that love for her and, thus, in that respect, I had ceased to be a factor in his life. I admired that strength within him; it was an integral part of his character, and his loyalty.

It was a little later that I asked:

'You saw Lionel Manning to-day?' Faint colour stole into my cheeks and a wave of thankfulness surged over me. At last I could be honest; there were no secrets to be kept from him; nothing to taint the shining brightness of a truth that suddenly seemed more precious than all else.

'Yes. There's a hope of disposing of the practice quietly and your money will be released, Lydia.'

I caught my breath.

'You wouldn't consider using some of it

for – Milbury? I cheated you of all that once, Stephen, and–'

He shook his head, but his voice was low, gentle as he replied:

'No, my dear; you'll understand if I say that ties such as ours have been, must be cut irrevocably, or not at all. No loose ends.'

I didn't speak. Looking at him, realizing anew how deep my love was for him became renunciation in itself. Yet mingled with anguish was a certain exultation... I had, at least, restored his respect for me and, in turn, regained in some measure that quality within myself.

I saw Stella and Stephen together the following day. Stephen had already acquainted her with my decision, and even as our eyes met it was as though many years rolled by and we stood as once we had done as children.

'Oh, Lydia,' she whispered, and was in my arms, clinging to me.

'I'm – forgiven,' I asked shakily.

The answer was in her eyes, shining with that brightness as of a spirit soaring beyond material considerations to a point of sublime self-abnegation. Stella, I knew, would be incapable of bearing malice, or a grudge; her heart was filled with far too great and divine a capacity for loving ever to allow of her stooping to petty vindictiveness.

I put her hand in Stephen's, held both

tightly for a second, and then managed to say:

'I shall come back to Milbury one day...' I glanced around at the gleaming whiteness of the hospital waiting-room where our meeting had been arranged. How much I had learned and suffered since last I stood in that same room.

'Where are you going?' Stella asked anxiously. 'Don't you see, Lydia, we must know that you're all right and–'

It was as though some inward power gave me strength to answer her; power to say:

'My darling, I shall be perfectly all right... I don't know yet where I am going; perhaps I've only just begun my journey; all I do know is that, at last I am on the right road... No, don't come with me; I want to walk along these old streets and remember...'

I turned as I reached the door and glanced back. Stephen's hand was still clasping hers and there was between them that emotion and fulfilment and love which took almost tangible shape in its passionate sincerity.

My vision was blurred as I reached the street and made my way through the town. No longer was I the cynosure of all eyes and no longer did I seek to be; for the world on which I was gazing was strange and new and a little frightening.

Yes, I should come back to Milbury ... when Stephen and Stella were married and

I could gaze without envy or jealousy upon their happiness and the fulfilment of all their cherished ambitions. Only courage and determination, the fortitude of a deep resolve could, for me, bridge the gulf between present and future ... a future in which I must serve.

It struck me that mine was a curious story and that it was poetic justice that, at this stage of it, I was unable to envisage its ending... I knew only that a fragile trend of hope remained to urge me on towards atonement.

The publishers hope that this book has given you enjoyable reading. Large Print Books are especially designed to be as easy to see and hold as possible. If you wish a complete list of our books please ask at your local library or write directly to:

Dales Large Print Books
Magna House, Long Preston,
Skipton, North Yorkshire.
BD23 4ND

This Large Print Book, for people
who cannot read normal print,
is published under the auspices of

THE ULVERSCROFT FOUNDATION

... we hope you have enjoyed this book.
Please think for a moment about those
who have worse eyesight than you ...
and are unable to even read or enjoy
Large Print without great difficulty.

You can help them by sending a
donation, large or small, to:

**The Ulverscroft Foundation,
1, The Green, Bradgate Road,
Anstey, Leicestershire, LE7 7FU,
England.**
or request a copy of our brochure for
more details.

The Foundation will use all donations
to assist those people who are visually
impaired and need special attention
with medical research, diagnosis
and treatment.

Thank you very much for your help.